Halley's Casino III: Return Trip

Written By

Mark JG Fahey

Library and Archives Canada Cataloguing in Publication

Fahey, Mark, author
      Return Trip / Mark J.G. Fahey.

(Halley's Casino ; 3)
ISBN 978-0-9948918-4-6 (paperback)

      I. Title. III. Series: Fahey, Mark . Halley's Casino ; 3

Fahey Mark 2019

Return Trip - Halley's Casino III: a novel by Mark JG Fahey

First Paperback Edition: November 2019

Cover design by Lanze Lee Langill & Mark JG Fahey
Back cover photo by Jonathan Vermeire (Frost Photography)
Edited by Helen Durrant, Lynne Penner & Mark JG Fahey*

Halley's Casino III: Return Trip

This book is dedicated to my parents

Anna Mary Patricia (TC) Kearney Fahey

(The original TeeceeFore) ☺

Gerald Oscar Fahey (we miss you)

1

For 500 years the family of Attalus of Sardegna had been purveyors of the finest olive oil and wine throughout the whole Mediterranean. His ancestors settled on the Island of Sardegna in 100 AD.

Handed down from generation to generation, Attalus and his son Felix continued this rich lucrative tradition but with Attalus's declining health Felix had found himself needing to take the reins of the family business from his father.

He could never imagine not having his loving father by his side. A father whose whole life was not just dedicated to producing the best wines and olive oils anywhere but a father who had taught him everything in life.

Felix's mother had died giving birth to him and though Attalus would remarry – and more than once – Felix would never enjoy having any siblings. Instead, he had countless cousins who also worked alongside him and his father in the family business.

Felix himself never married despite having many lovers over the years—both female and male. His paramours were either other merchants or visitors to the island who conducted both business and love affairs for themselves or – if employees – for their masters.

The world had opened up from the time when Felix's family had first arrived on the shores of Sardegna. Egyptians, Persians, Africans, Grecian, Roman, northern tribes once enemies and slaves, and envoys from the Visigothic kingdoms – anyone was a welcomed trading partner.

"Business is business," Attalus would remind his son, "no matter what they look like or where they come from." To Attalus, the world was a proverbial oyster. Attalus and his family thus prospered.

The Empire that was once Rome had now converted to Christianity, it was still a force to be reckoned with but it never would be the grand spectacle it had once been. Felix was none too fond of any religious uprising or any risings at all. He found himself to be more of a romantic sort.

Felix, though he always enjoyed hearing and reading about the tales of a long ago Rome that he felt a connection with, never forgot his Greek heritage (his father would have had a fit if he did.). Would Zeus himself come crashing down if I did? Felix would laugh to himself.

Attalus could always count on his son; never a day went by without the sight of Attalus beaming with pride for Felix. Grandchildren would have been nice but one cannot have everything. Felix had turned out to be a very capable business man in his own right and that was good enough for his father—to know that when he passed on from this life to the next all would be well taken care of.

Attalus's vast estate was the largest on Sardegna, encompassing a quarter of the island. A forest of olive trees and long paths of grape vines spread out, touching a part of the coast where ships could harbor close enough for easy transactions.

Felix was getting worried about his father the last few years, though. Attalus's strength and vigor began to slowly diminish and he was frequently kept indoors battling fevers that ran hot one day and cold the next, which meant he was kept away from working the soil which he so greatly loved.

"At 99 years of age, who wouldn't start to slow down?" Marliuse, Felix's cousin and now full-time nurse to Attalus, reminded him.

"I know but he has hardly ever been sick in his entire life," Felix mentioned, time and time again to Marliuse.

"Some young die old and some old die young," Marliuse mused. "We can only hope that we live as long and healthy as your father and who knows maybe he will fool us all and regain a posture of youth and hang on for a few more years yet. Perhaps we should join the Christians – don't they speak about life everlasting or something to that effect?"

"Don't get me started, Marliuse," Felix waved a finger at his cousin in a playful manner, though deep inside he had no taste for such a faith that would change his Roman heroes from gods to goats.

"Your father has outlived four wives and countless relatives and friends," Marliuse sighed, "it is hard to imagine a world without him."

Four wives! Felix thought. Somehow it felt like hundreds… No, somehow it felt that both he and his father had lived more lives than he could count.

It was an odd feeling he felt and something he kept to himself.

Three more weeks had now gone by and Attalus was none the better. Actually, he was getting worse. Visitors were becoming more frequent and – now bedridden, Attalus's end of days drew near.

"It's a part of living," Attalus tried to console his son. "Sometimes we live longer than one could ever imagine. There's nothing wrong with that, is there? Look at yourself, Felix. You are not the young man you used to be, are you? I see flecks of white in your hair and I know you dye it; no one wants to look or grow old and yet like a blade of grass we grow only to wither away as the season's end approaches."

"But Father, what will I do without you?" Felix cried, holding onto his father's hands. "You'll do fine, my son; you always have," Attalus pulled himself up from his bed.

"What are you doing, Father?" Felix helped his father sit up.

"Take me one last time out to the vineyards and olive groves. I want to feel the sun once more on my face. I want to take in the fresh air that I once so loved and now so greatly miss."

"Marliuse!" Felix shouted out.

"Yes?" Marliuse came running in.

"Please dress my father. I will be back shortly."

"As you wish." Marliuse proceeded to do as Felix had asked, without question.

"We're going to the groves." Attalus smiled as his niece took hold of him.

Felix soon returned with a horse and cart and was now sitting outside their villa's entrance, waiting for his father.

Marliuse appeared first, her head down as she walked slowly towards Felix.

"Where's father?" he asked.

Marliuse looked up with tears running down her face.

Felix didn't have to ask Marliuse any further questions, he knew straight away that his father had passed on to the next life. Felix looked up to the sky and wept.

He stepped down off the cart and embraced his cousin, each consoling one another. Felix wondered what the future would now hold, without his father.

****

One year later, on the anniversary of Attalus's death, Felix held a feast honoring his late father. Relatives and friends, years old clients and merchants attended; the whole island it seemed, was present.

Felix had finally decided to marry. His bride was no other than his cousin Marliuse (though, truth be told, she was a far distant relative). Tributes to Attalus and now marriage plans were being made.

There were many tears shed for Attalus at the feast and many stories shared of his long life. One story in particular noted how striking the resemblance of Felix to Attalus was. No one could remember any family, anywhere, where such strong genes prevailed and long life at that.

Felix said he could not explain it but when pressed, his answer was, "It's in the wine and olives!" At which response, everyone called for more wine, albeit with much laughter.

When all was said and done and with more tears – happy and sad – everyone went their separate ways. Marliuse herself, along with her parents, departed for the southern capital of Cagliari to attend to marriage arrangements; something Felix was happy to let her do.

The next day Felix needed to tend to his father's personal belongings. It was a task he had been lagging behind in.

With Marliuse away – and feeling very generous – Felix gave all his workers the day off. His father would likewise do so a few days during the year – after all, they weren't slaves. The family was well liked and loved, to say the least; they took care of their own. Some speculated that Attalus was deep down a secret Christian, though in fact he was far from it. He was just a man living life as one should. He had no need to be told how to live and how to treat another well – he just did so. It was something he also taught Felix to practice.

Attalus had always stayed as far away from any sort of religious fever or politics as possible. He had observed over his lifespan that the two seem to be entwined and not for the better good. 'Do as I say. Not as I do.' – was the thought that came to mind. No man should hold any type of power over anyone for personal gain or otherwise, he would remind his son time and time again.

Felix walked into his father's den. He looked around, wondering where to start. He did not want to give everything away but did not know what to keep or what not to keep.

He sat down on his father's familiar old rocking chair. It was an heirloom; he definitely would not be giving that away. He looked over the room once more.

As he rocked back and forth thinking, out of the corner of his eye he noticed that the sun peeking down through the upper skylight bounced off a blue-gold lined trunk that was almost hidden from view. In fact, if it were not for the sun's dancing ray that caught its gold reflection, he would have missed seeing the trunk altogether.

Felix rose and walked over. The trunk was half draped with clothing. He pulled away the garments to reveal the whole thing.

The sun now shone on the entire box. Felix had to cover his eyes momentarily, shielding them from the blinding light.

It stood three feet high and two feet across. Four long sleeves of gold crisscrossed the box. In between the gold there was a faded blue reddish colouring. There was also a vast assortment of pictographs of animals covering the entire trunk.

It took Felix a few moments to recognize the box. He then remembered it as another heirloom that had been handed down through the generations. It was of Babylonian origin, he recalled his father telling him.

The trunk stared up at Felix. It had a double padlock with a big black oval-shaped picture showing a majestic lion's head just above the lock.

He didn't want to break the lock. Maybe he shouldn't even open it, he thought. Felix drew out the trunk, set it in front of the rocking chair and then sat down. He rocked away looking down at it. There must be a key for it, somewhere in his father's belongings – but where? He scratched his head. Where?

After about five minutes he decided he would have to begin the search somewhere, so he might as well start with his father's dresser. Felix stood up and as he did so he stubbed one of his big toes on the trunk.

"YEOW!" he screamed out.

He bounced around on one foot, feeling the swelling in the toe.

"Damn trunk!" he yelled at it, "Why didn't you just stay hidden?" Then he laughed to himself and sat back down.

Felix rubbed at his big toe, it wasn't as bad as he first thought; it was more of a jolt than a stub but painful none the less.

He had almost forgotten about finding the key and had decided to leave things for another day when something extraordinary took place – the lock popped open by itself!

Felix bent forward and slowly lifted the lid of the trunk. His eyes could hardly believe what he was seeing. Inside the trunk there were hundreds of scrolls – each tightly rolled with a red seal. Also, there were gold and silver coins – none of which were a mint he had ever seen before.

He picked up one of the gold coins. It was called an aureus and it depicted an image of Augustus Julius Octavian Caesar. Felix held it up and immediately, without pause, knew who it was.

An ageless Apollo-like classic sculpture could be seen on one side and on the other, an image of a heifer. Felix could not believe what he was looking at. "Magnificent!" he muttered under his breath. He stopped for a second, looking around to make sure no one was watching him and then he dove back into the chest.

Silk scarves, gold goblets, knives and spoons, small hand painted frescoes and an open scroll that read 'Livia's Dream'... It couldn't be? he thought.

What would his father be doing with all of this?

Where did he get it?

Why had he never told him – his son – about it?

And why is the box deeper on the inside than it appears to be on the outside?

Was it some sort of trick chest?

Was this perhaps an inheritance that Attalus never got the chance to tell his son about before he died?

Felix sat back rocking, catching his breath. He rolled the gold coin of Augustus Caesar through his fingers, not even realising he was doing so. He thought again for a few more minutes before he tossed the coin back in the trunk. This would need some serious thinking.

He was about to close the trunk when he spotted what looked like the top of a pyramid sticking out above the coins. He reached in for it and pulled it up and out.

It was indeed a pyramid, one that stood twelve inches high and about two inches wide. It was black in appearance or only seemed to be, for as Felix pulled it up it changed color to a reddish yellowish greenish hue.

Unknown to Felix it was a Chameleon Stone.

He held it up with both hands, turning it around and upside down while it continued to change colors. My, those Egyptians sure were clever folks! Felix thought, believing it was of Egyptian origin. He had never seen anything like it; it kind of reminded him of the changing twirls of light in the night sky that danced during the harvest season.

As he was admiring it he fumbled the stone, sending it crashing to the floor. It shattered into pieces that went everywhere.

"No! No! No!" Felix cried out. "What have I done?"

He looked down at the floor and he could not believe what he was seeing. The shards of the stone were all moving, mingling – assembling the pyramid back together.

Felix stood and took a few steps back, watching in amazement what was taking place.

What type of magic was this?

Was it magic?

He was starting to realize there was more to his father – things that he did not know about. Felix found this idea unsettling and intriguing all at the same time. Of course his father would have come across and met all kinds of people in his lifetime of bartering, trading and the like.

But this?

After it had reassembled itself, Felix wasn't sure if he should touch it or pick it up at all but he wanted to return it to the trunk. He saw his father's walking cane dangling behind the rocking chair and grabbed it. Felix poked at the pyramid…

Nothing happened. He poked it again… Nothing.

He decided to just push it aside until later when he could find a set of prongs to use to lift it back into the trunk – or to just put it somewhere else, out of sight.

Felix then thought he heard the sound of bees buzzing about the room but could see nothing.

How strange, he thought.

He reached forward to close the lid on the trunk. The buzzing noise was coming from the inside of the trunk itself. Felix did not know what to make of it. What else was hiding within this mystery box? Felix took his father's cane once more and drove it into the trunk. As he shook the cane about inside the trunk, the sound ceased.

Felix then pulled the cane out but something was now attached to the cane. It was some sort of bracelet that was caught on a piece of the old cane's splintered wood.

What's this? Felix gazed at it and as he did, it gave him a sense of déjà vu.

He lifted the cane up further and as he did so the bracelet fell off. Felix stretched out his hand and caught it. What an odd piece of jewellery.

It was a type of black leather, or what he thought was leather, with three white pearl buttons to the right side of a centred soft, square shape of sorts and there was one larger white pearl button to the left of the shape. He slipped it onto his wrist without thinking. Nice fit, he thought, though not overly appealing to wear out in public.

He licked his thumb and proceeded to rub the pearl buttons with it. As he rubbed harder he could feel a pulse streaming through the bracelet.

"Now what?" he said out loud.

The next thing Felix heard was what he thought was a voice emitting from the bracelet itself.

"Master, is that you?" the ghostly voice asked.

Felix jumped like he had seen a mouse and threw off the bracelet.

"Master? Master?" the voice repeated.

What sorcery is this? Felix could not believe what he was hearing.

"Master, are you there?" the voice once again asked.

"There is no master here," Felix blurted out without thinking.

"Voice recognition confirmed," said another different, rather mechanical type of voice.

"Bio readings commencing," the voice echoed.

"Heart rate a little high, otherwise vital signs all working within normal parameters.

"Brain function and memory synapses fragmentized.

"Compensating.

"Unable to reconstruct.

"Initializing Medtronic transfer 4—336—6.

"Data transfer unsuccessful.

"Recommend immediate subject transport to nearest Med Bay.

"Transfer reinitiating," the voice ended.

"Master? Master? It's Eno."

"The computer has detected an anomaly in your frontal cranium memory lobe.

"Master? Please say something. It's me! Eno," he implored.

Felix rubbed his forehead. Sweat was dripping down the side of his face and he felt as though he was going to faint – and did. Eno heard a large thud.

"Subject immobilised," said the computer.

"Activating emergency transport.

"Commencing in five, four, three,…"

Within seconds, Felix vanished into thin air.

2

The Great Library of Atiox on Mastic 4 had been around in circulation for as far back as anyone could remember. It was said it housed more books than even the mythological planet of the Athenaeums – both were only a rumour.

The entire planet of Mastic 4 could quite literally be considered a library, four of its nine moons held special antiquities from across the vast universe including artifacts dating back to The Year of Conflictions and beyond.

On this day, down in the basement of the main library, Professor Gabriel Pheet was rummaging through a stack of books that reached twelve feet high and that was covered in dust. Gnits of Mastic 4 (the assistant librarian to the assistant librarian to the brother of the assistant librarian, 104 times removed) assisted the Professor.

Gnits stood three feet tall, if that. He was slender in appearance and fresh faced – like a new born. Clad in a type of lederhosen outfit, on his feet he wore hover shoes so as to help him find books no one else could find, high above the already giant stack of books that filled the basement hall.

And – oh yes, he had four eyes – two in the front and two in the back – which helped him tremendously while searching.

"Professor!" Gnits shouted down from high above the endless stacks of shelves. "Are you sure it's here? I do not remember ever hearing of such a title among any of the books we have – and that's a lot of books! It's not even listed in our data bases."

"I am positive it's here. I mean I have actually seen and read it," Pheet replied. "It has been a long time but I know it is here. It *has* to be here."

"How long ago was that Professor?" Gnits asked back.

"I don't know. Maybe… 120 years ago."

"120 years ago!" Gnits hovered down lower now, staring the Professor straight in the face. "We've been looking in the wrong place Professor," Gnits vented.

"How do you mean, we're looking in the wrong place?" Pheet threw up his hands.

"I remember it clearly as though it was yesterday – well, at least last week. I was down here researching tides and lunar movements when I came across it."

"I don't doubt that you did, Professor. The problem is that we rotate the collections every 100 years or so. It is very possible that the book you seek may be housed elsewhere here on Mastic 4, or it could be on one of the moons," Gnits informed the Professor.

"Well that is good news," said the Professor while closing up the books spread out across the desk he was working on. "I thought I was going crazy."

"Good News! We have just spent 4 days – or rather, *I* have spent 4 days-hovering up and down these dusty aisles looking for a book that is not even here," said a frustrated Gnits as he hovered up to meet Pheet eye to eye once more.

"And what a good job you have done Gnits. I could not have done it without you," Pheet replied.

"Good job! Good job! A good job is finding the damn book!" Gnits loudly remarked.

"Shhh. Keep it down Gnits, after all we are in a library. I should not have to tell you that." The Professor waved a finger at Gnits then popped him on the nose with his finger as though Gnits were a naughty child. Gnits waved the Professor's finger away from his nose.

"Very well then, Gnits. I will let you carry on and locate where the book might have been rerouted to. In the meantime, I am famished! Any suggestions where one might get a bite to eat?"

I have a few suggestions, Gnits thought to himself.

"I'm sorry Professor, I am a librarian not a restaurant guide," Gnits huffed.

"No need to get antsy about it, Gnits," Pheet shushed.

"I will get back to you tomorrow-or later on today," Gnits replied. "I should have a better idea about where the book could have been re-routed to then. I may have to charge you extra credits for the extra researching though," Gnits grumbled and hovered up and down one of the long dark aisles until he disappeared out of sight.

What do you mean you're going to charge me extra credits?! No one said there was a fee. Pheet said to himself as he packed his belongings into his small briefcase.

The Professor was learning that Mastictonians were not the sort to be trifled with – even at 3 feet tall or there about.

3

The Photon Ledger hung in space orbiting Mastic 4 and its nine moons. She had been brought out of deep hibernation for the extended journey and adventure that no one knew the ending to.

The word was that the Photon Ledger was an organic hybrid Marinian/Triopelian deep space vessel equipped with a long range Interstellar Thrust and now a recently installed Sonic Rhythm Drive. It was a medium-sized ship with three decks which in the past was used as a traveling laboratory but now was converted for more conventional uses. There was still a working lab on the ship but it now only took up one deck. The other decks were converted to personal quarters with the top deck used as leisure space along with the main bridge that was also located there.

Nebula Yorker – Neb to his friends – had never seen anything quite like it in his short stay within the greater universe. To say it was unique was an understatement.

It sort of resembled some kind of bird of flight but Neb wasn't sure what kind of bird. It was the brainchild of no other than Professor LeBeau and Professor Gabriel Pheet and was built over 100 years ago.

The explanation for it being in dry-dock for so long is in itself another story, best saved for another time. Suffice it to say that LeBeau and Pheet are lucky – if one can use that term – to be still above ground and breathing.

Neb thought of them as the Martin and Lewis (Dean & Jerry respectively) of their time(s), except they had extraordinary and brilliant minds when working for the good of all. In fact, they could only be outmatched by Neb, when he was on his game – which was most of the time.

Professor Pheet had just finished relaying to Neb and LeBeau the difficulties in finding the book – 'The Lost Door' – due to the fact he was looking in the wrong place and that he might need some extra credits – if anyone of them might have any extra lying around.

After figuring out what Pheet was talking about, Neb assured him that no extra credits would be needed and that he would speak personally with Gnits regarding the situation.

Neb had met Gnits two years earlier on Halley's Casino. Gnits could not get over being five foot nine inches when on Halley's Casino and being able to stand eye to eye with everyone he encountered. He and Neb had become fast friends during Gnit's stay on the Casino, due to Neb's kindness.

"If you say so," the Professor replied to Neb. "I don't think he's going to take no for an answer. He seems very determined about getting those credits."

"Don't worry about it, Gabriel," LeBeau joined in on the conversation.

"Are you sure, LeBeau? I thought Gnits was going to bite my ankles off there for a minute before he hovered off."

"If Neb said he would speak with Gnits and work something out then Neb will speak with Gnits and work something out," LeBeau replied.

"Ok, LeBeau," said Pheet. "But for such little beings, they sure are scary."

"Very well Professor, you go off and find something to eat and LeBeau and I will take care of everything up here. Neb out."

"But…" Pheet's voice faded as Neb cut the transmission.

"Has he always been like that?" Neb turned and asked LeBeau.

"Like what?" LeBeau replied.

"You know – the credit thing?" Neb looked at LeBeau.

"Oh that! Well he had at one time – many, many years ago – had a problem with one of the universities he worked for (or he thought he worked for) and credits were somehow involved though I am not quite sure how and why. He doesn't like to talk about it." LeBeau smiled and turned back to his console.

"I see," said Neb. "Glad I asked… I think?"

Meanwhile, down on Mastic 4, Professor Pheet had been able to find a nearby local establishment and he had settled in for an overdue dinner as he put it.

"Would you like to see the wine list?" the waiter asked. He was a non-looking Mastictonian, in that he must have stood close to six feet and reminded Pheet of Purell.

Pheet looked up and thought about it for a second but went for the ice tea instead.

"Very good sir, in the meantime please feel free to peruse the menu." He handed it to Pheet. "Then, when I return with your ice tea I won't have to wait and come back to take your order," he dryly remarked in a low baritone voice and walked way.

"Yep, just like Purell," Pheet smiled as he began to look through the menu.

And as he was doing so, a familiar voice called out.

"Why if I didn't see it with my own two eyes – Professor Gabriel Pheet! I thought you were dead?"

The Professor, with the menu now propped up below his eyes, turned slowly around to the table next to him where the voice emanated from.

"Don't play coy with me, Professor." Someone snatched the menu out of his hand.

There, sitting in full view was Kcils Ecarg, an old flame of the Professor's from a time in his life he deemed ancient history. He couldn't believe it. (Nor would LeBeau, if he were here and Neb too, would have been amused to learn that 'old smelly pants' had ever had a girlfriend.)

Pheet sat with his mouth wide open and said nothing.

"It's alright Gabby," ('Gabby'! Just as she used to call him!) "Your secret is good with me, honey."

Kcils Ecarg was a very pleasing sight for her species. She was a Melnarite.

She had deep dark shiny caramel skin and a sleek curving body. Her cat-like facial shape and her ears gave her away easily as a Melnarite.

"Meow," she purred. "How long has it been, Gabby? 100 years – give or take?"

"Is it really you, Kcils?" Pheet finally spoke up.

"It's really me, Gabby."

"Come join me." She patted the chair beside her.

The Professor jumped tables as the waiter returned with his ice tea.

"Changing seats are we? That's going to cost you extra credits."

The waiter laid down the glass on the table, "I hope at least you're ready to order."

"Oh, I am sorry, I didn't have time to...," the Professor replied.

The waiter cut him off, "Of course you didn't."

"Off-worlders!" he shook his head and walked away.

"What's with the credits deal?" Pheet asked Kcils, who ignored his question.

"So Gabby, what brings you back here? Oh wait. I bet you're on some secret mission to save the universe?" she flirted, rubbing her hand on Pheet's knee under the table.

"My!" the Professor blushed at both her flirting and the question and didn't quite know how to answer both. So he quickly reversed the question and asked her what she was doing on Mastic 4? He was *quite* sure she wasn't studying up on any academic endeavours.

"I am waiting on my boyfriend."

She took her vaporcig out of her purse and puffed away.

"And speaking of him – here he comes now," Kcils pointed behind the Professor.

Pheet turned and looked over his shoulder to see who Kcils was pointing to.

His mouth almost dropped to the floor.

It was no other than See-Ess – aka the 'Big Fish', one of Marine's most notorious, well-groomed, well-mannered and well-spoken gangsters. His six foot, five inch bulky frame slid inbetween Kcils and the Professor.

"Hello love," he gave Kcils a peck on the cheek.

"Gabby, you old moon crater, how have you been?" See-Ess asked.

"Do we know each other?" Pheet enquired.

"Do we know each other?" Guffawed See-Ess.

"Shame about Jipgoto, eh," he leaned in and whispered into Pheet's ear.

The Professor almost peed himself.

****

Gnits was busy surfing through the library's databases, searching for the Professor's book. He was having a very hard time locating it. Nothing was coming up to any of his queries, which he found extremely painstaking and odd.

It had to be here, he thought, unless it has been loaned out which is highly unlikely in that it would have taken forms upon forms upon forms upon forms just to request it and even after that there would be more forms. Not to mention the years it would take to print the forms in the first place. Gnits was starting to think something was not right.

He had finally located its last rotation as being 100 years ago; one week after the Professor had last seen it. After that, the trail went blank.

Though the name of the book was listed as 'The Most Coor' and not 'The Lost Door'. "'The Most Coor!'" he huffed. No wonder he couldn't locate it.

He decided he would visit Hall RV2C, the last place the book was shelved. Perhaps it was still there but had somehow slipped between the cracks, so to speak, which again was highly unlikely. However, Gnits was determined to find out where the book had gone to. It was his duty as a Librarian.

As Gnits was about to get up from his console and head for Hall RV2C he swerved in his chair to see an old friend standing before him.

"Neb!" Gnits happily called out.

Neb fell to one knee as Gnits ran to him and gave him a hug.

"It's so nice to see you, Neb. I never thought I would see you here on Mastic 4 even though you had promised to visit one day-but not this soon."

"Well I had to bring you your winning credits, which you forgot," Neb teased.

"Really? Credits? I had no idea," Gnits replied.

"I'm just kidding," said Neb. "You're the worst poker player I have ever seen, we should be returning your credits."

"Ok, I am good with that," Gnits held out his hand as they both laughed.

"So what bring brings you here, Neb?" Gnits asked, happy to see his old friend.

"Why a book of course," Neb stood up.

"Just a book?" Gnits laughed. "Well, you have come to the right place. What can I help you with then?"

"Actually, a colleague of mine is supposed to be here working on that right now but I guess he hasn't gotten back from dinner yet."

"You don't mean Professor Pheet, do you Neb?" Gnits said with a taste of disdain.

"Why yes," Neb replied, noticing the tone in Gnit's voice. "Ok, what did he do, Gnits?"

"It's not what he has done, so to speak, it's more his attitude, you know?"

"Yeah, that's our Professor alright," Neb agreed. "He does mean well but you will only realise that after you get to know him, Gnits. However, to be honest, he and I, along with another friend – Professor LeBeau – need that book ASAP."

"You know LeBeau?!" Gnits interrupted Neb.

"Oh, I see you have heard of him," Neb chuckled.

"Know him! Dear no. I have seen him though – along with the rest of the universe – talking to himself. Yes – during the seahorse race on Marine!"

Neb had to laugh some more, "Would you like to meet him?"

Just as Neb finished speaking, in walked LeBeau – as if on cue!

"So did we find that book yet?" LeBeau asked.

"We are still looking, I am afraid," Neb replied.

"I would say that time is of the essence but then you already know that. "Here," LeBeau handed Neb an isopad.

"What's this?" Neb took the isopad from LeBeau.

"It's Tict," he replied.

"Thank you," Neb grabbed the pad and activated it.

While Neb was about to speak with Tict, he said to LeBeau, "My friend here – Gnits – is a big fan of yours."

"Really? I did not know I had any fans," LeBeau puffed up his chest and held out his hand to Gnits, who shook it.

"You look different," Gnits looked up at LeBeau.

"Different from what?" LeBeau let out a chuckle.

"I don't know, you just looked shorter..." Gnits replied. "Hey, that seahorse race was a blast!"

"Neb!" Tict let out. "How goes the search. Have you found it?"

"We're on to it," replied Neb as Gnits and LeBeau turned their attention to the isopad screen and waved to Tict

"Who is that?" Tict asked.

"Oh, you remember Gnits, don't you Tict. The worst poker player that ever played on Halley's."

Tict laughed, "How could I forget?! We should be returning his credits."

"Ok! I get it! I am a bad poker player!" Gnits walked away and sat back down at his console.

"How is TeeceeFore doing?" Neb asked, concerned as ever.

"She is feeling much, much better, although..." Tict paused, "She lost the baby," he said with his head down.

Neb did not say anything. At the time of TeeceeFore's injuries Neb had consulted with Med Bay. They had told him there was a possibility that TeeceeFore might have sustained too much internal damage and that the child she and Tict were expecting might not make it.

LeBeau overheard Tict, as did Gnits. There was a long silence between the four.

"I'm sorry," was all Neb could muster.

"She's up and about now, though confined to a sealed off part of the docking bay for another week. Med Bay is running a few more tests before they will allow her to resume her transfigured humanoid state. She does say hello to you and LeBeau by the way and says too that you are not to worry about her, you have more than enough on your plate."

"Tell her we miss her and hope to see all of you soon," Neb replied.

"I will," Tict said while thinking – hoping – that Neb could reverse Earth's plight along with Marcus's scheme.

"Oh, by the way, someone else wants to talk to you," Tict moved away and suddenly, there, filling the isopad small screen, was Kel – soon joined by Purell.

"Kel!" Neb joyfully exclaimed.

"What about me?" Purell asked with a frown.

"Yes, hello to you as well, Purell," Neb looked over to LeBeau who rolled his eyes.

"Plus ça change, plus c'est la même chose, eh," Neb laughed.

"What was that?" LeBeau took a double take.

"French Language; Earth, I believe," Purell began, with Kel finishing off his sentence. "'The more things change the more they stay the same.'"

"Amen to that," Purell added.

"Did you know, LeBeau, that your name translated from French to the English language means…"

"Handsome man," Neb cut back in, "I have been meaning to mention that to you."

"Really? Well that does not surprise me," LeBeau grinned.

"I could have told you that," Purell quipped.

"Yep, nothing changes," LeBeau said out loud so that Purell could hear.

"Both Purell and I are fully functional and ready to report to work. We should be orbiting Mastic 4 in about five hours," Kel took over the conversation.

"So soon?" Neb asked. "It's been six weeks, are you sure you're up to it?"

"Quite sure, sir," Purell replied for Kel.

"Our new frames have been strengthened to withstand dragon ice, among other forces that we may encounter. We are like brand new! We have new updated data nodes, processors – I could go on and on," Kel said, almost sounding like Purell.

"We even have the same color eyes – deep blue," Purell giggled.

"Weren't your eyes both blue before?" LeBeau chimed in.

"Yes and no," Kel answered. "Blue but not deep blue."

"What is the difference?" Neb asked.

"Deep blue! Hello?" Purell sighed.

Gnits looked up from his console and muttered, "Androids!"

"Oh and we have new ears with impeccable hearing," Kel threw in, overhearing Gnits.

Gnits blushed red. "Sorry," he whispered.

Neb wasn't sure if he liked the new and improved Kel and Purell. Each one seemed to have the attributes of the other, a result of Airhert's fusing.

"Ok then, see you when you get here. Please put Tict back on, would you?" Neb asked.

Tict's face soon filled the screen once again.

"Are you sure they are 100 percent ok?" Neb asked Tict.

"That's what the Biotech Lab said," Tict replied.

Let's hope, Neb thought.

"Neb," said Tict, choking up a bit, "you take care and get back soon. I don't think I have the patience to train another assistant."

"Don't worry about me, Archibald Tict. You look after yourself – and TeeceeFore – she is your top priority – the Casino is second."

"What about the book, dear boy?" Tict asked.

"I think Gnits may be zeroing in on its last known shelving," Neb answered.

"Well, I must get back to the business of running the Casino. It can't run itself. Well, it could but where would all the fun be in that?! Be safe Neb, you know what sort of fellow Marcus is, there is no telling what else he has planned, or what awaits you. For all you know he may be expecting you."

"I am counting on it," Neb assured Tict.

Tict ended the transmission. He turned in his office chair looking out into deep space as Kel and Purell's shuttle zipped by heading out for Mastic 4. He wondered if he would ever see his friends again; he wondered what would happen if Marcus broke free of the Velexian Viper Reversal Vortex Bubble. Neb's parents had told their son to stay clear of Earth. Perhaps Neb has something up his sleeve that they did not know about, or they knew he would come anyway.

Neb had nothing up his sleeve…at least, not that he knew of.

Tict, at Neb's asking, had sent out a universal request (through the Guild of course) for all concerned to stay clear of the Milky Way Galaxy until further notice. Most of the time when such an order was issued it had to do more with quarantine measures than it did with a Velexian Viper Reversal Vortex Bubble which no one knew existed – well, most didn't.

Neb thought it best not to inform the Guild of the true reason for the time being, unless it became necessary and to meet that eventuality, Neb had pre-taped a video divulging the reason as well as his Triopelian identity – should all hell break   loose.

4

On the outskirts of Rome lies the Appian Way or the Via Appia, the queen of the long roads.

The Romans were master road builders. Some roads like the Via Appia were built to transport soldiers while other roads – such as the Via Ostiense, Via Labicana, Via Tiburtina or Via Nomentana all had their own importance in Rome's history – past, present and future.

Thus the saying 'All roads lead to Rome' was beginning to take on a new, larger meaning.

The date was March 4th,1990 and Emperor Marcus Attitpius was planning on expanding those roads to outside the boundaries of Earth itself.

Yet deep down beneath the volcanic layers of Rome, 40 feet down, outside the walls of Rome herself, in the ancient catacombs once used for burials and secret Christian gatherings – plans of another kind were taking shape.

These catacombs were long forgotten, as were the early Christians who had, for a short time, used them as a means to elude the Emperor.

Marcus had eventually wiped out the new faith entirely. In fact he had wiped out all religions, there could only be one god, one Emperor, one Rome and that was Marcus Attitpius.

For the last seven months, Victoria and Bancroft Yorker (Blulay and Ruban) worked feverishly below ground.

Their escape pod landed on the outskirts of Rome, unbeknownst to them at the time but fortuitous in now allowing them to keep tabs on Marcus.

Using the components from their escape pod from which they had stripped every last useful piece of equipment they could, they had managed to set up a force field and communication dampeners – to avoid being detected by Marcus's own technology.

They also had personal cloaking devices, to use whenever they would tread above ground when needing food and to also allow them to observe the populace – which they did, sometimes cloaked and sometimes not.

One needed to be extra careful as Marcus had spies everywhere. Knowing what he knew about the outside universe, Marcus knew that the possibility of extraterrestrial life reaching his Earth loomed and he wanted to be ready for it.

They had almost been captured 3 months earlier, by Marcus's guards so Ruban and Blulay knew they had to be very careful in treading this new world. Subsequently, they had sealed off a portion of the catacombs to any outside intruders who may try and find their way to them. The catacombs were a long forgotten piece of this Earth's history which for the time being they were thankful for and called home.

They knew though that Marcus would always be on the lookout for them or for any others that may have been caught up in this parallel conundrum and if what they had gleaned proved correct, Marcus did have a secret holding facility made just for the purpose of internment.

Ruban was able to equip their deep, dark and damp underground home comfortably using Triopelian means, along with Earth's own organic resources. They salvaged enough spare parts from the pod to build a small computer console with three camera monitors, one of which monitored the entrance to their home, another focused on an exit point should they be in need and the third was a long range scope lens pointed skyward that fed them data on the Velexian Viper Reversal Vortex Bubble's status.

The world which they now found themselves in was not without its own technologic know-how. Television was television, radio was radio and phones were phones – it was almost like being trapped in the 1960s.

Marcus though, of course had the entire advanced tech one could want and need. He kept important stuff to himself and no one knew about it, beside Eno that is.

Every now and then Marcus would let a little piece of new tech escape—to sooth the masses as it were – and at those times, he of course took all the credit and the subsequent adulation.

The planet was strewn with coliseum arenas. Marcus's earlier dream of having such was now fulfilled. Everything to anything filled the stadiums for the enjoyment of the people; every major sport: football, baseball, soccer, hockey, rugby, cricket, the list went on and on.

There were also the blood sports that gained the widest attention of all. Gladiatorial combat to the death and the DSFL (the Death Surprise Football League) were two such 'sports'. No one ever knew when a DSFL game would take place, thus the surprise – even to the players! The planet had not seen any type of war – civil or otherwise – since Marcus took dominion. He did away with countries and borders for the most part. What was once recognized as countries were now all provinces of Rome. Indeed, the planet was now deemed Rome not Earth.

Each province had its own little hierarchy overseen by its Governor placed there by Marcus himself. Should a dispute arise between say, neighboring provinces, where once upon time war would ensue, now all disputes would be solved by mortal combat in the arena with each presiding Governor – regardless of age, or whether male or female – would settle the disagreement one-on-one to the death.

It was always a ratings winner.

Ruban and Blulay detested the violence and the sheer inhumanity of it all. However, in some ways this version of the Earth was superior to their own but it just wasn't the Earth they had come to know and love.

There was no arms race, no nuclear arsenals, no hunger, no environmental problems, no racial issues, no unemployment and illness was kept to a minimum. Many of these very issues that plagued their Earth had been a deterrent for the Guild when considering Earth to be eligible for entry into the Guild. This new Earth though…

They knew from what Neb had told them that Marcus's initial plan was to take over the *whole* of time and space. When that plan failed, his second time scheme (which Neb thwarted) only involved taking over the Earth – which he now seemingly had achieved. Yet, as with all megalomaniacs, once they have their minds made up, achieving their main goal seldom ever changes. They may veer off in a different direction but the end result is what really matters in their twisted minds.

With the Velexian Viper Reversal Vortex Bubble in place, Ruban and Blulay felt comfortable enough to believe that Marcus's Rome would go no further than it already had.

They thought of Neb often and hoped he would stay away but they had a feeling he wouldn't.

5

Neb and LeBeau had returned to the Photon Ledger after unsuccessfully trying to find 'The Lost Door' with Gnits. All three had scanned every inch of Hall RV2C where the book was last placed or where it was supposed to have last been placed.

Gnits was not a happy librarian at all, it was incomprehensible to him that this book, or indeed any book at all, could be misplaced and not found in the great Library of Atiox. But not even a *digital* copy could be found. Gnits promised to keep looking into it and would send word to Neb as soon as he could.

Now on the bridge, Neb and LeBeau were waiting for the Professor to arrive back so they could start preparing to leave for Earth.

"I wonder where he has gotten to?" LeBeau sat down at the helm console and began inputting the coordinates that Neb gave him to navigate the Photon Ledger through the secret Triopelian space/time corridors.

"Well if he doesn't get here soon, we will leave without him," said Neb.

"Leave without me!"

LeBeau looked up from the console to see the Professor standing in the doorway to the bridge.

"How did you do that?" LeBeau quizzed his old friend.

"Do what?" Pheet replied, pulling a carrot stick out of his pocket and munching on it.

Neb looked the Professor up and down. There was no one on the bridge when they arrived back but himself and LeBeau but Pheet had suddenly appeared as if out of nowhere.

"Why, I have been here for hours," Pheet replied.

"Hours!" LeBeau stood. "We spent the last three hours looking for that damn book—and oh, by the way, it doesn't seem to want to be found. Thank you very much," LeBeau protested.

"Really?" Pheet answered.

"So Professor, where have you been?" Neb asked.

"I was having dinner and bumped into two old acquaintances. I couldn't just leave them, could I? That would have been downright rude of me," Pheet answered.

Hmm? LeBeau thought. Who could he have run into?

Neb walked over to Pheet and began sniffing at his breath.

"What are you doing?" Pheet took a step back from Neb.

"Just checking, Professor," replied Neb and then said to LeBeau, "He's ok."

Neb thought the Professor might have started drinking again and that was the last thing he needed, an imbibed Pheet.

Everyone involved in this mission had to be able to provide a tip top performance with clear minds at all times— their thinking abilities were key to the success of the mission. Marcus was no fool and the last thing Neb needed was a fool on the team.

"Incoming message," the ship's Interface interrupted.

"On screen," said Neb.

"Howdy all!" Purell's and Kel's faces filled the screen.

"Howdy?" LeBeau cocked an eyebrow.

"It is an expression of 'How do you do'," Kel answered.

"What?" Pheet barked.

"They are saying hello," Neb turned to LeBeau and Pheet to explain.

"Well, why didn't they just say that in the first place," Pheet said, unamused.

"HELLO EVERYONE!" Purell waved excitedly.

Pheet waved back then caught himself doing so and lowered his hand.

"We should be in view of Mastic 4 within the hour," Kel relayed.

"Very good," Neb replied. "We are in the process of starting our calculations for the jump."

"I must say, sir," Purell began, "my data nodes are overjoyed at the prospect of our mission to save the Earth from tyranny and villainy. It gives me goosebumps – if I could have goosebumps. I think you will be pleased with the upgrades that both Kel and I have had-thanks to you no less, Neb," Purell finished.

"What is he talking about? What kind of upgrades?" LeBeau asked Neb.

"Neb has been so good as to have our data processors Triopelian supersized with a litany of information spanning all of Earth's past, present and future," Kel answered for Neb.

"Future?!" Both Pheet and LeBeau were taken aback.

"Yes," Kel replied. "Based on what we know thus far on parallel conundrums we can now ascertain the possible outcome should the Velexian Viper Reversal Vortex Bubble burst—and so, in effect, infect the rest of the universe."

"And let me tell you, it might get a little messy," Purell added, in a very downcast mode.

"Triopelian supersized?" LeBeau turned to Neb.

"I owed it to them, didn't I?" Neb answered. "After all they saved my life back on Marine. Their upgrades have incorporated not just Earth's history but also the history of all other known worlds throughout all of the universe (or universes!). I gave the Bio Lab techs a day off before we left and did the upgrades myself. Even though all of this information is now embedded in their data processors, accessing it is another story. One does need a failsafe should they fall into the wrong hands. For now though, all they need to know about the Earth has been activated."

"Such a clever fellow, isn't he?" Purell remarked.

"He is," Kel nodded to her robotic counterpart.

Neb still wasn't used to Kel's and Purell's new symbiotic relationship and wasn't sure if he ever would be. At first, he and the Bio Lab techs thought the fusing caused by Airhert would be temporary.

"After all, they are *just* androids," one of the techs had said, which landed the tech in some hot water with Neb who assigned the tech lavatory cleaning duties for a couple of weeks. This actually turned out quite well in the long run as the tech improved all waste stations by 200 percent. You see, for the most part when guests are transfigured that does not mean that their bodily evacuations are transfigured too. The tech was able to devise – or invent as you like – a slipstream vaporizer that conflated the waste into minute particles that actually gave the Casino an extra boost in its fuel cells. Suffice to say, the tech was so happy (as was Tict and Neb) that she decided to change professions and was promoted to 'Head of Waste Management' for Halley's Casino.

As well, she did thusly apologize to Neb and Mr Tict for the remark about Kel and Purell.

She also actually became a close friend of Desfannie 417...

After separating Kel's and Purrel's structural body frames it was assumed that if their individual data components were intact then there should be no problem while reconstructing any burnt out data nodes. However, what was found flabbergasted everyone. Not only did they not find any dead nodes – they found new ones.

The only explanation Neb could think of (and one he kept to himself) was that they were evolving. And why not? Androids had been around for as long as the Casino – and who knew how long a time before that?

He wondered if Kel and Purell knew?

Neb let Kel and Purell believe too, that there was a failsafe mechanism implanted, when in fact there was none. He had a theory and wanted to see if it would come true.

"Looking forward to seeing you all again in the flesh," Kel waved out from the screen.

"Flesh! That's a good one," Purell retorted.

"Very good, Kel," said Neb, waving back, "we await your arrival. Neb out."

"Such a thoughtful fellow," Purell was heard to say as they faded from the view screen.

As smart as Kel and Purell were, they were also like children, Neb thought and smiled.

"So – new and improved, eh?!" LeBeau remarked.

"Yep," Neb replied.

"I don't see why we need them. Androids this. Androids that! La. La. La, La. La," Pheet said, as he plonked himself down at his science console.

"What was that?" Neb looked over to the Professor.

The Professor didn't hear Neb or didn't want to; he was still in shock at meeting Kcils Ecarg after all these years. And The Big Fish – well, that was another story!

"Are you ok Gabriel?" LeBeau whispered over to his old friend, "You seem a little out of sorts."

Pheet looked up from his console, blank faced – staring at LeBeau.

"Gabriel?" LeBeau was getting a little worried.

Neb, though not eavesdropping, could not help overhearing their exchange.

He decided to remain silent.

It took Pheet a couple of minutes to answer LeBeau and all the while his deadpan face glared out, as if looking right through LeBeau.

"I bumped into Kcils Ecarg at the diner," Pheet finally awoke.

"Kcils Ecarg!" LeBeau gasped as goose pimples ran up and down his arms.

"Who's Kcils Ecarg?" Neb turned around to face the Professor.

Pheet tried to pay no attention to Neb's question. Instead, he swerved his chair around back to his science console and started inputting imaginary data.

"I think you touched on a vein there, Neb," LeBeau walked over.

"Me? I just asked him a question!" Neb replied.

"Yes, yes I know. It was a long time ago and the Professor still hasn't got fully over it," said LeBeau. "Kcils Ecarg is an old girlfriend of the Professor's".

"Girlfriend?" It took a minute or so to register with Neb. His eyes widened as he looked back at Lebeau. "A girlfriend?!"

"Sorry," Neb called out to the Professor who was still ignoring him.

"How long has it been?" Neb whispered to LeBeau.

"I think close to over 100 years."

"Over 100 years!" Neb bellowed then covered over his mouth as Pheet looked over at Neb and LeBeau, staring in Neb's direction.

"What?" asked the Professor.

"Nothing. Everything is honky dory." They both waved over at the same instance.

"I am going to head down to the laboratory if that is ok with you," Pheet rose and left the bridge.

"Testy, isn't he," Neb remarked.

"Yeah, well, old flames – some old flames – can have that effect on you, especially Kcils Ecarg," LeBeau said as they watched the door swoosh closed behind the Professor.

"I'll say," Neb shook his head. "I thought something was off when he just suddenly appeared on the bridge. You can fill me in later on this mysterious Kcils Ecarg but for now I don't want to waste any more time. Kel and Purell will be here soon and once they are aboard, we are out of here, pronto!" said Neb.

"Oh she's quite the story – that Kcils Ecarg is," LeBeau said under his breath.

"What was that?" Neb asked.

"Oh nothing," LeBeau smiled and slowly walked back to his console.

Kel and Purell soon arrived, docking with The Photon Ledger, where it was now in orbit around the fifth moon (known as Hacckett) of Mastic 4's nine moons.

****

Gnits was still searching the Library on Hacckett for 'The Lost Door'. Neb decided to make one last trip down to the moon before heading off for Earth.

"No luck eh?" Neb sighed.

It is quite remarkable that it has not been found or even located Neb," Gnits shared. "I did some extra researching on this book 'The Lost Door' and it seems to refer to parallel or mirror worlds of myth and legend – much like Airhert on Marine," Gnits laughed.

"Yes, myth and legend," Neb half smiled.

"You know Neb, we librarians don't usually ask our clients their business as to why they are looking for a particular book and the like – but just out of curiosity…" Gnits paused, looking up at Neb inquiringly.

Neb was taken a little aback at Gnits query and wasn't sure how to answer. He did not want to give anything away that might then be gossiped about to another fellow librarian, then to another – and so on and so on.

"It's for a movie I am planning on shooting," Neb replied.

"A movie?" Gnits was puzzled, wondering what a movie was. "One other thing I found, Neb. The Professor wasn't the only one to have taken a look at this book."

"Really?" Neb asked. "Who might the other be?"

"We only have the initials logged and it was quite a long time ago – 500 years to be exact."

"Wow, a book taken out twice in 500 years, I would say that is rare, isn't it?" Neb pondered as he asked Gnits.

Gnits then read out loud the initials, "'M. A'."

Neb didn't react; instead he thanked Gnits for all of his hard work and asked Gnits to contact him ASAP should the book be found. And with that Neb left.

Neb now did not think the book would be found.

****

Outside of the Earth, the universe continued as it was. As usual no one paid much attention to the blue planet that was now quarantined by The Guild at Tict's request, through TeeceeFore. However, within any political type body, rumor will inevitably swirl and leak out.

"'Loose lips sink ships' comes to mind," Tict told TeeceeFore.

Neb was aware that this may well happen, thus time was of the essence – as only Neb could appreciate, he having always to battle with its variances.

What was it about time?

Neb sat alone in his quarters aboard The Photon Ledger thinking yet again about the question. Why was time always at the heart of the matter? Why couldn't time be just left alone, to let itself play out, to unveil whatever time had in store for him – others – everybody? How was it that time could be manipulated in the first place? And why did it seem he was always a player in these schemes that time machinated? How many times could he actually save time or did time really need to be saved?

Only time would tell…

Neb knew his parents were alive and safe for the time being – he could feel it. As LeBeau might say, 'it was a Triopelian thing'. He laughed to himself.

And what about the Triopelians?

They must have some kind of inkling as to what was going on in the greater universe and with Earth, it wasn't like them not to know.

Would they swoop in at the last minute and save the day as when they did with Membob Koop? He got the feeling from his parents that there would be no interference or intervention this time around – or were his parents trying to tell him something else? Why did they tell him to stay away from the Earth?

So many variables. So many outcomes. So much to think about.

Was this 'The Lost Door' the opening to reversing Marcus's plan or just the beginning?

Did 'M. A.' mean Marcus Attitpius took out the book 500 years ago?

But who wrote this book? Where did it come from in the first place?

Neb closed his eyes and leaned back in his chair, he began to clear his mind and to focus on the 'here and now' and not the 'then and why'.

He thought about something Airhert had told him before he left for the Plexus Rim.

Each planet has its own tri dimensional span; Nixibonc and Marine were thrown together in a symbiosis not of their own doing.

Could Earth's own tri dimensional span hold the key?

Would not a parallel world and its counterpart somehow reverse each other?

It was indeed an equation to contemplate.

As Neb went deeper and deeper into meditation his body, spirit and mind relaxed so much he did not know he was floating above his chair.

Yes, another Triopelian thing.

Neb also did not realize that Kel had entered his quarters; she watched in fascination, marvelling at what she was witnessing. Who indeed was this Nebula Yorker? She quietly backed out of his room, leaving her trusted friend to himself and his gentle hovering.

Neb opened his eyes; he thought he felt a presence. Triopelian?

In an instant, he was back sitting in his chair, his mind completely refreshed and ready to take on the next task at hand. It was all or nothing – and nothing was not an option. With or without any Triopelian help, Neb would see this through. His parents' lives were at stake. The Earth, that he considered his home world more than Triopelia, was in peril. He knew what he had to do – he must keep a 'take-no-prisoners' attitude.

A change in tactics was required. If he wanted to defeat Marcus he had to start thinking like Marcus – as unsavory as that may be.

6

The Emperor Marcus Attitpius stood on the upper deck of the hangar, looking down at the work being done below. He grinned that evil grin he was so well known for.

Everything he had planned thousands of years ago was now coming to fruition. Mind you, there had been more than a few little interruptions by Tict, Neb and Lafil.

Lafil.

He let out a sigh. If only you could see me now father.

"You were no father of mine," he then spat out, loudly.

A few workers below heard Marcus venting his anger but supposed he was talking to someone and they continued on with their work.

Marcus looked down as finishing touches on his new ship were being conducted.

There were about 100 men running up and down the sides of a magnificent huge purple-sheened vessel, working frantically in order to have it ready for its inaugural launch 10 days hence: March 15th.

The Emperor did not take much notice of the date and those who thought 'The Ides of March' cursed. His brazen cockiness, as with all things, allowed him to challenge even history. Marcus took no historical note.

He had christened his ship 'The Anvilus'. It would forge ahead out into deep space bringing Rome and his vision, to the universe.

Marcus turned quickly on hearing footsteps behind him. He would usually have his Praetorian Guards with him but he kept them away from the hangar and its workings. They had been told it was a private temple for Marcus and Marcus alone; that only he, the Emperor, was allowed to enter.

"What do you think?" Emperor Marcus beamed with pride as Eno showed up.

"The Guild will not know what hit them," Eno, now the Proconsul of Australia, answered.

Marcus smirked and patted Eno on the back and as he did so Eno's mobile transfiguror flickered on and off, revealing his true lizard appearance for a brief moment.

Marcus gave Eno a slight swat to the left side of his head.

"You fool!" he lashed out. "How many times have I told you to have your mobile transfiguror updated?"

"Sorry, master," Eno stepped back, his head down, looking at the ground.

"You may well be able to go about as freely as you do in Australia – and YES, I have heard accounts of missing people out in the desert. Skins and bones, eh. But when you are here!" Marcus leered into Eno's terrified face.

"I sincerely apologize, master. It won't happen again," Eno replied fearfully.

"It better not, though it seems to happen over and over again with you, doesn't it? Why I keep you around is beyond me."

"Maybe…" Eno stopped, "…because I saved your life," Eno took three steps back.

Marcus glared at Eno. "You have a flair for reminding me of that, don't you? I guess that's why I like you, Eno. You are the pet I never had as a child."

Eno couldn't wait to get back to Australia.

Marcus turned and headed for the lift with Eno following a few steps behind him.

They entered the lift silently.

The doors closed and the lift ascended. Marcus looked down at Eno.

"When the doors open I want you to stay put."

"But master, all of the Proconsuls from all around the planet will be present, won't it look out of the ordinary if I am not there?" Eno protested a little.

"And what if your mobile transfiguror should fall offline again? How will I explain that? Eh? 'Sorry folks I forgot to tell you that Proconsul Eno is actually a being from another planet. Hide your bats, rats and cats.' No. The populace is not ready to know about the greater universe. Not just yet – but soon."

"I don't like cats," Eno muttered.

"What was that?" Marcus replied.

"Nothing, master," Eno pouted.

"Good, go and get it fixed now! Then come and join us."

"At once," Eno slipped in front of Marcus before the doors opened.

Marcus grabbed Eno, throwing him forcefully back against the walls of the lift.

"Not now stupid! After I make my entrance."

Marcus tugged at his toga and patted it down, making sure to brush away any creases.

The lift doors swooshed open. Marcus stepped out of the lift to a musical fanfare and applause. He was immediately flanked by 24 Praetorian Guards – 12 on each side of him – as he slowly walked down a flight of stairs between them.

One of the guards thought he saw Eno flicker between his humanoid and true form as the lift doors swooshed closed. He brushed it off to having too much wine the night before.

The Grand Receiving Hall applauded Emperor Marcus Attitpius. All 200 Proconsuls (201 once Eno returned), from around the globe were in attendance to hear the Emperor on this most auspicious day.

No one was sure why the Emperor had gathered everyone. (That is no one except Eno, of course.) Some thought the Emperor was going to either merge or do away with another province or perhaps add another new one to his Empire.

Or was he once again going to pit one Proconsul against the other when there was no need, to play out before the cameras and the planet for his own selfish pleasure?

To be summoned to Rome by Marcus was seldom (if ever) a good thing, as good things go.

The Grand Receiving Hall was actually the exact duplicate of the Senate of Rome though perhaps a tad larger – to add to Marcus's tad larger ego.

He had done away with the Senate when he overthrew Augustus. He had needed to time it just so, knowing that if he did not, Lafil would once again appear as would Nebula Yorker. Suffice to say that he was able to manipulate the time stream by using Eno's ship that he encased in a time bubble on the moon.

Marcus had begun introducing bits and pieces of technology for his citizens' use from that time onward. Television and radio came first and then, every ten years or so he would introduce something else new to sooth the populace – but never too much, in case it would somehow work against him.

There were no factories or even hired labor to manufacture any one of these new gadgets. They would instead just suddenly appear and frequently enough to have everyone eating out of Marcus's hands. The people believed he was doing all that he could, as a god should, to look after them.

"Good citizens of Rome," Marcus addressed his Proconsuls. "Thank you so much for agreeing to my invitation today."

Marcus now sat centered for all to see in the round.

"You may all be wondering why I called you here. Be assured, it is not to have anyone thrown into the arena," Marcus laughed, as a sigh of relief washed over the room.

Marcus felt it and did not approve of it.

He paused as his Praetorian guards walked over and proceeded to guard each exit.

"Gentlemen, let us not waste time on quips. The point of the matter is this," Marcus snapped his fingers.

The room went dark. Everyone had a bad feeling.

A hologram appeared. Now no one had ever seen a hologram, it was one of the many technological advancements that Marcus had kept to himself – but now all of that was about to change. All eyes focused on the hologram.

It was The Anvilus – now hung in midair and slowly turning for all to see. The Proconsuls were in awe (as were the guards!), they were not sure what was more impressive – the hologram itself or the vessel that was appearing as a hologram.

Marcus remained silent for some minutes, to let everyone take it in.

"What is it?" the echo murmured throughout the Grand Receiving Hall.

Soon, The Anvilus was replaced by the Earth spinning in space. The stars started to race by as the hologram projected deep space. Stars, planets, giant gas nebulas, swirling faraway galaxies all swooped and finally a bright luminous icy comet sped by and exploded.

The lights of the Grand Receiving Hall started to inch back on as the hologram faded.

Marcus stood up and as he did so the floor of the Grand Receiving Hall began to retract revealing The Anvilus far below.

Everyone stood, not sure what to make of it all. They all looked at each other confused and somewhat speechless as to what they had all just witnessed.

Even the guards were frightened. What did this all mean?

Eno then arrived, having made sure his mobile transfiguror was now functioning 100 percent. He entered the hall and made a beeline for Marcus who had not noticed his arrival. Two of the guards stopped Eno before he reached the Emperor, which set some of the other Proconsuls to thinking that Eno was going to attack Marcus. (Which some had already thought about and some – unknown to those others – were thinking about and planning to do.)

Marcus finally caught sight of Eno and waved him over. Without thinking (as he did at times), Eno hovered over the gaping hole and then over to Marcus.

Marcus looked up at his invitees as Eno hovered; most of their mouths were agape as they had never seen anyone hover let alone anyone wearing hover shoes.

Had it been another time, Marcus would have down right killed Eno on the spot but as he watched Eno glide and the Proconsuls' expressions on their faces, he felt it all fell right into his plans.

Three-quarters of the way across the open floor Eno realized what he had done and was *still* doing but he could not stop his forward progression. He thought he was done for, for sure. He reached Marcus and stopped. To his surprise Marcus patted Eno on the back and said, "Well done."

Eno wasn't sure what to make of Marcus's response. Was he just toying with him or perhaps he would deactivate his shoes and let him fall into the hole, for all to see? Eno waited but Marcus did nothing of the sort.

"Friends!" Marcus shouted out. "What you have just witnessed is the future – your future – our future –" he paused, "– *my* future."

"Today, Rome reaches out to touch the heavens, the stars above and beyond. Your Emperor has waited for this great day for as long as he has had breath. Today, Rome finally achieves what she has always wanted – the Universe!"

Murmuring and whispering began rippling through the room as Marcus watched in glee. Eno stood by Marcus's side wondering how it was now going to play out.

"Yes gentlemen, space travel!" Marcus opened his arms wide while walking back to the center of the hall, the floor now closed.

"Is he mad?!" the Proconsul of Greater Britain, Gaius Rulle, leaned over to Timus Gra, Proconsul of Russia.

"Quiet," Timus shushed, "he will hear you."

"I don't care," Gaius replied back, with an air of defiance.

"Gaius! Ruban told us to expect the unexpected. Granted space flight is totally so! Why are you so upset?" Timus Gra tried to calm his friend down.

But Gaius Rulle ignored Timus Gra and made his way down to the floor.

"Gaius, no!" Timus Gra called out to his friend – but it was too late.

Marcus watched Gaius Rulle's descent onto the floor, it was a most unprecedented move on Gaius Rulle's part. No one had ever seen this happen before.

Was Gaius Rulle challenging the Emperor?

A hush swept through the hall, as all eyes followed Gaius.

The Praetorian Guards inched closer to Marcus as they too took notice of Gaius Rulle. Marcus waved the guards off with a nod. They froze, awaiting their Emperor's next command.

Gaius Rulle walked quickly toward Marcus without pause. Marcus stood his ground.

"SIC SEMPER TYRANIS!" screamed Gaius Rulle as he pulled out a dagger from beneath his toga, now rushing toward Marcus.

Marcus rolled his eyes. Really? Where have I seen this before? He mouthed to himself, yawning.

Every one of the Proconsuls was on their feet, some wishing for Gaius Rulle's success, others horrified at what they were witnessing.

A blue stream of light suddenly whistled out, hitting Gaius Rulle head on. He let out a scream that lasted all but seconds, though long enough for everyone to hear and to feel fear as the now ex-Proconsul of Britain dissolved in front of them all.

Marcus smiled, returning his phaser into his toga.

7

Ruban and Blulay sat in stunned silence, reading the secret communication from Timus Gra.

"What was Gaius thinking?" Blulay looked at her husband in sheer disbelief.

"Humans," Ruban said, shaking his head.

Ruban and Blulay had formed a small underground 5th column to keep an open ear and eye on all things Marcus. They knew it was only a matter of time before Marcus headed back into space and now with Timus Gra's message, all was verified.

For the time being Marcus was unaware of the Velexian Viper Reversal Vortex Bubble. This ignorance suited Ruban just fine but once Marcus found out about it, the jig would be up for he would then know that other forces were in play on the ground – and perhaps waiting in space too.

Then there would be an all-out war to find not just them but any other aliens also trapped within the parallel conundrum.

Oddly enough however, he and Blulay did not meet or find any aliens themselves, even though they knew they existed as they also knew Marcus's 'secret' prison existed.

Ruban and Blulay had an idea that Marcus was enslaving these beings to help with his ship building. He was using their advanced knowledge of such procedures by promising them their freedom once they were done and back out into space.

Though again, with the Velexian Viper Reversal Vortex Bubble in place that was going to be a tough sell once they were sky born.

Sooner or later everything was going to collide for better or for worse.

They both wondered – and as long as Neb stayed away – they hoped and prayed for the better outcome.

If they could somehow diffuse Marcus, there might be a chance to bring some kind of normality back to the Earth though even that might take hundreds if not thousands of years.

Or could the clock be turned back?

"We need to get a look at that ship," Ruban said to Blulay.

"At least we know where it is now – under the old Senate."

"Then what?" asked Blulay. "Do we try to sabotage the ship? Or take it for ourselves?"

"Well first, I want to see what type of tech is aboard the vessel. We then might be able to determine what beings

Marcus has locked up and then we can find a way to help them escape and to join our little party," Ruban replied.

"That is going to take a lot of effort and planning," Blulay replied.

"Did Timus Gra give an indication of when Marcus plans to launch the ship?" she added.

"No he did not. But if Marcus felt so comfortable as to release this news to his Proconsuls, I imagine he isn't going to wait much longer.

"At least we have the Velexian Viper Reversal Vortex Bubble to stay him off for the time being." Ruban stood up and walked over to the console and turned on the camera, showing the bubble in place around the earth. The Earth's bottom half sat in a trans-luminous bubble while the upper half of the planet looked exposed. However, an invisible ring encompassed the whole of the bubble keeping the parallel conundrum at bay.

Blulay joined Ruban. She stood by his side, her head resting on his shoulder as they both looked at the screen.

"It's hard to believe that time inside of the bubble is locked as if nothing has happened and that the universe is unaware of what is taking or *has* taken place here on the Earth. Besides Nebula, no one knows," Blulay said sadly.

Ruban wrapped his arms around his wife, comforting her.

"What would happen if a vessel were to try and penetrate the bubble from the outside?" she asked, "What would be the effect to the bubble then?"

"The bubble would draw out the energy from any vessel, absorb it into its matrix and actually intensify the strength of the bubble. The ship would disintegrate of course. On the other hand a ship trying to penetrate from the inside would have the reverse effect it would just bounce off and go nowhere," Ruban replied.

"So no one gets in or out," Blulay sniffed.

"That is about the size of it, it would seem. But..." Ruban paused.

"But what?" Blulay asked.

"This is only the second known deployment of a Velexian Viper Reversal Vortex Bubble that I know of. The first was breached by some unknown force and caused the planet to implode on itself before it was able to expand out. It's all here in this book."

"What book?" Blulay asked.

Ruban opened a drawer beneath the console and pulled out a slim book that he then handed to his wife.

"'The Lost Door'," Blulay read out loud from the old rustic cover.

"Where did you get it?" she asked.

"I don't know," Ruban replied. "I found it in The Traghip years and years ago. How it found its way into the escape pod, is beyond me."

Blulay leafed through the book. It was only about 100 pages in volume.

"How then did you know how to deploy the bubble? Did the book give instructions?"

"That's the funny thing. No, it did not. As I said I found the book years ago – decades in fact, the more I think about it. After I had read the book I scanned our Triopelian data archives to find any history of parallel infringements that may have taken place."

"What did it say?" Blulay grasped Ruban's hand intensely.

"As I remember, it read that the only known occurrence of a parallel conundrum took place on the planet of Anthem."

"Anthem?" Blulay cocked an eyebrow.

"The planet of Anthem was located in the Plexus Rim Galaxy, its closest neighbors being Pratt, Dirk and Lerxst. Anthem was part of the Quadopeleian of planets – made up of Pratt, Dirk and Lerxst."

Blulay's eyes almost bolted out of her head. She could not believe what Ruban was saying.

"Quadopeleian?" Blulay asked, stunned. "Why have I – we – never heard of this before?"

"Are you sure, Blulay?" Ruban replied. "Think back to your childhood days. Remember that song we were taught in pre-school?"

Blulay thought about it and slowly began to sing.

One, two, three, four, three, two, one

Four was found no more

Where did it go/where did it hide

Forever away from our eyes.

Blulay stopped and looked up at her husband who was nodding his head up and down.

"Yes dear, they were talking about Anthem."

"Why would something as important as this be kept from us?" Blulay asked, realizing the importance of the song. "And all these years I thought it was about flower pettles and seed replanting!"

"Well in some ways that still holds true," said Ruban. "If you think about it, Anthem's demise set new protocols, when it came to terraforming new planets, expansion and the like. Planting new seeds through time and space exploration, as we did, when we came upon the Earth all those years ago."

Blulay thought about what Ruban had just relayed. She thought deeply about his words as she paced the cave.

"That still leaves a myriad of questions as to how Anthem slipped into a parallel conundrum and why it was hidden from us in – of all things – a childrens' song!" Blulay stomped her feet angrily.

"Slow down there girl!" Ruban laughed.

"Girl? Hmm I like the sound of that," she replied.

"You'll always be my girl," Ruban gave her a peck on the lips.

"Though, to answer your questions, when I came across the archive I had to ask myself the same sorts of things. From what I could fathom it seemed as though the information on Anthem was imputed into the The Traghip's data archive, just as the time and space anomaly hit us back in 1910 and that's what stranded us on Earth. Also imputed, was the blue print of the Velexian Viper Reversal Vortex Bubble and how to deploy it," Ruban finished.

"Why didn't you tell me about this before, Ruban?" Blulay asked.

"At the time I thought it was some kind of joke. I tried to find any other data on Anthem but nothing came up so I let it pass, thinking it was a piece of galactic fiction. That is until seven months ago, when the birds stopped singing."

"But how was it you were able to deploy the Bubble so quickly?" Blulay asked, wonderingly.

"Well, that's another funny thing. It was already set up and ready to deploy when I opened the data archive and running across the screen were the words: 'Break Glass in

Case of Emergency'. I broke the glass – so to speak – pressed the button and up it went!"

"Providence?" Blulay asked.

Ruban shrugged his shoulders and thought that something more than parallel conundrums were at play but he couldn't put his finger on what that something was.

"Well, let's be thankful to whoever did supply us with that information," said Blulay, falling into Ruban's arms.

8

Neb, Professor Pheet and LeBeau sat in the lounge area adjacent to the bridge where Kel and Purell were busy conducting tests regarding the Velexian Viper Reversal Vortex Bubble. They were employing simulations as to how to penetrate the bubble.

Neb, the Professor and LeBeau were all enjoying a meal in relative quietness, although each was wondering what the other was thinking about. Which was odd actually, since – for example – Professor Pheet was actually thinking about the stowaways that were hidden in the lower deck of the Photon Ledger. They being of course, Kcils Ecarg and See-Ess – aka, The Big Fish.

At the sound of the bridge doors swooshing open, everyone turned to see Kel and Purell walk into the lounge. They made their way over to the three seated companions and Kel laid down a small coin-like object on the table in front of Neb that was in fact a hologram receiver.

"Active," Kel said aloud.

The hologram receiver shot up a projected hologram of the Earth sitting in and surrounded by the Velexian Viper Reversal Vortex Bubble. They all watched as the Photon Ledger made its appearance, as it approached to try and penetrate the bubble.

Time after time they watched the simulation fail as each time the Photon Ledger folded into the bubble and disintegrated.

"How disappointing," LeBeau sighed.

"Indeed!" Purell agreed with his friend.

Neb stood without saying a word. He replayed the simulations a few more times, making mental notes. Each time he replayed the hologram, he stood and watched from a different angle of the room.

"What are you thinking, Neb?" Kel inquired, knowing that Neb was trying to work it all out in his head. She had come to know all too well Neb's reluctance to not finding an answer. She found Neb's tenacity always refreshing.

Neb rubbed his chin, as he usually did when deep in thought. Though, as he was doing it this time, his chin started getting longer and longer – like Pinocchio's nose!

"What in the…?" LeBeau pointed to Neb. Only to find his finger stretching out, like a rubber band.

The Professor was, at this point, fast asleep.

"Encountering a spacial fluidity dimension graviton field," the ship's Interface alerted.

"Fascinating!" Purell quipped as his lips seemed to drop to the floor.

"Indeed," Kel replied, as they both swayed from side to side.

The Photon Ledger had now entered a space time conduit on its way to Earth.

"I think we are on our way now." Neb's eyes rolled about, then seemed to pop in and back out as he looked out of the port window of the lounge.

The ship shook violently as it weaved its way through the twirling void. At one point, Neb thought the ship was going to pull itself apart. Just as he thought it would though, the ship came to a soft halt. What seemed like seconds had actually been over a four-hour jump through time and space.

"Look!" Kel pointed over to the port window.

The Photon Ledger had parked itself and was now orbiting the dark side of the moon. From this position they could clearly see the Earth hanging in space, encased in the clear gloss of the Velexian Viper Reversal Vortex Bubble.

Purell, soon followed by LeBeau and Neb, stood by Kel and all four gazed out in awe at the Earth.

"Professor!" LeBeau called out. "You have to see this!"

A loud belching echoed through the lounge. The four turned to see the Professor down on his knees. He was grabbing his stomach, in wrenching pain.

Purell hurried over to help the Professor and did a quick med scan as he lifted him up and back onto his chair.

"It's ok," Purell said to the others. "He's experiencing a temporal fidget. He'll be fine, just give him a few minutes to adjust."

"Thank you, Purell. Though, what just happened?" Pheet asked groggily.

Before Purcell could answer the Professor, the Interface cut in.

"Intruder alert! Intruder alert! On deck three."

Pheet looked up at Purell and said. "Oh shit!"

"What was that, Professor?" LeBeau came walking over.

"I think he may have shit himself," Purell backed away, holding his nose.

"I didn't shit myself!" Pheet shouted at Purell.

"Intruder alert! Intruder alert!" The Interface bellowed once more.

"What? How? Where?" Neb called out to the Interface.

Just then the doors to the lounge swooshed open and out stumbled Kcils Ecarg and See-Ess (aka: The Big Fish).

"What in the name of…?" Neb's jaw dropped. "Who are they?"

"Oh shit!" The Professor muttered under his breath again.

"What was that, Professor?" Purell asked, taking yet another step backwards.

"What was *that*?" See-Ess jumped up and down, getting his space legs back in order. "That was something else. Talk about your turbulence," said See-Ess.

Kcils Ecarg's fuzzy ears popped up. "Meow!" she said, agreeing with See-Ess. "That was one hell of a ride!"

"Gabby!" Kcils said, suddenly noticing the Professor, who was not looking quite himself.

Gabby? Neb looked over to Pheet and back again over to Kcils.

What is going on here? Neb thought.

LeBeau turned about to face these intruders. He recognized both their voices though he wished he didn't.

"If I wasn't seeing it with my own two eyes," See-Ess cried out happily as he walked over to LeBeau. He gave him a great big bear hug.

Neb was now definitely confused and not amused. "This isn't the Love Boat!" Neb was heard to say.

"Elvis Cash you old sod! How long has it been?" See-Ess embraced LeBeau, almost knocking the wind out of him.

"Elvis Cash?!" Kel, Purell and Neb all said at the same time aloud.

"OK .OK. OK. OK. OK. OK! What is going on here?" Neb yelled at the top of his voice, so loudly that it made the room feel like it vibrated.

See-Ess let go of LeBeau and LeBeau slumped beside the Professor.

"I don't like your tone of voice," See-Ess turned to Neb.

"Really?!" replied Neb, sarcastically.

"Do you mind telling me who you both are and how you happen to be on this ship?"

"Gabby offered us a ride to Marine. Though by the looks of it I don't think we are anywhere near Marine," Kcils interjected, now looking out the port window. "Hey that's a nice looking watery planet out there. Still, I don't think it's Marine, too much land."

See-Ess charged forward, making a beeline for Neb but Kel stepped in his way and stopped him. He bounced off of her and found himself on his ass.

"Damn androids," See-Ess picked himself up.

LeBeau took hold of See-Ess's arm. "Take it easy big fellow, Neb's not your enemy."

See-Ess almost threw LeBeau across the room but stopped when he saw it was him."Sorry, Elvis. I didn't see you there for a second. My apologies."

"Apologies accepted," LeBeau nodded.

LeBeau called over to Neb. "Let me take this one."

"Sure Elvis, why not? Is there anything else anyone wants to tell me, that they haven't yet told me?" Neb asked, looking about the room.

"I believe the Professor may or may not have shit himself," Purell offered up.

"Not now!" Pheet glared over at Purell.

Kel stood beside Neb and whispered into his ear. "And two boiled eggs."

"Indeed," Neb cocked his left brow in response and forced a smile.

Nothing surprised Neb anymore when it came to Pheet. He had learnt not to be, after going through the last fiasco with the Professor. However, now wasn't the time for more surprises. Then again – consequences and coincidences seemed to count for something always.

"Where are we, by the way?" asked See-Ess.

"You – we – are presently hidden in the shadow of the dark side of the Earth's Moon—in the Milky Way Galaxy, to be precise," Kel answered.

"Why did you tell him that?" Neb asked, a little perturbed. "He doesn't need to know anything."

"Earth!" See-Ess mused. "I thought Earth was off limits. Something about quarantine, or something to that effect."

"How does he know that?" Neb turned to Pheet.

"I didn't say anything," Pheet said.

"I didn't get your name," See-Ess queried Neb.

"Nebula Yorker," Purell answered for Neb, his android chest pumped out.

"What are you doing?" Neb turned to Purell.

"Was it something I said, sir?" Purell tilted his head robotically. It was almost as if he did it purposely, to egg Neb on. Neb wasn't sure.

"Oh yes. I've heard of you," See-Ess paused. "Assistant Concierge of Halley's Casino, I believe. You have a very fine reputation, Mr. Yorker." See-Ess walked over to Neb and held out his hand.

Neb wasn't sure what to make of See-Ess, yet. He automatically shook See-Ess's hand. It was something that came with the job. Sometimes he wished he could stop but he couldn't. His parents had taught him to be always polite, regardless of the situation.

"Who knows," his father would tell him, "Any hand that you shake, even one you don't want to, might just be a life saver one day."

Neb gritted his teeth and nodded as they shook. "So, Mr. Ess what do you do for a living, if I may ask?" Neb asked diplomatically.

Before See-Ess could answer Purell blurted out.

"See-Ess. Aka… The Big Fish.

"Marinian.

"CEO of Big Fish Industries.

"Arrested and charged with 2199 counts of embezzling and racketeering, gambling, water fraud and bribery. Also, first prize winner of the Get A Foot Up Dancing School's inaugural championship – 'Two Step Three Step Back Flip Blow Out Dancing Contest'."

"Ah. Those were the days," See-Ess smiled proudly.

"Which days were those?" Neb wondered out loud.

"Why all, of course," See-Ess laughed, giving Neb a good hard slap on his back.

Neb was not expecting the hard slap and lunged forward, falling into Kcils chest.

"Meow," purred Kcils, batting her eyes.

"I am sorry. Excuse me," Neb blushed red, getting his footing back.

"So Elvis? How is it you find yourself with this odd crew of misfits?" See-Ess turned back to LeBeau who had been thinking about how he was going to explain 'Elvis Cash' to Neb. LeBeau did the only thing he could think of and changed the subject back to the Professor.

"So tell us Gabriel, why did you offer See-Ess and Kcils Ecarg a ride again? Neb's waiting for an answer."

Neb was just about at his wits' end. Since meeting The Professor and LeBeau, he wondered if anyone was who they said they were, besides Kel and Purell. Then again, Neb wasn't sure if Kel and Purell knew who they were after they had been merged back on Marine. Hell, he was starting to wonder who he himself was – which wasn't good, no, not good at all.

"MOVE FORWARD," he heard his father's voice in his head. "MOVE FORWARD."

He took a deep breath, inhaled, then exhaled and then said, "Ok people. Listen up. We have a job to do, so let's do it. We will worry about our newly arrived guests later. If I had a brig, I would throw you all into it but as it is, I do not have that option. See-Ess and Kcils Ecarg. I would kindly ask you to stay out of our…," Neb paused. "My business for the time being; unless called for. I have come to realize that your being here is no mere coincidence – or at least that is my experience and I am usually correct in these types of matters."

"Really?" said See-Ess defiantly. "Who put you in charge?"

"See-Ess, now is not the time," LeBeau raised his voice.

See-Ess grumbled but heeded LeBeau.

Neb was taken aback at how quickly See-Ess listened to LeBeau; or was it 'Elvis Cash' who he paid attention to? Neb guessed that he would sooner or later find out what was up with that. But for the time being he was grateful for LeBeau's input and his take charge demeanor over this very large and scary type of being. Not that Neb was scared, as it were, it was just that he had a bigger fish to fry that awaited him on Earth, that being Marcus.

"Our first priority is finding a way through the Velexian Viper Reversal Vortex Bubble," Neb said.

"What's a Velexian Viper Reversal Vortex Bubble?" Kcils asked.

"That!" The Professor pointed out the lounge window toward the Earth. "See that blueish hue surrounding the planet."

"You mean the atmospheric ring?" Said Kcils.

"Why yes, Kcils," said a surprised Pheet. "Have you been studying again?" he asked.

"No," she replied. "See-Ess has been teaching me a thing or two about the universe you know."

"Has he?" Pheet looked over to See-Ess who was across the room chatting with LeBeau. "He is full of surprises, I will give him that," Pheet eyed The Big Fish.

Anyhow, Pheet went on in great length explaining the Bubble to Kcils and the reasons why Neb's parents activated it.

After the Professor had finished he thought he may have given Kcils too much information on the subject and asked her not to broach the topic with Neb. Though that would not stop her from telling See-Ess later on.

Neb returned to the bridge with Kel and Purell, leaving Pheet and LeBeau with See-Ess and Kcils in the lounge along with specific orders not to let them anywhere near the bridge.

"Understood," LeBeau assured Neb.

"You are quite the protean, aren't you, LeBeau," Neb said to LeBeau. "Or should I say – 'Elvis Cash'!"

"I can explain that, Neb," LeBeau quickly answered, almost red faced.

"I am sure you can and I look forward to hearing all about it," Neb replied, knowing it was going to be one story for the ages. "However, now is not the time. Just keep Pheet's guests out of our way. Ok?" Neb patted LeBeau on the shoulder with a smile then made his way to the bridge.

Neb wished John Lennon was around to speak with. He always found their chats to be soothing and helpful.

Purell and Kel sat side by side working the science console as Neb continued watching the simulated hologram of the Photon Ledger crashing into the bubble again and again.

"Anything?" Neb called out to Purell and Kel.

"Nothing, sir," Purell replied.

Kel and Purell whispered together, which Neb took notice of. It was so odd to see them working in tangent the way they now did. Since the merge and reconfiguring of their synthetic organismic frames, along with their internal mechanisms, Kel and Purell were as one. These were definitely not your Disneyland-type automatons he once saw with his parents when on a visit to the magical kingdom, he laughed to himself.

Disneyland, he reminisced. It all seemed so long ago and not even real anymore.

Kel turned around and looked at Neb – or Neb thought she was looking at him.

"What's that?!" she said

"What's what?" Purell asked.

"There on the moon," she pointed out towards the viewing screen.

Neb fixed his eyes on the screen. "I don't see anything."

"Neither do I," Purell affirmed.

Kel worked her console frantically, as frantically as only an android could.

She magnified the viewing screen until a spot of a gleam sparkled out from the moon.

Neb and Purell also saw it.

"What is it?" Neb walked over to the screen, staring down at it.

Purell ran his fingers over his console keypads looking up at Neb and Kel every now and then. His fingers danced over the console. Kel had never seen him work so fast and she was *very* impressed.

Finally, Purell stopped and looked down over the data that began to appear on his console screen. Kel leaned in to look as well. "Very good, Purell," she said.

"What? What is it?" Neb ran over to the two.

"It seems we have a cloaked ship on the moon," Purell answered.

"A cloaked ship?" Neb said, surprised.

"That's not all," Purell continued. "Look here!" he said to both Kel and Neb.

Neb's eyes couldn't believe what he was reading and seeing. Not only was it a cloaked ship but its fuel cell's signature originated from Halley's Casino.

"How can that be?" Kel asked, looking up at Neb, who was as equally puzzled by this revelation.

"Indeed," Purell also wondered.

"Another mystery," Neb said aloud.

"Perhaps we can transport it aboard the Photon Ledger and find out more about this mystery," Purell offered.

"Do it!" Neb ordered without hesitation.

Purell turned to Kel. "Be my guest, Kel."

"Why thank you good sir," Kel replied.

"Good lord," Neb rolled his eyes. "If you two were human I would tell you to get a room."

"Get a room, sir?" Purell asked, puppy-like.

"Never mind," Neb said. "Just begin the transport."

Kel began to code in the transport coordinates.

"I can't seem to get a lock on it," Kel tried again, as did Purell.

Just then See-Ess entered the room (although actually he had already been in the room for sometime, observing the goings on).

"You can't get a fix on it because it's sealed in a time welt."

"What?" All three said, looking up to see a smiling See-Ess standing over them.

"He's right," said Kel.

9

The Emperor paced back and forth on his luxurious palace garden balcony. In fact, it was the same balcony that saw Caesar Augustus and his wife Livia witness Marcus's and Neb's fall from the sky that night thousands of years ago.

The same sky that Marcus now stared up to.

A falling star did catch his eye as he gazed above. He sometimes wondered what omens they brought, if any at all. His now over four thousand years of existence, counting the before and after meeting of a one, Nebula Yorker, had caused Marcus to grow increasingly superstitious – though he would deny it.

Neb though, was the least of his worries for the time being. He knew that eventually they would meet again. Perhaps one day after he returned to space? Or of course, he could and might wait until 2061-2062 Earth time to settle accounts with Neb and Mr. Tict.

Tonight though his thoughts weighed on getting The Anvilus in order for its launch in the next few days. His Proconsuls for the most part seemed enthused. Though his encounter with the late Gaius Rulle of Great Britain did give him pause.

Where there was one dissenter, more were sure to follow.

Marcus should have known better. If history had taught him anything…

His guards were now tripled around the clock since the incident. Nothing was going to stop him in his ultimate pursuit.

He walked over to one of the supporting columns on the balcony and looked around to see if anyone was watching or nearby before pressing hard with his hand on the column. The floor opened and gave way to stairs leading down into a hidden vault. Marcus slowly descended the stairs as the floor above him closed.

A light automatically switched on as he reached the bottom and there in the center of the room was Livia (once wife of the Roman Emperor Augustus), encased in a clear glass suspended animation field.

"Good evening, my dear Livia," Marcus sneered up at her.

Livia was dressed all in purple from her veil on down to her feet. The look on her face was one of shock and terror.

Marcus had thought many times of releasing her but she was too much of a trophy to do anything more than think about it.

"So my dear," Marcus began. "Soon the dream that once was Rome will be spread throughout the known universe and how you laughed and spat in my face when I first told you so. Though, you quickly changed face when I slit the throat of your dear Augustus. Those were the days," Marcus laughed out loud, gleefully.

"If only you could see what I have done with the Empire! Rome is just not Rome but the world is Rome and I, its warm tender loving Mother and Father. You had your chance, Livia. Oh yes you did. Eternal youth could have been yours and the admiration of the galaxy," Marcus spat at her.

"But no. You called me a madman and insane, though that title was reserved for Caligula. What a shame it was when I had to have him executed along with your son Tiberius. Can you believe they were outed as secret Christians? Why yes, Livia. I too was shocked and surprised – just like everyone else. You should have seen the crowd that filled the Colloseum that day. It was full to the rafters and the spectacle was broadcast planet wide."

"What was that Livia?" Marcus pressed his ear up against the glass casing. "Planet wide? Oh that's right, it happened after your time, though not much after. It was the highest ratings ever. Although of course it did help that I gave everyone their very own brand new television to watch it all in glorious Technicolor. The blood was spectacular!" Marcus raised his hand to his chest. "I'm getting choked up just thinking about it.

"I do have it recorded; I'll have to show it to you one day. I think you will like it. Tiberius and Caligula were on fine form that day. I have never seen grown men cry and plead for mercy quite so passionately, as they both did. We even set up a voting line, asking our viewers if we should spare their lives. The stadium crowd won out over the viewing crowd."

"Just between you and I," Marcus looked about the room, even though there was no one else there. "I think it was fixed," he winked at her.

Beep. Beep. Marcus's wrist com went off.

"What is it?!" Marcus lashed out, knowing it was Eno.

"Your presence is needed immediately, master," Eno replied.

"Can't it wait? I'm in the middle of something."

"Sensors have picked up an incredible force field surrounding the planet."

"What kind of force field?" Marcus barked.

"We sent up six probes to investigate and each one vaporized on impact!" Eno said, alarmed.

"Why are sensors only detecting this now?" Marcus demanded.

"Our energies have been so focused on getting The Anvilus ready, master. As per your orders," Eno replied.

Marcus fumed.

There was a long silence as Marcus mused over the situation. "I will be right up."

Marcus closed off his wrist com as Eno said. "Up?"

"Well my dear," Marcus turned back to Livia, "The Empire beckons. We will see each other soon enough. I promise." Marcus kissed his hand and placed it on the glass in front of Livia's mouth.

As Marcus ascended the stairs a single tear ran down Livia's face.

10

Ruban slid into the underground hangar superstructure where The Anvilus sat unseen, waiting to be unveiled to the world. He wore a long white lab-type coat, white pants, white shoes and a cap to identify him as one of the many maintenance workers that were constantly running back and forth along the long hull of the ship. His plan was to get inside The Anvilus, find out what type of alien technology it was being fitted with and then to get out as quickly as he had got in.

He tapped the outside of the hull lightly and then placed his ear against it. Ruban's Triopelian auditory range picked up a Hiliponian resonance. The first thing Ruban thought was... A Hiliponian must be being held captive somewhere in the facility. But what would a Hiliponian being be doing on Earth before the pre-Marcus parallel conundrum event? Of course there were always a few off worlder's buzzing around Earth when they knew darn well that they shouldn't be but then again who was Ruban to judge.

"What if you get caught?" Blulay had said to her husband when they were working out the plan.

"Then my dear you find an isolated island somewhere and live out your life quietly."

"The hell I will!" Blulay shot back. "It's together or nothing."

Ruban assured her that he would be back without fail. He would have his personal body cloaking device at the ready, should he be in need. Getting in is always the easy part he said, it's getting out that sometimes can be tricky.

"You! What are you doing?" A voice barked out at Ruban from behind him, knocking him back to the present.

Ruban didn't move or flinch, his ear still stuck to the ship's hull. "Testing for echo," he responded. Ruban stood still, afraid to lift his head up from the ship. His eyes shifted though, to see a very large brute of a man staring down at him. It was Gecoo Chin, the Quarter Master of The Anvilus.

Of course Gecoo Chin had no idea what Ruban was up to. He was in a foul mood and Ruban just happened to be the first person he saw to vent his anger on.

"Testing for echo?" Gecoo Chin harshly replied.

"Yes, come listen for yourself," Ruban blurted out without thinking and immediately regretted it. To his complete and utter surprise, Gecoo Chin leaned up against the ship and pressed his ear to its side. He now faced Ruban, only inches apart from each other's nose.

"What's that cologne you're wearing? Ocean Breeze?" Ruban blurted out.

He was starting to sound like Neb. Or was Neb just like his father?

"What?" Gecoo Chin asked.

"You know," Ruban sniffed the air. "Scent. Fragrance. Aroma. Perfume. Toilet Water."

"Toilet Water!" Gecoo Chin lifted his ear from the ship's hull.

Now I have done it. Ruban cringed.

Gecoo Chin's fiery eyes burned through Ruban. Why did I have to say anything? Ruban now waited for the blow to come down.

"I'll have you know my wife bought me this cologne. It is called 'Mist of Avalon' and it's not cheap. Ocean Breeze is garbage," said Gecoo Chin. "You might as well splash fish sauce on yourself than Ocean Breeze!"

"My mistake. Sorry!" Ruban replied, his ear still against the hull.

Gecoo Chin looked Ruban up and down, "You're new here, aren't you?"

Before Ruban could open his mouth Gecoo Chin continued, "You must be one of the new recruits from Australia? I've heard about you lot. Always trying to be funny, eh." Gecoo Chin let out a hearty bellow, slapped Ruban on the back and walked away.

Did that just happen? Ruban stayed put for several minutes until he was sure Gecoo Chin was gone and out of sight.

I don't sound Australian, do I? Ruban was still trying to get his head round his encounter with Gecoo Chin. Ruban shook it off and went back to the task at hand. He now lightly tapped the hull. It made no sound whatsoever – to the human ear, that is.

"Definitely Hiliponian," he whispered to himself.

As he conducted more tests he heard footsteps heading his way. Perhaps Gecoo Chin had done some checking up on the new recruits?

A tall skinny man in a long white lab coat with an isopad in his hand walked briskly by Ruban, his head down – engaged in the figures on the small screen. He was about six feet away when he came to a direct stop, turned slowly and head up, he looked straight at Ruban. He moved forward a few steps, stopped again and sniffed the air. Ruban did not know what to make of it, they both stood silently, staring at each other until the tall skinny man cocked his left brow, smiled, turned and went on his way.

"This is indeed a strange day," Ruban said to himself aloud, thinking he was thinking it. He decided he had enough information for the time being. He took out a small metal vial and scraped off micro dustings from the ship into the vial. He was positive now of the Hiliponian resonance and wanted to get back to Blulay, who he knew would be worrying every second he was away.

He pocketed the vial and was about to leave when the tall skinny man showed up with two other tall skinny men in white lab coats.

"You're not human are you?" the first tall skinny man said.

"Take him," he said to the two others.

They grabbed Ruban and whisked him away.

11

Neb looked over to See-Ess. Didn't he ask the Professor to make sure his guests stayed put in the lounge?

"Why does no one ever listen to me?" he said aloud.

"I do," replied Purell.

Neb had to crack a smile. Purell was always at the ready with a good quip or two. And he was right, both he and Kel were always there for him.

"But See-Ess is correct regarding the time welt," Purell ventured.

"Is he?" Neb huffed to himself.

"You may not be able to transport that ship into your docking bay but that doesn't mean one can't go down there and take a peek," said See-Ess, looking at the shiny glimmer on the view screen. "And perhaps, even find a way in."

"How do you know so much about time welts and finding a way onto a cloaked vessel?" Neb walked over to See-Ess. Neb was not intimidated by See-Ess. He was more rather intrigued by his knowledge of such things. Perhaps there was more to this big brute than meets the eye.

"I get around," See-Ess replied. Standing his ground as Neb stood toe to toe with him, now looking up at See-Ess as See-Ess looked down at Neb.

"You're a brave lad, aren't you?" See-Ess said.

"More than you know," Neb replied.

See-Ess let out a hearty laugh.

"I like you, Nebula Yorker!" See-Ess grabbed Neb and gave him a hug. He lifted Neb up off the ground and twirled him about laughing. Neb pounded See-Ess on the back. "I can't breathe," he let out in a whisper.

"What was that?" See-Ess let go of Neb who then fell to the ground.

Neb sat on the floor of the bridge catching his breath.

"You could give TeeceeFore a run for her money," Neb coughed as he eased himself back up on his feet.

"What's that's? TeeceeFore? Money?" See-Ess's ears perked up.

"It's nothing," Neb replied. "Anyhow, getting back to my question. How do you know so much about time welts?"

"I've picked up a few things here and there in my line of work. Also..." See-Ess paused, "My father was a colleague of the Professor's some time ago and I listened in on quite a few sessions he had with the Professor when I was a young tadpole."

"And who might your father be?" Neb asked.

As See-Ess was about to answer, the Interface cut in with another Red Alert.

"Red Alert! Red Alert! Incoming sonic shock wave."

"Kel!" Neb yelled out. "Intensify force field to the ship!"

"Doing so now," Kel replied, keying in the data.

The sonic shock wave shook the Photon Ledger once, twice and a third time; almost knocking everyone off their feet.

"Damage?!" Neb called out.

"None," replied Purell.

LeBeau, Pheet and Kcils came stumbling through the bridge doors from the lounge.

"What was that?"

"Were we hit?" Pheet asked, worried.

Kcils was now hanging onto him like a scared cat would.

LeBeau rushed over to his science console.

"Incoming!" The Interface rang out.

"Hold on everyone!" Neb called out.

Three more times the wave hit the ship.

"That's odd," LeBeau looked up from his console towards Neb.

"Odd?" Neb asked.

"This sonic shock wave has a bio signature attached to it. I have never seen this before in my entire life."

"Are you sure there's a bio signature?" Pheet asked LeBeau.

"Confirmed," Kel cut in.

"Incoming," the Interface rang out once gain.

This time the sonic shock wave hit the ship with a thunderous thud.

"It's penetrating the shields," Purell shouted.

Just as Purell alerted everyone, a white blue mass of energy came through the bridge's hull. It hovered like a cloud of bees and inched closer toward the crew. It first floated over to Purell and Kel who were seated side by side. It crackled with static as it did so.

Purell and Kel gazed at it intensely but remained motionless so not to disturb the entity. After thirty seconds it moved away from Purell and Kel, stopping next at LeBeau.

"Fascinating!" LeBeau quipped.

It next went over to Pheet, Kcils and See-Ess-each time spending more than thirty seconds at each one.

Finally it turned to Neb.

Neb watched it closely as it approached him. The mass expanded, now covering Neb.

"Neb!" Kel cried out.

"Its ok, Kel," Neb replied. "Everyone stay calm."

While the white blue energy engulfed Neb, LeBeau was busy scanning the mass. That's interesting, very. LeBeau said to himself as he viewed the scanning results. But can it be? LeBeau quietly sent the results over to Kel's and Purell's work console.

They both looked down at the message on the screen. Fascinating! Purell typed back to LeBeau, who raised a brow at Purell's reply.

Meanwhile Pheet, Kcils and See-Ess watched, each one thinking the same thing, "I'm hungry."

"Neb?" LeBeau spoke up as the mass continued to swirl around Neb. "You know that bio signature we were getting from the sonic shock wave? It's yours."

Neb looked over to LeBeau, "Fascinating!" Neb replied.

"But how?" Lebeau asked.

Then without warning Neb and the white blue mass disappeared.

"Where did he go?! Where did he go?!" LeBeau yelled out.

Kel and Purell frantically tracked the mass and Neb's bio signature. LeBeau rushed over to assist. All three worked feverishly.

"Damn!" Lebeau punched the console. "Nothing."

And as he did so the bridge's view screen flickered on.

"Hello everyone. I'm good," Neb's face filled the screen sitting in the cockpit of a vessel.

"Where are you?" Kel asked.

"I'm on the moon.

"Prep the docking bay. I am coming in," Neb ordered.

See-Ess turned to Kcils, "This is a weird place. I love it!"

"Agreed," Kcils smiled back. "But do they have any food on this ship?"

12

Ruban sat on a cold steel chair; his hands tied behind him and a thin brown cloth bag covering his head. He heard feet shuffling and whispers in the distance. The room was frigid – 4 or 5 Celsius he reckoned. He must have sat there for over an hour. His thoughts turned to Blulay. She must be over worrying about him by now, though he did tell her that he would be no more than three to four hours and that time was almost up. He moved his rump back and forth trying to generate some heat-any heat at this point. Then he heard a door slowly crack open.

By the sound of the footsteps there must be four others in the room with him now. "Take the hood off him," a raspy voice said.

Soon Ruban was confronted by four tall skinny men in white lab coats. They had long drawn out, pale faces; all had jet black hair and deep hazel eyes.

"You're not human are you?" The rasping voice was heard but whoever was speaking was not visible to Ruban.

Hmm, five. Ruban thought. How did I miss that?

"What are you talking about – not human? What do you mean by that?" Ruban replied, squinting his eyes, trying to refocus.

"What I mean is you're not human, as we too are not human."

The man with the rasping voice appeared from the back corner of the room, out of the shadows. Ah? The alien slave workers that Ruban had heard rumors about perhaps. He kept his thoughts to himself.

"I really don't know what you are talking about," Ruban answered.

"It's just that we don't know what species you are. We know everyone else who's here but you're something altogether very different." The rasping voiced tall skinny man in his white lab coat made his way around Ruban. His back was now turned to him.

What's the end game here? Ruban wondered. Was this all part of Marcus's interrogation tactics employed to force the truth out of you before death or enslavement?

Ruban felt a cold touch breeze his hands. Goosebumps crept up his arms as he realized that his captor was untying him.

Ruban pulled his arms up, rubbing his wrists. "Thank you," he said.

"We are going to be blunt with you, whoever you are. First of all, you need not worry about us, we are not the Emperor's henchmen. My name is Komi Koop of Themosjustic. These men with me are what is left of my crew. We and 15 other species have been enslaved by the Emperor Marcus Appitius. He has embedded transfiguror's and tracking emitters into our arms." Komi Koop and the four others rolled up their sleeves, showing Ruban the red round markers.

"But you. You have no such tracks in your arms," Komi Koop said, pointing to Ruban's arms.

Ruban shed a tear, his head down. "I am sorry for your confinement," he slowly raised his head up.

"Why do you cry?" Komi Koop asked surprised. "Who are you?"

Ruban stared straight ahead thinking about his next words. "My name is Ruban of Pr..." He was cut off, at the sudden sound of alarm bells ringing.

"Inspection! Quick, hide Ruban of Pr in my room now before the Praetorian get here," Komi Koop ordered his men.

"What's going on?" Ruban asked as they hurried out the door.

"Secret inspections. We never know when they are coming. Most times they are in the middle of our sleep cycles—most times. You'll be safe in my room. I assure you," Komi Koop nodded. "Go now quickly, before they get here or we're all done for."

"Thank you," Ruban said, as they whisked him away, out of sight.

Where did he say he was from, this Ruban of Pr? Komi Koop asked himself.

They all lined up against the wall of the mess hall — forty two in total. Six Praetorian Guards all dressed in black and red fatigues and each holding white sixteen-inch stun sticks stared at the workers.

They included:

Five Hiliponians—including Komi Koop.

Ten Dregonions.

Six Themosjusticians.

Seven Oootopopahians.

Five Chocxivxixians.

Four Lanoishullonians.

And Five Telvonians.

Each were implanted with transfiguror's and trackers. Their true shapes and origins were unknown to the Praetorians. To them they were all humans, just as Marcus had planned. It was enough that he had the Earth under his control; revealing alien life to the masses wasn't on the docket, yet.

Each worker had a name tag attached to their white lab coats that they had been given. Komi Koop's name was George and as the designated Supervisor he was called out first.

"George!" screamed out the Praetorian. "Here!" He pointed to the ground in front of him with his stun stick. Komi Koop/George broke line and walked over to the guard who then proceeded to stun him, laughing at him as he fell to the ground.

He next called out Phil, a Telvonian, "You! Come here."

He did the same again, though he raised the level of the energy in his stun stick knowing Phil (the Telvonian) seemed to always need an extra boost. The Praetorian loved giving pain for no reason whatsoever. Leaving Komi Koop/George and Phil slumped on the floor, the guards exited the mess laughing.

"What's that human term?" Tim, a fellow Hiliponian helped Komi Koop up.

"You mean, 'bastard'?" said Phil, as everyone gathered round Komi Koop and Phil.

Ruban had been watching the event unfold through the keyhole of the old door to Komi Koop's room. He didn't know whether to come out now or stay put. "Bastards indeed," Ruban said under his breath as he waited.

As he continued looking through the keyhole he saw what looked like Komi waving him out and then remembered how keen the eyesight of a Hiliponian was; much like an eagle's on Earth. "It's ok Ruban of Pr," he heard Komi say.

Ruban slowly opened the door. It creaked, as he did so. Besides the Hiliponians, who had met Ruban earlier, the rest of the group were seeing him for the first time.

He rushed over to Komi Koop's side. "Are you ok?" he asked.

"It was nothing that I have not been through before," Komi replied.

"You get used to it," Phil said.

"Can we continue the conversation that we were having before we were so rudely interrupted by our Praetorian tormentors?" Komi now asked. "You say you're from Pr. I don't think I have ever heard of such a planet. Have any of you?" Komi looked around his fellow captives. They all shook their heads and answered, "No."

"Not Pr," Ruban gave a little chuckle, "No, no. I am Ruban of Pratt."

A hush came over the room.

"You're telling us you are a Triopelian?" Komi's eyes almost popped out of his head.

13

Neb took over the controls, manually landing the shuttle inside the Photon Ledger's docking bay. He was greeted by Kel, Purell and LeBeau at his request.

Pheet was not invited and was none too happy. Nonetheless, he understood Neb's reluctance to include him, due to the two new crew members Pheet had signed on without telling him.

Neb had been able to disengage the time bubble's override system to free it from its position on the moon once he had figured out the energy mass's origin and why his bio signature was attached to it.

The shuttle wasn't much bigger than the submersible on Marine; it could sit five easy though six would be pushing it.

Once the shuttle was secure within the docking bay, Neb opened the shuttle's hatch to find Kel, Purell and LeBeau eagerly awaiting the hows and the whys. Neb stepped out of the shuttle onto the docking bay's floor and said, "One small step for man. One giant leap for mankind."

"What?" Said LeBeau.

"Neil Armstrong, man," Neb replied. "You know – the first man to step onto Earth's moon."

"If you say so," LeBeau answered, a little bewildered. "What is he on about?" LeBeau leaned into Purell.

"I'll fill you in later, it's one of those Earth things, but I think it has something to do with a moon dance," Purell replied.

"Neb, are you well?" Kel approached him with a medical scanner.

"You won't need that Kel; I am fine. I assure you."

None the less, Kel continued with her scan. "Your bio signature is off by point 01, Neb?" Kel raised a brow. "I agree that it is nothing to worry about for a Triopelian," Kel stated, "But the point 01 is human DNA and not yours."

"Interesting," Neb rubbed his chin. "May I see the scanner?" he asked Kel.

Kel handed him the scanner.

Neb went over the readings twice to make sure. He had an idea but kept it to himself.

"Let's run a few more tests on this and find out whose DNA it is, just to be safe," he returned the scanner back to Kel.

"So are you going to tell us what the hell just happened to you and how it is you piloted the shuttle back here?!" LeBeau asked testily.

"You have been hanging out with Purell too much," Neb winked in Purell's direction.

"That's what I have been telling him," Purell glanced over at LeBeau with a chiding look.

LeBeau tried to ignore Purell, though that was never ever going to happen.

"Before I start," Neb began, "Professor, are you listening in?"

Of course Pheet was, having tagged LeBeau with a listening device.

"What was that Neb?" LeBeau asked.

"You don't think the Professor would miss out on this, do you? Even though I banished him from coming to the docking bay. It's alright Gabriel," Neb spoke out into the air. "But please, please, do not tell the others about this conversation, will you?"

The Professor's ear piece buzzed, he understood and excused himself from Kcils and See-Ess and headed for the lavatory. Cramps. He rubbed his stomach.

"By all means," See-Ess cringed.

Though the player that See-Ess was, had also planted a listening device on LeBeau—unknown to the Professor and even to Neb.

"This should be good," See-Ess said to Kcils. "We might make some profit out of this yet."

"I kind of hate to do this to poor old Gabby, but momma needs new shoes," Kcils meowed.

Neb now started to explain.

"First of all, the white blue energy mass with my bio signature was an echo of the Vegastriopelia."

"The Vegastriopelia!" See-Ess and Kcils heard Pheet scream it out from the lavatory.

"What's a Vegastriopelia?" Kcils asked.

"I don't know but I am sure we're about to found out," replied See-Ess, rubbing his hands together.

"The Vegastriopelia!" Screamed LeBeau.

The Vegastriopelia! Kel and Purell looked at each other.

"How is that possible?" Purell enquired.

"It's a long story; suffice to say the shuttle is from another time frame."

"Another time frame!" Pheet screamed out again.

See-Ess and Kcils silently lipped it to each other.

"You see," Neb continued, "it should have dawned on me when we detected the shuttle on the moon but with so much on my mind these days it escaped my notice until the energy mass whisked me away."

"What am I missing here?" LeBeau asked.

"The Vegastriopelia? Another time frame?"

"If I may?" Kel looked to Neb. Neb nodded.

"You see, Mr. LeBeau. The Casino was destroyed in this other time frame by Marcus but not before Neb was able to change the past into the future."

"That's not quite correct, Kel. It was Lafil who changed the time frame and – by coincidence – Marcus did too. He played a part when he injured Lafil," Neb interrupted.

"I stand corrected," Kel acknowledged.

"Yes, Mr. LeBeau," Purell picked up the narration from Kel and Neb.

"The Casino picked up on Lafil's bio reading distress signature and transported him back to the Casino, then promptly left Earth's orbit. Now with the knowledge Lafil obtained from Neb – about the future from 1986 where Neb hailed from and also said events regarding Marcus's future history with the Casino, he was forearmed with the knowledge that Marcus would kill him in 1758. So, Marcus was caught and placed in confinement – until he escaped in 1986. Marcus then travelled back in time to 12 BCE to change time and his first encounter with Lafil, by trying to murder him in 12 BCE rather than centuries later. There was only one variable that Marcus did not consider – Nebula Yorker," Purell finished.

LeBeau slowly sifted what Purell had just related and found himself out of breath at Purell's explanation.

"What does that all have to do with the shuttle on the moon?" LeBeau finally said after all that.

Before Neb could reply Kel picked up on where Purell ended.

"When Marcus escaped from the Casino in 1986 he had an accomplice – Eno Low."

"President Eno?" Pheet screamed out from the Lavatory.

"President Eno?" See-Ess and Kcils laughed.

LeBeau just thought, President Eno?

"Eno piloted a shuttle; this shuttle," Kel pointed to it.

"The plan was for Eno to await Marcus's signal while waiting on the moon encased in a time bubble. The plan was also for Marcus to overthrow Rome and then conquer the rest of the Earth with all the advanced technology he would need at his fingertips, to continue his original plan. However, Eno left the Casino before Marcus could place his plan in operation and again – the one variable he overlooked was Nebula Yorker.

"Marcus took Neb with him to Rome of 12 BCE thinking Neb would perish. Neb was born in 1960 and going that far back in time should have killed Neb. As you know with time travel you can only travel as far back as your age or to the time of your being conceived on your home world. Neither Marcus nor Neb at the time knew that Neb was not born of Earth but rather was *conceived* on Earth yet born in space. His parents being Triopelian."

"Triopelian!" See-Ess and Kcils shouted out loudly enough that Pheet heard them. Oh dear! This could be a problem, Pheet thought. They too must have bugged LeBeau.

"Neb did not die on his reentry back to Earth in 12 BCE and Marcus ended up with amnesia. That is, until he regained his memory. Marcus did end up destroying the Casino back in 1986 – the shuttle here is from that time frame," Kel now finished.

"Eno waited and waited through time. For him it would have been nothing, perhaps minutes and yet somehow Marcus managed to appear and re-evolve," Neb continued. "The only explanation that comes to mind is that Marcus somehow regained his memories that we had wiped. In doing so, we had hoped that he would have, under Lafil's guidance, lived out his life with Lafil on Earth – remaining none the wiser."

"You wiped his memories?" LeBeau asked, surprised.

"Yes, that is correct, LeBeau," Neb replied. "I will fill you all in when you fill me in about Elvis Cash."

"Fair enough," LeBeau acquiesced.

Neb continued. "As I was saying, the energy mass is an echo from the Vegastriopelia, from that time frame and it zeroed in on me when we – I – came in to close enough range for contact."

LeBeau began to pace away from Neb, Kel and Purell, to the other end of the docking bay. LeBeau was trying to wrap his head around all of this new information. He liked Neb – he really liked him. He felt a bond, a kinship with him, but Neb had never told him about this other time frame or about wiping people's memories. "Triopelians," he said under his breath as he continued his pacing, staring down at the floor and looking up every now and then, over to Neb.

Finally, after five long minutes he joined Neb, Kel and Purell who were standing beside the shuttle.

"So how did that work out for you, Neb? Marcus's plan, that is. It seems to me that time frame or no time frame, Marcus seems to have succeeded."

Neb scratched his head and replied. "Time is a somewhat unknown variable depending how one looks at it – say, as though time were flesh and blood, so to speak. Time is always moving forward and yet time can be unlocked moving backwards thus changing the events of the future from within a certain time frame such as we have encountered with Rome of 12 BCE."

Suddenly Professor Pheet burst into the docking bay, followed by See-Ess and Kcils, "I'm sorry, I'm sorry! I didn't know that they also bugged LeBeau."

14

Ruban was two hours late in returning to a worried and distraught Blulay. Thoughts of him being tortured had been running through her head. She did not know how she could survive without him. It was bad enough that she would never see her precious son Nebula, or even her home world again – although if truth be told, Earth was her home now, for better or for worse.

She remembered Ruban's words about finding a secluded island or place far away from Rome. She just did not want to think it would become a reality. She sat with her hands over her face crying, overwhelmed with grief and the unknown. Her demeanor was very un-Triopelian by Triopelian standards.

She stood and wiped away the tears, took a deep breath and straightened out her smock when suddenly she heard running feet coming from the tunnel entrance. She ran over to the computer console.

"Interface enact self-destruction sequence," she calmly said.

"Commencing," replied the Interface.

Her eyes widened as she looked towards the room's entrance for there, standing with a half grin, was Ruban.

"ABORT SELF DESTRUCT!" he yelled out.

"Aborting," the Interface rang out.

They both rushed into each other's arms, crying and laughing at the same time.

"I thought you were..." Blulay couldn't finish her words. She buried her head into Ruban's chest, sobbing.

"It's ok. It's ok. I'm here now and I am not going anywhere without you, anymore. I promise," Ruban finished, squeezing Blulay even closer.

They stood together embracing for more than 30 minutes, not saying another word and letting their Triopelian bodies' rhythms compose one another.

"You were pretty quick there on the trigger finger, wouldn't you say?" Ruban asked Blulay as they came out of their embrace.

"Really? That's all you have to say?" Blulay replied, eyeing her husband who felt like a lightening beam had run through him.

"I'm sorry. I'm sorry," Ruban apologized profusely. "But – you *were* a little quick there," Ruban wouldn't give up.

Blulay continued with her steely look, staring straight at Ruban.

"Where were you?

"What happened?

"I thought you were captured by Marcus.

"When I heard the footsteps echoing in the tunnel I thought for sure they were coming for me.

"You didn't want our entire tech to fall into Marcus's hands did you?

"You can be such, such…" Blulay paused, "A man!"

Ruban at this point knew he should just shut up; he also knew when Blulay was right.

"So what did you find out?" she now asked.

"Well for one thing, our information about off-worlder slaves was correct. I sort of was kidnapped by them."

"Kidnapped?" Blulay asked.

"Yes, that is why I was delayed in getting back to you. It was quite the eye opener. Suffice to say we have some new allies."

"Tell me more!" Blulay said excitedly.

"Let's make something to eat and I will tell you all about it. I am famished," Ruban replied.

"You bet," Blulay grabbed her husband by the hand and they headed for the galley.

15

Marcus inspected The Anvilus for the hundredth time with Eno by his side. Komi Koop led them both through every nook and cranny of the vast ship. They were now in the engine room.

"She should be ready to be space bound by the 15th as requested," Komi Koop reported to Marcus.

"She? Should?" Marcus sneered in Komi's direction. "Why does one always refer to a ship as her and not him?"

"If I may," Komi Koop interrupted. Marcus glared at Komi Koop while he continued. *"The early term for a ship, specifically in Latin, was the word 'navis', which was a feminine term which translates as 'ship'. By extension, when referring to a sea-going vessel, crew and captains came to use feminine pronouns when referencing the ship directly. So, rather than a gender neutral pronoun like 'it', the ship became 'she'."*

"Who gave you permission to speak, Themosjustician?!" Eno prodded Komi Koop with a stun stick.

Hmm? Marcus thought. Eno has become quite the barbarian.

Komi Koop fell to his knees. Blood started coming out of his nose and ears as Eno grinded the stun stick into his upper body.

"ENOUGH!" Shouted Marcus, pulling the stun stick out of Eno's hand and thrusting it into Eno's side.

Komi Koop smiled on seeing Eno fall to the floor.

"How *do* you know this?" Marcus quizzed Komi Koop.

Komi Koop slowly pulled himself up, wiping his black blood from his face. "I have become a student of your planet's antiquities before and after the change."

"What change?" Marcus enquired, now standing eye to eye with Komi Koop.

Komi Koop swallowed hard. He knew he should have said nothing but he was fed up with Marcus. Death would be a welcome friend at this point, he thought to himself. Komi Koop now stood, defiant. He closed his eyes waiting for the final blow to hit him.

Marcus was waiting for Komi Koop's answer when the klaxon started to ring, sounding through the entire ship.What's going on? Marcus thought, as he pulled Eno up from the floor.

'Incoming message', ran the ship's Interface. 'Spacial anomaly detected from the moon-post on long range sensors.'

"Define," Marcus replied to the Interface. "And turn off that damn alarm!"

"Which actions do you wish to proceed with?" the Interface replied.

Marcus scratched his head and sighed, "The alarm first," he moaned angrily.

The klaxon immediately ceased at Marcus's request.

"Now Interface, about the spacial anomaly," Marcus waited and looked over at Eno, who shrugged his shoulders.

"Did I ask *you* something?" Marcus said.

Eno looked away from Marcus's gaze, his head down.

Komi Koop wondered if Ruban may have something to do with the situation.

"Please direct your attention to the monitor," the Interface began.

All three looked down at the monitor, now displayed on one of the many consoles in the engine room. From the moon's vantage point the Earth hung 466,000 kilometers away – or 289,800 miles, give or take.

"I do not see any anomaly?" Marcus questioned the Interface.

"Magnifying now," answered the Interface.

As the Interface magnified the Earth frame by frame it slowly came into view. The Velexian Viper Reversal Vortex Bubble revealed itself. The Earth's lower bottom sat in a translucent half bubble while the remainder of the planet appeared to be surrounded by a glowing protective shell.

All three stared at the monitor, each one wondering what it was they were seeing. Neither Komi Koop nor Eno could remember seeing anything like it in their lives. Ruban had not divulged the Bubble's presence to Komi Koop. He had only told him that the Earth was kept in check; safe from Marcus's plans for its future. Komi Kopp now thought that perhaps this is what Ruban had been referring to.

Marcus looked intently at the monitor. "Elaborate," Marcus told the Interface.

"Working," answered the Interface.

"Do you know what this is?" Marcus turned to Komi Koop.

"I do not," said Komi Koop.

Marcus wasn't sure if Komi Koop was telling the truth or not. Marcus had a hard time believing anyone but himself. He leaned over the monitor to get a closer look, blocking the view from Eno and Komi Koop. "Interface!" Marcus howled. "What is *this*?"

"Summarizing. Evaluating. Extrapolating. Configuration in process," replied the Interface.

Thirty seconds later the Interface relayed, "The object is a sub-structured trans-dimensional span reversal force field anti-folding space time corpuscle."

"A what?" Marcus said.

Eno and Komi Koop mouthed the same words.

"The structure is in line with the planet's push and pull gravitational field, locking the Earth's trans-dimensional span," the Interface continued. "The circular atmosphere of the planet has been effectively sealed. The containment is isolated to the planet which means all space and time outside of the Earth is non parallel and remains constant within its normal parameters," the Interface finished.

Marcus stood silently, confused by what the Interface had relayed. He was having a very hard time wrapping his head around it. For as much as Marcus had an unlimited knowledge gleaned from and about the universe(s) – digesting it and formulating it all was another story altogether for him. If truth be told, that is why he kept Eno around and alive – for Eno to figure out that which he – Marcus – did not know. Eno, for his part, tried his best to extrapolate – to make it easier for his master to understand things whenever this type of situation arose.

"Well?" Marcus glared at Eno.

"I will need to further investigate the anomaly before I can give you an answer," Eno replied, as his transfigurer started to fade in and out – revealing his true identity yet once again.

Komi Koop eyed Eno in amazement.

A Repoocian Reptilian! So Proconsul Eno is not an Earther! Interesting, he thought.

"What did I tell you about that?!" Marcus was about to stun Eno again who had already balled up, waiting for the pain to begin again.

"If I may?" Komi Koop interrupted.

Marcus turned to Komi Koop whom he had forgotten about temporarily. This new revelation it seemed, was beginning to work against him. Nebula Yorker came to his mind.

"If I am correct, your majesty," Komi Koop now addressed Marcus as so. "I would surmise that nothing is going to get in or out of this force field at present. Including this ship."

Marcus eyed Komi Koop with discontent. I never did like Themosjusticians.

Marcus turned his anger on Komi Koop, stunning him instead of Eno.

"We will see about that, won't we," Marcus laughed. As did Eno, who was happy it was not him being stunned.

Komi Koop lay on the cold floor of The Anvilus's engine room. He was curled up, yet laughing to himself.

Marcus threw the stun stick down, close to Komi's feet. He looked over at Eno.

"Order the arsenal team to strengthen the current of these sticks. They do not have the desired effect that they once had," Marcus growled at Eno, kicking Komi in the back as he walked away.

Eno shuddered to himself. That's all he needed, a stronger stun stick in Marcus's hand.

"And get that damn transfiguror fixed! I will not tell you again!" Marcus was heard shouting back at Eno as he exited the engine room.

Eno closed his eyes, wishing he was back in Australia.

16

Neb was busy going over the logs of the shuttle he had piloted from the moon onto the Photon Ledger. LeBeau was at his side, assisting. LeBeau had gotten over the shock of Neb's revelation of the shuttle's true origin and the time frame where it came from.

"Is it any wonder there is a distrust of Triopelians throughout the universe?" he said.

To which Neb 100 percent agreed, though he had lived his life thinking he was just another human being from Earth and had never met any other Triopelians – aside from his parents. Subsequently, he did not think LeBeau's observation of Triopelians pertained to him.

"Everyone fibs now and then," he told LeBeau. "Some for a useful purpose and some not."

LeBeau agreed but then asked, "What is a fib?"

Neb tried to put in to words what he had been thinking.

"I may be Triopelian but I have never set foot on Pratt, Lerxst or Dirk. In fact I have never met another Triopelian other than my parents and it was only a little over three years ago that I found out about my true heritage. For all intents and purposes, I do not associate myself as

Triopelian but as an Earther, from Earth. That being said however, I guess I am not your typical Earther."

"You think so, do you?" LeBeau laughed.

"But back to the work at hand. We need to figure out whether the shuttle's logs can give us a clue on how to at least try and find a way past the Velexian Viper Reversal Vortex Bubble," Neb said to LeBeau. He then paused for a moment before continuing. "I am worried about See-Ess," Neb entrusted LeBeau with this thought. "I know that the Professor is your friend and I too have come to like him as such. Yet, there are so many unknown variables with him, you know. And Kcils? What's up with her?" Neb shook his head as he updated the shuttle's data nodes.

"Well yes, I must agree with you regarding the Professor, Neb. He certainly did lead us-and Mr. Tict-on a wild chase both on Marine and on Halley's Casino and…" LeBeau stopped. "However, do you think it was wise locking up See-Ess and Kcils in that makeshift holding cell? It has only made them angrier; well at least See-Ess."

"I see, Elvis Cash," Neb smiled. "What do you propose I do with them? There is a lot at stake, LeBeau. I can't trust them after they bugged you, to listen in to what didn't concern them. Still…" Neb paused. "I feel there must be some part they are to play in all of this. As I mentioned earlier, coincidences have repercussions in my experience. And it's not just my parents I am worried about. The Earth and the entire universe is in peril. My gut instincts tell me that See-Ess and Kcils are here by no mere coincidence. But for what end?" Neb confided to LeBeau.

"How can you be so sure?" LeBeau asked. "Is that another one of your Triopelian things?"

Neb laughed. "Yes and no. You see, when I first met Tict he mentioned that there was no such thing as coincidence – though alluring to believe that there is. But ever since, coincidences keep springing up – as if they were meant to."

"That is an odd equation," LeBeau answered. "It would almost seem that – if that were the case – that anything or everything we do has already been planned out and is waiting to reveal itself. Which by the way, I do not believe, Neb. I believe in the 'One Step at a Time Theory'," LeBeau rambled on.

The 'One Step at a Time Theory'? Neb raised a brow, musing. "You sound like my parents. Oh and what exactly *is* the 'One Step at a Time Theory'?" Neb asked.

Before LeBeau could answer, however, Purell and Kel suddenly appeared alongside.

"If I may?" Purell interjected, "The 'One Step at a Time Theory' is as follows…" Purell then stopped and looked at LeBeau.

"Please go ahead, be my guest," LeBeau motioned to Purell. "This should be good!" he whispered to Neb.

"No need to whisper, you know. I can still hear you," Purell tilted his head at LeBeau.

LeBeau let out a heavy sigh. "Just get on with it, will you please, Purell."

"Testy, isn't he?" Kel turned to Purell.

"Quite," Purell answered.

"As I was saying," Purell now finally continued, "The 'One Step at a Time Theory' is…" Purell cleared his throat, as if he needed to and started his explanation.

"We are born.

"We eat.

"We defecate.

"We die.

"No variables.

"No equations.

"No Prophetic questions or answers.

"And lastly…" Purell paused for effect, "No coincidences."

"End of story," Purell finished, crossing his arms and looking quite proud of himself.

"That's it?" Neb laughed. "You have to be kidding."

"He kids you not! What is a kid by the way?" LeBeau first replied and then asked.

"Kid. A young goat. A child or young person," Kel added to the conversation.

"Not now," Neb rolled his eyes. "Honestly! You two!" Neb shook his head at Kel and Purell, exasperated.

"But sir," Purell tried. However, Neb cut him off and shushed him.

Kel also tried to speak, though to no avail.

"This is how you live your life, LeBeau?" Neb asked.

"It's not a question of how one lives his life, Neb; it's the way of the universe. How it folds or unfolds is a matter of how it is, my friend. 'One step at a time.'" LeBeau answered.

Hmm? Neb pondered, rubbing his chin as he nearly always did when he mulled something over.

"What about all the bits in-between?" Neb began. "We all are born; we all then eat, defecate and die at some point. I think. But what about life, love, adventure and – yes – coincidences? Do you really think we have been thrown together by mere happenstance? Look around you. One step forward, two back is where we are if there are no coincidences, as Mr. Tict would presume. However, my own experiences with coincidence is that it is not just a word or a concept – it is fact."

"He does have a point," Purell looked to LeBeau.

"I was not born, nor do I eat or defecate or die and yet here I am," Kel joined in. "Corporeal beings such as yourselves can be quite clever – creating intergalactic casinos, androids and yes even beings such as yourself,

LeBeau. Yet, you discard the truth. Or at least, some of you do."

"Which truth is this?" LeBeau asked Purell.

"We are here. We are now. And we are all in deep shit unless Neb here can diffuse the situation with the Earth and Marcus."

"And… if he cannot, neither coincidence nor 'The One Step at a Time Theory' will save any of us and/or the universe," Purell finished speaking for Kel, while staring straight at Neb.

"You never cease to amaze," Kel said to her sidekick.

"Undoubtedly," Purell cocked an eyebrow.

Neb laughed, uncontrollably.

"With that said and done!" Neb walked over to Purell and gave him a hug, "Let's get back to work, shall we?"

"Look here. I think we might be able to interface into the shuttle's time bubble and plot an alternate course, if I am correct," Neb handed the isopad to LeBeau. "What do you think?"

LeBeau scanned over Neb's equations. "Interesting," LeBeau now rubbed his chin.

"May I?" asked Kel.

She reached for the isopad, to take it from LeBeau. Purell was now by her side.

"Yes, very interesting," they both said at the same time while rubbing their chins – mimicking Neb and LeBeau.

Neb now cocked a brow wondering if they – Kel and Purell – knew what they were doing?

He clocked it up to android evolution for the time being.

17

Ruban and Blulay, along with Timus Gra (the Proconsul of Russia), Nivek Htims (Proconsul of the Greater United States) and Bor Rekab (Proconsul of the Northern Border of Canada)met secretly at a small hidden bistro situated off The Appian Way, outside of Rome – off the beaten track, one might say.

The owner of the 'Red Riders Bistro', known as Mr. Gdown, ushered the five guests to a lightly lit back room that was beside the kitchen.

Mr. Gdown was a huge man, standing six feet tall. Some might call him a brute of a man. He was an ex gladiator of Marcus's games who had won his freedom two years earlier and one of only a handful of combatants that Marcus had ever freed.

He had no love for the Empire, nor Marcus for that matter, and he had been quite easily recruited to the resistance group by Gaius Rulle, the now deceased Proconsul of Britain. Mr. Gdown did his part for the 5th Column – the Resistance – the Underground – whatever you wanted to call the group. He had become close to Ruban and Blulay and trusted them with his life – as they him.

"If you need anything," he said and winked as the five sat down at a table.

"Maybe some water?" Blulay replied.

"Coming up," said Mr. Gdown with a smile as he closed the door.

"Such a nice man," Blulay said to the others.

The five, now all seated, turned to business immediately. Ruban relayed the information from his reconnaissance mission the day before. There was no longer the need to hide from everyone the technological knowledge that Marcus possessed since the Emperor had played his cards by showing off The Anvilus's hologram imagery and Eno's hovering. Ruban felt though, that breaking the news of *alien* slaves was probably a story best kept for another day – as was that of his and Blulay's origins. Sooner or later, though, they would need to come clean if they were to defeat Marcus.

"He is truly mad!" said Timus Gra, referring to Marcus. "How *can* one rule the stars, for heaven's sake?" He pointed skyward.

Space travel of any sort was never discussed nor had it *ever* been brought up during Marcus's reign. Marcus had made sure that all and any such talk never made it into any of this Earth's literature, or media: the radio, television. All had remained clear of such knowledge – until now. Of course there was limited tech available but nothing that would cause any sort of trouble for Marcus. Computers and the like were reserved for the military. Television, radio and communications such as the telephone had been 'invented' (but nothing else – not even digital watches). The Emperor had everything planned out to a T.

Blulay looked over to Ruban and gave him that look – a look that said, 'we have to start being honest with these people.' Actually, it was more of a Triopelian – I can read your mind thing than just a look.

"Have any of you ever dreamed what it might be like to travel into space? Perhaps go to the moon, for example?" Ruban asked.

"Go to the moon?" Nivek Htims laughed out loud. "Why would anyone want to go to the moon? If the gods wanted us to go to the moon don't you think they would have given us wings?"

The funny thing about this culture was that Marcus – though he did away with any and all religions – had kept the notion of the gods. But not to worship them, no – he was the only one who was to be hailed as a GOD and to be given complete devotion.

"Why to explore!" said Ruban to Nivek Htims. "Don't you see, it's (wo)mans' birthright to explore beyond his/her own world – given time that is. You should have long ago started to invest in such possibilities but Marcus has weakened your drive to strive and survive. And now you find yourselves dumbfounded by Marcus's drive to the stars and ask yourselves whether Marcus is – as you say – mad or actually a god? Which answer do you want – if any?" Ruban asked.

"We want a world free of Marcus and his maniacal ways. So, perhaps if he leaves this world, as he says he can, then so be it – good riddance," Timus Gra vented.

"I agree, but what happens when he comes back; if he comes back?" asked Bor Rekab.

A thought surged through Ruban like a cutting knife. Does Marcus, once free of the Earth, need the Earth? Ruban did not like the feeling he was feeling – not one bit.

Knock, knock, and knock. Followed by ten seconds of silence then one more knock. It was Mr. Gdown carrying a tray of glasses with a large jug of cold water and a few edible treats.

"Thank you Mr. Gdown," Blulay said, patting Mr. Gdown's hand as he laid down the tray.

"You're most welcome," replied Mr. Gdown.

"Why don't you join us?" Nivek Htims asked.

"Yes, please do, Mr. Gdown," Timus Gra insisted.

Mr. Gdown looked about the five, his eyes steady – not blinking even once. After a lengthy minute or two he said. "Ok, for a little. Someone has to run this dive," he smirked and sat beside Blulay.

"Tell us Gdown. What do you think of this whole spaceship scenario?" Bor Rekab asked.

"Well, from what I know – or should I say from what you have told me – it sounds very exciting!" replied Mr. Gdown.

Ruban turned to Mr. Gdown, "That's what I want to hear. You see, gentlemen, we have an explorer in our midst," Ruban stood, reaching for a glass and then the jug of water.

He poured the water into the glass, raised it in salute to Mr. Gdown and then raised the glass to his lips and took a big, refreshing gulp of the cold water.

"I don't know about myself going into space," Mr. Gdown said, "but if it can get Emperor Marcus off the planet, well I am all for it," he chuckled loudly.

Everyone got a good laugh out of Mr. Gdown's comments.

After the levity had passed, Ruban let it be known they would need to put their plan of action into play soon – before the 15th of the month, the day of the launch of The Anvilus.

Ruban had decided now was not the time to tell the others about the Velexian Viper Vortex Reversal Bubble that currently was saving the planet and the universe from complete chaos. He knew deep down though that he would have to spill the beans about everything he knew – about himself and Blulay, the Bubble and the existence of outside world(s). And the time frame they all now found themselves in. Perhaps better to do so, sooner rather than later he thought – maybe now was the right time?

He looked at Blulay.

She knew too.

As Ruban reached his decision to spill everything, a ruckus was heard from within the bistro.

"Excuse me," Mr. Gdown stood and exited the room quickly to see what the disturbance was all about.

"What do you mean you have no pigeon?! I want pigeon!"

There stood Gecoo Chin, the Quarter Master of The Anvilus, yelling at the top of his lungs, screaming for pigeon.

"But sir, it's only Tuesday. Our pigeon special isn't until tomorrow," said the young waiter, terrified of Gecoo Chin.

"What seems to be the problem here?" Mr. Gdown appeared, towering over Gecoo Chin who was now seated and looking up from the table at Mr. Gdown. He stopped thinking about the pigeon he wasn't going to get and thought that there was something oddly familiar about this giant of a man standing before him.

"It's ok, I will take care of this," Mr. Gdown said to his waiter, who quickly took off to the kitchen.

"As my waiter mentioned good sir, our pigeon special is every Wednesday and we will not be serving any today. May I offer you the fish instead? We have a tremendous shark soufflé," Mr. Gdown said in a calm, low tone.

Gecoo Chin stared and said nothing.

Mr. Gdown waited for an answer.

Gecoo Chin's eyes grew wide as he now remembered the man standing in front of him. "You're Germanus!" he spat out.

"Germanus the Great, to be correct," smiled Mr. Gdown.

"Sorry about what happened to your brother – Rufus," Gecoo Chin added.

Mr. Gdown remained silent, glaring down on Gecoo Chin with an unfavorable look. "Thank you," was all he said. "Now, how about the shark soufflé?"

"Yes, yes, of course," Gecoo Chin replied, knowing he had touched a nerve with Germanus (Mr. Gdown) in mentioning his brother, Rufus.

Rufus was unceremoniously put to death, live on prime time, for the entire planet to see. It had happened two years earlier.

Now Germanus and his brother Rufus actually came from a long line of gladiators but when Marcus overthrew and murdered Augustus Caesar he had cloned these two men who were in Caesar's employment at the time and who were ex gladiators. Neither Germanus nor Rufus – nor all the long line of Germanuses and Rufuses – knew they were clones and neither did each subsequent Germanus know that the original Germanus and Rufus had been free men. Marcus never, in fact, freed anyone. For the time being, he just let Germanus think he was a free man. After all, Marcus had to, once in a while, give the masses what they wanted and seeming to free Germanus made him even more of a god to the people – or at least he thought so. A tyrant always thinks they're ahead of the game – but is the game ahead of them? Marcus intended to one day call upon Germanus to fulfil a duty.

As for Rufus, a memory frame had activated. How many times *could* you clone a clone and not have a memory frame crop up – and one had for Rufus.

Rufus's memory frame had to do with Nebula Yorker no less, a name that the Emperor despised with every fibre of his being. Rufus had warned his brother, Germanus, of the situation but in typical Germanus fashion, he had waved it off as a bad dream.

Night after night, for weeks, the memory frame would not let go. It had come to a point when Germanus mentioned it to Eno, who had just happened to be present during one of Rufus's arguments about Nebula Yorker – whether he was real or not real. Unfortunately, this was just as they were about to go out into combat in the Great Colosseum.

Eno immediately rushed to Marcus's side to inform him of said predicament. Germanus was pulled from the games and freed. Since when he had always feared that he too may find himself affected by memory and indeed he was. However, he kept it to himself but it was the reason why he now found himself aiding the Resistance.

He never told one soul about his memory frames even when Marcus had him checked out for the anomaly. Germanus still had no idea he and his brother were clones. It was like a puzzle Germanus still had to figure out.

Who was this Nebula Yorker?

A red thief?

A mother they never knew?

A hole in the roof of a barn?

Who was Lafil?

And a different Marcus?

And to top it off – though unknown to Germanus – his good friends, Ruban and Blulay, were this Nebula Yorker's parents. But then also unknown to Ruban and Blulay, Mr.Gdown was a clone and he knew of their son.

Above everything else that had occurred to Germanus, his greatest loss was that of his dear brother, whom he felt he had let down as Rufus had subsequently died a horrible death at the hand of Marcus.

Germanus was now a man on a mission and if Ruban, Blulay and a handful of Proconsuls could help him seek revenge then so be it.

"Germanus? Germanus?" Gecoo Chin caught Germanus daydreaming.

"What?!" Germanus/Mr. Gdown hollered back, not realizing where he was for the moment.

"I will try the shark soo-flay," Gecoo Chin brought Germanus back to the present.

Germanus inclined his head and said, "Right choice. "Michael!" Mr. Gdown called out.

Michael, the waiter, came running out of the kitchen.

"Our dear patron here is ready to order," Mr. Gdown said to the waiter and then left the room to rejoin his friends, who had been listening in closely.

"Does the shark soo-flay come with any hint of pigeon by chance?" Gecoo Chin asked the waiter, who rolled his eyes and said, "NO!"

"Ok. Ok. I get it," Gecoo Chin finally settled into the thought, no pigeon would be served today. (Though he thought he might look out for any pigeons on his way home!)

"What was that all about?" Ruban asked Mr. Gdown, once he had returned.

"Customers eh," he shrugged. "It happens all the time. All they need do is read the menu board at the front entrance before they come in."

"Oh, I see," replied Ruban. "So back to business then?"

Mr. Gdown sat, taking his place back at the table.

"As I was saying," Ruban continued and as he continued, each of the three Proconsuls Cell-Comms went off-all at the same time.

Now at this point it should be mentioned that only Proconsuls were equipped with Cell-Comm technology – though, if truth be told, the Cell-Comm was more of a pager. When it beeped, you jumped.

They each opened their Cell-Comms to read the exact same message. Marcus had ordered all Proconsuls back to the Senate immediately.

"Oh my! What can it be?" Blulay asked.

The three Proconsuls present looked up. Concern showed on their faces.

"This is indeed, very odd," replied Timus Gra.

"Usually it means bad news for someone," Bor Rekab added. "Though, actually, our last meeting wasn't all that bad as Marcus finally unveiled The Anvilus," he finished.

"I would say this is highly unusual, for certain. Though again – with all the proconsuls still in Rome, perhaps not," said Nivek Htims.

"That may be true; he had to unveil his plans sooner or later. It's just too bad Gaius Rulle went rogue on us. It has led to Marcus beefing up his security."

"It's never easy," sighed Ruban. "Let's stay positive and meet back here tomorrow afternoon. Say around 2:00 pm?"

Everyone nodded in agreement and left the room in single file.

Ruban and Blulay left last.

Gecoo Chin was enjoying his shark 'soo-flay', though he still wished it was pigeon. As he bit into the last few morsels of shark, he looked up just in time to see Ruban walking by his table. He hadn't paid any attention to the Proconsuls as he was too busy filling his stomach, besides he would not know what a Proconsul looked like – except for Eno, who was always slithering around The Anvilus.

Ruban did not notice Gecoo Chin (he was always looking ahead) until he felt a tug on his sleeve. He looked down at a grinning Gecoo Chin. Ruban almost felt like he was going to faint and did wobble a bit.

"Are you ok, dear?" Blulay asked, holding Ruban steady, a little unnerved herself.

"I am fine," Ruban replied.

"If it isn't my Australian friend," Gecoo Chin stood, wiping his mouth with a napkin, "I didn't think you guys were paid well enough to eat in a place like this," he laughed. "Who is this lovely lady?" Gecoo Chin turned to Blulay.

Blulay was at a loss. Who was this odd, perfume smelly person? And how did he know Ruban? She had never seen him before. Ruban tensed before he came up with an answer. Blulay could see the tension in Ruban's eyes. She decided to play along and find out what this was all about. Ruban was relieved that when he had first encountered Gecoo Chin, he had not divulged his name and he wasn't about to now.

"How was the pigeon?" Ruban changed the subject.

"Pigeon? Don't get me started on that!" Gecoo Chin vented, "I thought the pigeon special was today but it's tomorrow."

"Yes, I thought that also," Ruban replied. "Well, it was nice to see you again," Ruban grasped hold of Gecoo Chin's hand and shook it frantically. "Yes. We must be going," Ruban continued shaking. "Come dear, we must be going," he ushered Blulay with his eyes.

"So very nice to see you again," Ruban released Gecoo Chin's hand at last.

"See you at work."

With that Ruban took Blulay by her hand and hurried her out of the bistro as fast as they could go.

"What was that all about?" Blulay asked, as they quickened their pace.

"That, my dear, was Gecoo Chin-the Quarter Master of The Anvilus," Ruban replied, turning his head, to see if Gecoo Chin was anywhere behind.

"What? Who?" Blulay followed her husband's lead and turned her head about as the bistro started to disappear from view.

"I will fill you in once we get home, Blulay. Right now, let's just get as far away from here as possible."

Gecoo Chin scratched his head, wondering what had just taken place with the Australian. How rude he thought – and odd.

Mr. Gdown suddenly appeared and asked if Gecoo Chin had enjoyed his shark soufflé?

"Yes, it was quite good," he replied. "Do you happen to know those two who just left?" he then asked.

"What two?" Mr. Gdown looked about the bistro.

"Those two who just left."

"Those two?" Mr. Gdown waited for a few moments, "I've never seen them before in my life," Mr. Gdown answered, turning back to the kitchen just as Michael the waiter emerged with the bill for Gecoo Chin's meal.

"That's ok," Mr. Gdown shouted back to the waiter, "It's on the house."

"Really? That's a first," the waiter shrugged his shoulders and turned on his heel.

Gecoo Chin was left sitting and very confused.

18

Marcus sat alone in the dimly lit Senate chambers. It would be another 30 minutes before all the Proconsuls would arrive for the gathering he had called. The sound of the gold rings on his right hand tapping against the marble armrest of his throne echoed throughout the chamber as he thought about the force field surrounding the planet and how it was temporarily thwarting his plans.

Where did it come from?

How had it got there?

Who was working against him who had such technology?

He had personally interrogated all the off worlders rounded up over the years and who were presently imprisoned.They knew nothing about the force field. He could get no information, even after killing a few in front of the others.

There had to be someone else – or even a group of others – working against him. Someone knew something. But who? Who had the means, the tech? Whoever it was knew that Marcus had manipulated the time stream. He thought and thought until it hurt his head. Eno? He then thought. No. He couldn't be that bright? Could he?

Marcus did give it some serious consideration for a second or two then laughed to himself, just as Eno himself walked into the chamber. Eno walked toward Marcus slowly. He had made sure his mobile transfiguror would not time out on him. He was especially anxious that it didn't happen in front of the other Proconsuls, once they had arrived.

Marcus eyed Eno, as he slithered towards him. He was still musing to himself over the thought that Eno might be a traitor. He again, brushed it aside.

"Master," said Eno, as he reached Marcus and bowed. "Everything is prepared as you ordered."

Marcus leered at Eno, "Any more news on the force field?" he asked.

"Nothing yet," Eno answered.

"Did you try contacting the shuttle on the moon?" Marcus enquired.

"It would seem, Caesar – that for the time being, no signal is able to breach the force field. Eno replied.

Marcus did not like this answer. He knew deep down that he should have returned the shuttle back to Earth long ago but he had not felt it to be necessary at the time. He now was having second thoughts on that. Being that only he and Eno had any memory of their original time frame he wondered if the shuttle itself had some play with this force field as it too was from the same time frame.

Did it activate a defense mechanism?

Or was the shuttle in no way responsible?

Did Nebula Yorker have something to do with it?

He could never get Nebula Yorker out of his mind.

Neb was etched so deep, so gratingly deep.

He was a scratch you couldn't get at.

A pimple ready to explode.

A mosquito you could not swat.

An awful smell that lingered for days.

Eno watched Marcus as these thoughts pressed upon his master and thought. Gee, is this guy taking a seizure? He wasn't of course and Eno let the thought pass.

"We have continued sending up probes to investigate the force field as requested Caesar but the probes keep being absorbed into the field itself and by the looks of it are strengthening the field with each try we make," Eno informed Marcus.

"Why aren't the orbiting satellites affected?" Marcus asked.

"It would seem that the satellites are drawing power from the field and keeping them functioning for some reason that we cannot explain," Eno said.

"So the satellite signals can pass through the field yet we cannot get through. Something does not make sense," Marcus replied.

"Komi Koop is calling it a reverse vortex," Eno added.

A reverse vortex? Interesting. Something about that rings a bell. Marcus mused.

"Very good, Proconsul Eno. Take your seat. The others should be here soon. We will discuss this further, after the meeting."

Marcus settled back into his throne, his mind racing more than ever.

19

Neb and Kel worked endlessly on Neb's equations and hypothesis for using the shuttle to help them penetrate the Velexian Viper Vortex Reversal Bubble. LeBeau and Purell along with Professor Pheet, who had joined them, worked out the Schematics for the plan. See-Ess and Kcils sat in their makeshift holding cell trying to figure a way out. In all, everyone aboard the Photon Ledger was working on trying to better the situations at hand.

"What do you think our chances of this plan working are, Kel?" Neb asked as they both sat side by side at the science console on the bridge of the Photon Ledger.

"I would estimate 4.2 trillion to 1," she answered.

"4.2 trillion to 1! How exhausting," Neb smiled. "How did you come up with such a number?" Neb asked. He did not think the odds would be so high, maybe 1 trillion to 1-but 4.2.

"Since this procedure has never before been utilized and to the best of my knowledge – and that's a *lot* of knowledge –" Kel said in a Purell kind of way which did not go unnoticed by Neb, "I could have easily reached the conclusion that it may have been 100 trillion to 1. Though odds are a tricky item when such elements have never been observed or noted," Kel ended her line of reason, then finished by tilting her head robotically.

And there it was. Neb thought, that KEL-345 glint he first met all those years ago. Even though she had been re-animated into a new body construct and her data node processers fused with Purell's, there *she* was, the ever so evolving android.

"Of course depending how this experiment goes, the odds could rise or fall depending on the outcome," Neb just had to add.

"Obviously," Kel replied, matter-of-factly.

Neb and Kel moved back to the shuttle to continue their work, now sitting in the cockpit of the craft as LeBeau, and Purell with Professor Pheet, set up a work station in the docking bay adjacent to the shuttle.

The intensity of the work had everyone using their scientific abilities to the fullest. It filled them with a rush of exuberance that LeBeau and Pheet had not felt in years. Working alongside one another brought memories long forgotten to the fore. Memories of when LeBeau and Pheet had done their best work.

Purell could feel the energy between the two which also made him feel as though he was an equal in the task at hand and for an android who usually felt he was above most, if not all, beings – especially when it came to such advanced thinking – this inclusion almost made him feel human is some respects. And indeed, Purell was an equal to both LeBeau and Pheet, even if they had not told him so, Purell could feel it in their body rhythms.

As for Kel, she had come to feel about Neb the same as Purell did about LeBeau and Pheet. Neb had nurtured her abilities right from the very beginning of their acquaintance. With her inadvertent fusing with Purell back on Marine, Kel's capacity to feel emotion was greater than the inklings she had previously felt but had not understood until now, notwithstanding the Triopelian upgrades Neb had made to both androids.

Purell looked up from his console and waved to Neb and Kel who were both peering out of the shuttle's cockpit window at that precise moment. Neb and Kel looked at each other, smiled and waved back to Purell. LeBeau and Pheet also caught the moment and smiled to themselves. The positive vibes were doubtlessly flowing with each one feeding off the others as they all worked in unison. They would need to stay positive to tackle what lay ahead.

The only thing missing was the presence of John Lennon, Neb thought.

Neb stepped out of the shuttle and walked over to the 'Three Stooges' his codename for LeBeau, Pheet and Purell, though they were far away from being anyone's stooges.

"How goes it?" he asked happily as ever.

"We're making incredible progress!" An upbeat Pheet replied.

Neb had been very pleased with Pheet the last few days. Pheet's mind was working again as it should for a man of his calibre.

No more impel berry wine cobwebs remaining, Pheet thought. Though his momentary lack of reason and judgment concerning See-Ess and Kcils did bother him – and he was planning on apologizing to Neb – he just didn't know what to say.

"We have found the most extraordinary piece of information that may help us penetrate the Bubble," Pheet motioned Neb over to his console monitor where all four huddled, looking at Pheet's discovery.

"Oh, by the way," Pheet turned to Neb, "I am sincerely sorry about See-Ess and Kcils."

"Thank you, Gabriel," Neb smiled, patting Pheet on the shoulder, "I appreciate it."

They all turned their attention to the Earth with the Velexian Viper Vortex Reversal Bubble on the screen.

"Do you see how the Bubble's outer field is pulsating?" Pheet pointed to the screen. "The pulsating is what keeps the Bubble shell intact, thus holding back the parallel conundrum and stopping it from spilling out. But that is *not* what is interesting," Pheet smiled widely. "Here," he pointed.

"What?" Neb replied. "I only see satellites."

"Neb. Neb. Neb," said Pheet. "I thought you Triopelians were smart. Can't you see it either, LeBeau? Purell, can't you?" Pheet asked again.

Kel had joined the four and looked, "I see it," said Kel.

"See what?" Neb shook his head, a tad dumbfounded, as the rest were.

"Professor, shall I?" Kel asked.

"Be my guest," Pheet replied. He gave way to Kel.

"Firstly, I am not sure why the satellites are not encompassed by the Bubble but I will figure that out shortly," Kel began.

Neb's left eyebrow rose. He had finally got what Pheet was alluding to but let Kel continue.

Kel pressed a few buttons on the console then said. "Computer activate."

In the center of the docking bay, a large holographic projection of the Earth, surrounded by the Bubble appeared, with all of Earth's satellites positioned outside of the Bubble's range.

They all walked over to a get better view. Kel pointed upwards and said, "Do you see how the satellites' signals are penetrating the Bubble?"

"How can that be, Kel?" LeBeau stepped closer to the hologram, eyeing the satellites. "I thought that nothing could get in or out?"

"Precisely!" Pheet jumped in. "Having never seen the real thing before, except in theory, we thought that nothing was able to get in or out. Computer enhance the satellites tenfold and extrapolate a visualization of the Satellites' carrier waves."

"I would not have believed it if I did not see it with my own eyes!" LeBeau said and his mouth dropped open. "The signal is penetrating the Bubble!"

"A back door," Purell let out.

"A *lost* door," Neb said, turning to everyone.

"By the moons of Marine!" Pheet cried out. "Can it be?!"

"Kel, have you figured out how this is happening?" Neb asked her.

"I cannot," Kel replied.

"Anyone?" Neb looked at the three others. No one knew.

"Let's just say…" Neb began, "When the Velexian Viper Vortex Reversal Bubble was initiated by my parents, the parallel conundrum had just taken hold. Within mere seconds the whole of Earth's history had changed as in the blink of an eye-as one might say. Now Marcus would have started to change history as far back as 12 BCE Earth time and by the look of things it took its time in getting a firm hold on what is now the present Earth time 1990."

"Why so long?" LeBeau cut in.

"Because of the Earth's tri-dimensional span," Neb replied

"How does that explain the satellites then?" LeBeau further asked.

"The Velexian Viper Vortex Reversal Bubble only contains the Earth as a whole, not what surrounds the Earth."

"The orbiting satellites are not on the Earth, they are in space," the Professor answered before Neb could.

"Ok, I get it," LeBeau said. "However, it still does not explain the satellites' signals that are getting through."

"The satellites' frequency modulation and that of the Bubbles are polar opposites: reverse sinusoid oscillation," Purell said, taking his turn in the fun.

LeBeau was starting to feel left out in that it seemed everyone was getting onboard with the equation solutions but him. This was something that did not escape Neb's notice.

It was then and there that LeBeau came up with the answer to everything. By all accounts his inspired perception was the motherlode, revealing the final solution to their problem of how to penetrate the bubble.

"Do you think it will work?" Pheet asked.

"I must say LeBeau, without fail your equation is very androidian – if an android had come up with your idea," Purell marvelled at what LeBeau had just told everyone.

Even Neb had not thought of it, though given time he would have, he thought.

"When do we start?" Kel enquired.

"One has to be very precise in seeing this through," LeBeau said. "It's not something to be taken lightly and tests will need to be conducted before we subject ourselves to the procedure."

"You're quite right," Neb added. "Shall we get started then?"

"Absolutely!" LeBeau concurred.

LeBeau's solution to penetrating the Velexian Viper Vortex Reversal Bubble was as follows:

LeBeau came to the conclusion that by utilizing the satellites' carrier waves' frequencies, he could loop in the transfiguror transporter bio stream filter into the waves. It was something akin to what Sy Dyloup had done with The Rolling Stones, when they appeared on the Casino three years earlier. Though Sy Dyloup's procedure utilized brain waves and an REM filter with holographic enhancements while LeBeau's procedure would be dealing with real live flesh and blood. It was only a matter of tweaking the transfiguror transporter filters he said. The only gremlin in the procedure would be that once the transport was complete there was no way of knowing where the subject would materialize. There was no pin-point destination. They could find themselves stuck somewhere on the North American Continent, or Antarctica – or anywhere in fact. LeBeau though, was fairly confident he could find a signal beacon and transport through the waves and so locate where it was transmitting to. This could at least ensure they would materialize on the European continent.

In theory, anyhow.

It was hard to test the theory without conducting any tests. How could they send a test subject through and not know that it made it safely?

"Can we send the test subject down and then re-beam it back immediately for verification?" Pheet asked LeBeau.

"I believe we can," LeBeau answered. "But what type of test subject?"

"How about a chair?" Neb chimed in. "It's a solid structure."

After some hours of configuration, upgrading the transfiguror, locating an ample satellite signal and imbibing a few glasses of cold green tea with a twist of lemon everything was ready to proceed.Neb stationed one of the docking bay console chairs on the Photon Ledger transfiguror transport pad. It was a heavy, white leathered chair – about 15 kilos in weight.

"Count down to zero, has just begun…" Neb sang.

LeBeau entered the computations in the computer, "Ready," he said, as a few drops of sweat dripped from his brow. "It's now or never," LeBeau pressed down on the transport key.

A twirl of red-blue hued energy engulfed the chair and in an instant it was gone. LeBeau now counted ten backwards.

Everyone else mouthed the count; only LeBeau was heard, "Ten, nine, eight, seven, six, five, four, three, two, one."

Once again LeBeau pressed the transport key and —
poof! The chair was back. Everyone began to clap; the
procedure was a success it seemed. All were still looking at
the returned chair when it suddenly swivelled round to reveal
a very large potted plant sat centered. It was a tomato plant,
its lush vines covered with hanging tomatoes.

"I think we may have hit gold," Neb walked over and
pulled off one of the fruits. He brushed it up against his shirt,
held it up to his mouth and bit into it, to the total shock of all.

"Mmm, kind of sweet," said Neb.

20

Ruban had to explain his previous encounter with Gecoo Chin to Blulay. He had glossed it over before, which was not like Ruban at all. He put it down to feeling overwhelmed by meeting Komi Koop and his fellow prisoners and the worry of being able to escape without notice.

Would Gecoo Chin now spill the beans though and search him out? And when Gecoo Chin could not find Ruban, he would most likely make enquiries about the new Australian recruit. Then what would happen once Gecoo Chin found out there was no new Australian recruit?

Ruban felt everything was getting muddled; plans or no plans. First, it was Gaius Rulle and the unexpected turn of events when he attacked Marcus as he did. This led Marcus to beef up his security and also, no doubt, raised his suspicion that there was quite likely a resistance movement. (Marcus was, in fact, even more suspicious than they anticipated, with the revelation of a force field surrounding the Earth. Ruban and Blulay did not know that he knew but they would soon find out.) There was also now the problem of Gecoo Chin and then, to top it all off – what was that meeting with all the Proconsuls about?

Perhaps it was a blessing that their meeting at the Bistro had been cut short before Ruban divulged anything more. His gut instinct told him such. 'Gut instinct', he laughed to himself.

"Why the smile?" Blulay asked, noticing the glint of humour on her husband's face.

He laughed out loud, "Just something Neb once told me."

"About?" Blulay asked and as she asked, both of them wondered what Neb was up to – as they knew he was also wondering about them.

"Gut instinct," said Ruban. "Nebula said it was often more precise than one thought. It wasn't a Triopelian way of thinking or acting but more a human thing," he said.

"And what does *your* gut instinct tell *you*," Blulay smiled, grabbing hold of Ruban's hand.

"That perhaps we are best to keep some things to ourselves. Though our first priority is to help free Komi Koop and the others before Marcus kills them all – because he will. With The Anvilus almost ready for launch, what need will he then have of them?"

Beep. Beep. Beep. The sound of their console went off, activating the 17 inch monitor.

What can that be? They both thought. Ruban and Blulay turned to the screen.

A MESSAGE FROM THE IMPERIAL SENATE, scrolled across the screen followed by a voice.

"In five, four, three, two, …"

A camera panned the Imperial Senate, every seat was filled. Proconsuls from around the globe were accounted for.

Most fidgeted in their seats as they always did when called before Marcus.

Marcus loved it – to see them squirm and for all to see – though for some odd reason, Marcus was not presently present. This absence frightened all in attendance much more. Even Eno did not know where Marcus had gone to. He had been there a moment ago. Eno looked on.

The image of the Senate faded and was replaced on the screen with the words 'STAND BY'.

"This is all very odd indeed," Ruban said.

"Yes, I believe my gut instinct is kicking in," Blulay replied, wryly.

"Mine too," said Ruban. The picture on the screen was paused and they were left waiting with the rest of the planet. It really was highly unusual to say the least.

One minute went by that turned to twenty before the image of the Senate once again came in to full view on the monitor. The camera panned out and back in again as Marcus walked across the floor of the Senate before taking his seat in the center of the hall.

As Marcus sat down, out walked Gecoo Chin. Ruban's and Blulay's faces dropped – along with their gut instincts.

The Senate remained silent for a few more minutes as Marcus's eyes darted back and forth across the room.

"It has come to my attention," Marcus stood, "That a certain element of the Senate has been plotting against me."

Proconsuls Nivek Htims, Bor Rekab and Timus Gra each felt their skin crawl.

They had no idea who the man standing alone in the senate chamber was. It was Gecoo Chin. They had not noticed him at the Bistro earlier that afternoon.

"Bring in the prisoner," Marcus shouted.

Chains could be heard before anyone saw anything. Two Pretorian guards prodded the prisoner forward with two long lances. Clang, clang, clang, sounded the chains. The man was bound from head to toe. The guards pushed him ahead and he fell to his knees. He looked up at the camera that was now aimed directly in his face. It was Mr. Gdown, aka Germanus.

A gasp was let out across the Senate floor and around the planet at the sight of one of the greatest gladiators ever to have grace the Colosseum's hallowed ground.

Ruban and Blulay watched in terror and pity.

"Ruban!" Cried out Blulay, "What are we going to do?"

It would be only a matter of time before both she and Ruban would also be sought out and hunted down. Just as Ruban thought this, there on the screen in front of them was both of their faces-plastered on a planet-wide wanted poster for all to see.

Back in the Senate, Timus Gra stood up and yelled out, "Tyrant!" He pulled out a blade from underneath his toga and proceeded to plunge it into his heart.

Marcus cocked a brow and let out a venomous smile as Timus Gra fell forward.

Nivek Htims fainted. Bor Rekab sat with his head down, crying.

Soon more Pretorians arrived. It started to look as if there were now more guards than Proconsuls; which there were.

The planet was glued to their screens.

Six guards rushed over to Nivek Htims, yanked him from his seat and dragged his unconscious body over before Marcus, throwing him down hard on the cold floor.

For some reason they left Bor Rekab alone and instead took Proconsul Plump Trott of Lower Mexico who was sitting beside him. Procunsul Plump Trott was also flung at the feet of Marcus.

Bor Rekab sat stunned. Was he actually going to let Plump Trott take the fall for him?

A guard with a large bucket of cold water dumped it all over Nivek Htims, instantly waking him.

Plump Trott looked up at Marcus who was leering down at him, "I don't understand," he pleaded nervously, his entire body shaking uncontrollably. "What have I done, Caesar?" he begged before Marcus, now on his knees before the Emperor.

"Whoever finds these two," (At that moment, Ruban's and Blulay's faces flashed across the screen again.) "I will reward with the Proconsulship of these traitorous men," Marcus pointed to the two men grovelling a few feet away from him.

"Don't worry I have not forgotten about you Bor Rekab."

Marcus glared over Bor Rekab's way.

Bor Rekab somehow slipped out unseen – quite literally as only his toga remained, slumped over his seat.

"How did he do that?" Marcus seethed. Nonetheless the show must go on, he said to himself.

Ruban and Blulay turned off their screen. They had seen enough!

They sat opposite each other; eyes closed, with hands extended, their fingertips touching. A warm, green and yellow glow passed between them as the calm seeped in.

21

LeBeau continued to send a few more test subjects through the new adapted transfiguror satellite signal transport.

The chair proved to be a success but where had the potted tomato plant come from?

As it turned out the chair had materialized on the balcony of one Mary Trespass who lived 10 kilometres outside of Rome. She was rearranging her herb and vegetable garden and hadn't remembered there being a chair on the balcony before. She had shrugged it off though and lifted the potted tomato plant onto the chair to make more room. It was only seconds while she turned her back to reach for another pot to place it also on the chair. To her great puzzlement, on completing the movement, she found that the chair *and* her tomato plant were gone.

She wasn't quite sure what to make of it seeing that the chair was not there the night before and also that there was now one missing tomato plant. She decided to brush it off as one of those unexplained phenomenon – like the time her husband had vanished five years earlier.

Though, truth be told, Mary Trespass had never had a husband. Her discombobulation was in fact due to the heavy hangover she was now experiencing from the party the night before.

LeBeau carried on with the tests, alongside Purell and Kel who were assisting him. Professor Pheet and Neb were discussing what to do with See-Ess and Kcils.

A part of Neb did not feel like keeping them locked up but what choice did he have? He could not leave them alone on the ship while they were all down on the Earth trying to save the universe.

"Why not?" Said Pheet. "They are not going anywhere while they are confined behind the walls of the force field cell.

"I know," Neb replied. "I just have a bad feeling about trouble from those two. My gut instinct tells me to be worried."

"Your gut instinct?" Pheet asked. "Is that a Triopelian thing?"

Neb gave a little smirk and said, "No. It's an Earth thing."

"Fascinating!" Pheet replied.

"I can only surmise that having spent all those years on Earth, your body rhythms must have been absorbed into the Earth's tri-dimensional span."

"Something like that," said Neb.

"You and LeBeau have more in common than you know," the Professor continued.

"I heard that said before, though I doubt LeBeau has any Triopelian DNA strains running through his body. If that is what you are alluding to, Professor?" Neb responded.

"No, it's not that, Neb. Though that would be an amazing discovery. I am sure I would be able to write a paper about that indeed! Just imagine the press it would get," Pheet smiled. "Having known LeBeau as long as I have and only knowing you a short period, you're almost like one person in your thinking and attitude to problem solving. Though I will admit you are much quicker than LeBeau; sometimes even quicker than Purell and Kel too, come to think of it. How is that, Neb? Wait, don't tell me. It's a Triopelian thing," Pheet let out a little chuckle.

"You're catching on, Gabriel. You're catching on," Neb replied.

Hmm? The Professor thought. I think that's the first time Neb has addressed me by my first name. Though he wasn't sure, due to impel berry wine syndrome. It did make him feel very good about himself. Nebula Yorker sure was one of a kind. Or better yet, one of his kind. He wondered what the Triopelians would make of young Neb, if and when he would ever finally encounter his people. He'd hope and would love to be around to witness that meeting!

"I think we have the transfiguror satellite signal transport set!" LeBeau happily shouted out to Neb.

He, Purell and Kel put everything they could find and think of through the signal. From dirty socks to more dirty socks – that funnily enough, came back clean. Purell and Kel had replicated two life size humanoid mannequins down to a tee. They also came back in one piece, safe and sound.

LeBeau was now also 95 percent sure he could transport them near enough to Rome that they did not have to worry about materializing on the other side of the planet. Though again he could not guarantee where they would materialize around Rome.

It might be on hard ground.

It might be on water.

It might be on top of someone's roof.

Transporting Purell and Kel was a risk that Neb felt uneasy about. A transport beam in itself was one problem when transporting your normal type androids. (But Purell and Kel were certainly not your run-of-the-mill androids.) Transfiguring flesh and blood though a satellite signal would be another.

"Then again a chair or socks or mannequins are not flesh and blood either and they seem to have made it through and back just fine," Purell protested.

"Fair enough," Neb replied.

Perhaps Neb, LeBeau and Pheet would make it through – maybe they would not. However, it did solve the problem Neb had with See-Ess and Kcils and who would watch over them while they were planet side. It was determined that Purell and Kel would babysit See-Ess and Kcils.

"Babysit?!" Purell exclaimed.

Who's baby? What baby? Why would they need to watch a baby sit? Would the baby eventually do a trick or something or was the baby's trick in the sitting?

"For an enhanced android you can be a pain in the ass, Purell," Pheet retorted.

"Pain in the ass?" Purell retorted.

"My bottom is not experiencing any nerve end nodes."

"It will be if you don't shut up," Pheet shouted.

"Enough!" Neb blasted. "Purell," said Neb in a soft mellow tone. "I am putting you and Kel in charge of watching over See-Ess and Kcil while we are away."

"Oh," replied Purell. "Why didn't you just say that in the first place?!"

"He did," Pheet let out.

Neb pointed a finger at Pheet and said nothing.

Pheet dropped his head and walked away, pouting.

Neb could feel it was part impel berry wine withdrawals and part nervousness about the upcoming mission to save the Earth and the Universe. He could sense everyone's body rhythms, much like Kel and Purell could read theirs. LeBeau's was heightened with more excitement than fear, whereas Pheet was the other way around. Neb wondered if he should leave him aboard the Photon Ledger. And strangely enough, Kel was very mute.

"Is there something bothering you Kel?" Neb asked.

"What if you don't come back?" she answered and then added, "I will miss you."

"Kel," said Neb softly. He walked over and hugged her.

"I am feeling sad, am I not?" she whispered into Neb's ear.

"Yes, Kel. I can disengage your emotion node if you want?"

"No, that will not be needed," Kel rebounded. "To have that which I have not had – it would be sad not to have it at all. I will adjust to this new experience and learn from it. For what else is an emotion but a part of expanding self knowledge? I will only miss you if you do not come back Nebula Yorker. Until then I believe you have work to do, as we all do," Kel then tilted her head and smiled.

"Now you are playing with me," Neb smiled back. "Ok, then," Neb clapped his hands. "Purell can you work the controls? Can we all transport at once, LeBeau or do we need to be individually transfigured?"

"Individually," LeBeau answered.

"Ok, I will go first," Neb stepped up to the transfiguror pad. "LeBeau, Pheet," Neb nodded, "see you down there."

Purell worked the transfiguror controls as LeBeau and Pheet looked on.

"In five, four, three, two, one…"

Neb winked to everyone and was gone.

22

A few seconds later Neb materialized on, of all places, Mary Trespass's balcony.

Neb's head felt a little woozy and he was mildly disorientated so he hadn't noticed that LeBeau had followed him 60 seconds behind and that he too was feeling the same effects while standing at the other at end of the balcony-with both his feet stuck in potted plants.

For the time being, neither of them knew where they were or who they were. Professor Pheet was nowhere to be seen. After a few minutes, Neb and LeBeau regained their mental capacities.

"Wow! That was some transport," said Neb while checking himself, to make sure all his body parts were intact.

"You're telling me," replied LeBeau, looking down and seeing his feet encased in the pots which caused him to go in to a temporary panic as he thought his feet were cemented in. The feeling of the wet soil soon told him as he looked down that he would be fine and he pulled himself out of the pots.

"Where's the Professor?" Neb looked around, worried.

Indeed, where was the Professor?

"I hope he did not materialize inside a wall or something," LeBeau replied.

Neb and LeBeau looked out at their third story view. The sun was just coming up. Neb took a deep breath of fresh air. He let it fill his lungs and then he exhaled.

"There is nothing like fresh air," Neb told himself, remembering the first time he met Tict.

LeBeau likewise did the same.

"What do you want to do about the Professor, Neb?" LeBeau asked.

"Let's wait a little longer. It's too bad we don't have any way of communicating with the ship. Maybe he's still waiting to transport down?" Neb said.

They waited and waited but no Pheet turned up. After 30 minutes they decided they had to go. Each knew the risks of transporting through the transfiguror satellite signal and each also knew that they may not materialize in the same spot, even though LeBeau tried his best to make it so. Just in case though, they had made a plan to meet down by the Tiber, near the Imperial Palace, should they materialize in different places.

Neb wasn't sure what style of clothing they would need to wear in this Earth's Rome. Would it be togas and tunics, sandals? Prior to departure from the Photon Ledger, Neb went over a video feed his parents had sent. It would seem they wore both Rome-ish style clothes and contemporary style garments on this Earth.

Neb decided jeans and a black T-shirt, along with a light jacket, would be fine for himself. LeBeau chose light green linen pants and a short sleeve purple tunic. Pheet liked the idea of a toga but decided to go with black slacks, a white long sleeved shirt and a short white lab coat. They all wore black hover shoes, just in case they needed a fast getaway.

The sun was now making its way over the horizon, brightening up their surroundings. Both now got a better look at where they were.

"Ok, how do we get down from here?" LeBeau asked and as he asked, Mary Trespass walked onto the balcony from her living room, her morning coffee in hand.

Mary did not notice Neb and LeBeau at first but when she did, she let out a little gasp that was followed by her full cup of coffee crashing to the floor. Neb and LeBeau were caught off guard, as Mary was.

"Good morning," was the first thing that came out of Neb's mouth. "Balcony Inspector," he quickly said.

Balcony Inspector? LeBeau eyed Neb, wondering what he was up to.

Neb nodded to LeBeau. Yes Balcony Inspectors.

It then dawned on LeBeau what Neb was doing.

"Yes, Ma'am," LeBeau thrust out his arms, grabbing hold of the balcony's ledge with his hands. He gripped the ledge and gave it a good shake. "Yes. Yes, Yes. Very sturdy indeed," he said.

Neb followed suit and started to jump up and down. "Hmm, excellent concrete; very spongy," Neb observed.

"Spongy?" Mary Trespass said. "A concrete floor, spongy?"

Neb forgot he was wearing the hover shoes but rebounded with "What I meant to say, Ma'am, is that the floor is good enough to mop up with a sponge."

"Oh, yes. I can see that," Mary said. She looked down at her shattered cup and the pool of coffee at her feet.

"Hey! What has happened to my pots?" She had noticed the two pots near LeBeau's feet that were now half empty. There was dirt everywhere.

"Squirrels, Ma'am," Neb answered.

"What are squirrels?" Mary looked at Neb as if he was crazy. "You mean roof-rats don't you?"

Neb had no idea that there were no squirrels on this Earth.

"Yes, of course!" Neb slapped his forehead. "Roof-rats! That's what I meant to say."

LeBeau cut in, "Well everything looks in order, Maam. Thank you for your time but we must be getting on to the next balcony. Shall we?" LeBeau nudged Neb and motioned with his hand in the direction of the balcony door.

Mary Trespass moved over and blocked their path out. "Just a minute!" she said, eyeing them suspiciously. She moved closer to Neb, looking him straight in the eye and said, "Would you like a cup of coffee?"

Neb looked over to LeBeau with relief and shrugged his shoulders. "Yes, please. That would be so kind of you," Neb replied.

"Can we get it to go?" LeBeau smiled.

"Go where?" Mary Trespass replied.

Mary proceeded back into her condo apartment to make her guests some coffee. Neb and LeBeau offered to help clean up her balcony while she made the brew. After all, it was their fault that her pots were now in disarray and there was the broken cup and coffee staining her floor. It was the least they could do after startling her.

Neb and LeBeau entered her abode from the balcony which led into her living room. It was a modest size condo: three bedrooms, two bathrooms, and a large dining area.

"Just sit yourselves down and I will be with you in a moment," Mary called out from the kitchen.

Neb's nostrils picked up on the smell of the coffee that was wafting in. Real coffee! he thought. It had been a long time since he had tasted real coffee brewed from genuine beans. His supply that his parents has given him as a gift had long run out and there was something about replicated coffee that didn't quite do it for him.

The living room was bright and sparsely furnished. There was a blue four seater sofa, on which Neb and LeBeau now sat. Two small well-padded oak armchairs accented the room, with a small table between them. An oval coffee table separated the chairs and the sofa. There were a few pictures hanging on the walls; mostly of family it seemed. There were also two landscape paintings and one picture of Marcus hung in centre space. Neb eyed the picture with great disdain.

"Here we are!" Mary came into the room holding a tray with coffee and cookies.

She put the tray down on the table and poured each of her guests a cup.

"Thank you," said Neb as he reached for his cup. He closed his eyes and took a slow sip, savouring the flavour.

Likewise, LeBeau took a cup from Mary, though he did not close his eyes as he sipped away. "Hmm, very good," he said politely.

"Cookies?" she held out a plate with the cookies.

LeBeau gave Neb a look that said, 'we have to get out of here'.

Neb understood the message.

"Maybe just one," Neb smiled, accepted her offer and added, "Though we must be going soon. More balconies to inspect."

Neb and LeBeau bit into their cookies.

"Hey, not bad!" LeBeau quipped as he pocketed a few more when Mary wasn't looking.

Beep. Beep. Beep. Rang out.

"What is that?" Neb and LeBeau looked at each other.

"It's the television screen silly," Mary laughed. "Don't you have one?"

She pulled out a remote from the apron she was wearing and pressed down on the little box. Down rolled a screen in the far end of the room. A 52 inch screen, to be exact.

"Don't you just love these new viewing screens the Emperor released just last year?" Mary said as she popped a cookie into her mouth.

"Very," Neb smiled unconvincingly.

"I wonder if it's an update on the two fugitives?" Said Mary, all giggly and crunching down on another cookie.

Neb could not believe what he was seeing, for there – in all their 52 inch color glory – were the faces of his parents – Ruban and Blulay, aka Mr. & Mrs. Bancroft Yorker.

****

Meanwhile, Professor Pheet had materialized somewhere in a pitch black room. Or was it a room?! He could not tell. It was so very dark that he couldn't even see his hand in front of his face. Pheet started to panic. After a couple of minutes he started to feel better and thought maybe he should open his eyes. D'oh!

When he opened his eyes all was still pitch black.

After getting his legs back in working order and wondering where the hell he was, he yelled out for Neb and LeBeau and as he did so he tripped forward hitting a wall and inadvertently – a light switch. He covered his face from the light for a moment until his eyes adjusted.

There standing in full view of him was Livia, in suspended animation.

"What the…" the Professor mumbled.

23

Ruban and Blulay decided to stay put for the time being. Here in the confines of their catacomb home they could monitor what was going on up above. They felt terrible about the loss of Timus, and deep concern for Nivek, Bor and Mr. Gdown's safety and lives. They feared what the likely outcome would be. It would be the same outcome for them, if they were found. They were sad at this untimely circumstance and somewhat relieved that they had not divulged their home base as Ruban had been moving towards doing.

Their pictures being flashed across the planet were taken at the Bistro. As far as Ruban knew there were no cameras in The Anvilus's hangar bay that could have recorded his visit. Otherwise, Komi Koop and his fellow beings would be facing Marcus's wrath as well.

Ruban prayed it wasn't so.

Blulay was busy going over data from the Velexian Viper Vortex Reversal Bubble, something both she and Ruban did twice daily – once in the morning and once in the evening.

"Look here," Blulay called her husband over to her.

"The upper inner shield at the top of the Bubble is registering a frequency modulation," Blulay pointed to the console screen.

"That's odd," Ruban said, now sitting down beside her as they both peered at the screen.

"Let's run a diagnostic," Ruban began punching figures in the computer.

A graph of the Bubble appeared on screen showing three carrier signals points emitting from the top of the Bubble down.

"That can't be," Ruban shook his head.

"Pull up last night's data readout," he asked Blulay.

"Working," Blulay replied, doing her best Interface impression with a smile – trying to find some relief in the situation at hand.

"Good one," Ruban winked back at her.

Everything was registering the same as it had every morning and evening since they had arrived and implemented the Bubble.

Ruban and Blulay did not know that the Bubble did not encompass the satellites surrounding the Earth. They assumed, like many, that the Bubble did, though Pheet's discovery along with LeBeau's said otherwise.

Without knowing what was going on outside of the bubble and the universe, Ruban and Blulay had to rely on the tech they salvaged from the escape pod, it was mediocre at best, yet functional. Obviously, it was more advanced than some of Marcus's technology but not as accurate as they thought.

Why the blip all of a sudden and after all these months? Ruban wondered. He was also becoming wary, anticipating that Marcus may have discovered the Bubble and that he was trying to disrupt it somehow. It was the only explanation he could think of, though his gut told him otherwise. Could Neb be the culprit? After all, they had told him he was to stay away from the Earth. But then again, this was Nebula. And if it *was* Neb, what was he doing?

"Blulay, run a Triopelian Bio Rhythm scan of the planet," Ruban asked.

Blulay looked at her husband a little bemused, it hadn't entered her mind that Neb could possibly be behind the blips.

"Why?" she asked.

"I have a gut feeling," he replied.

"Oh, one of those again, eh," she turned to the console and imputed the Triopelian bio codes into the computer. They waited as the computer coordinated the scan.

After a few minutes the scan detected only two Triopelians on the planet.

"Well it was worth a try," Ruban sighed.

24

Neb spat out his coffee. It went flying all over him and the coffee table.

"Oh dear!" Mary let out. "Are you ok?" she asked Neb.

"I'm fine, fine," Neb coughed.

Mary rushed back to the kitchen and returned with paper towels and a sponge. She handed Neb the paper towels and he quickly cleaned up the mess on the table.

"I am so very sorry," Neb apologized.

"Are you sure, dear? You look quite pale. Maybe I should get you a glass of water?"

"Please," Neb replied.

Mary rushed off to the kitchen again.

LeBeau stayed silent, he also could not believe what he was seeing. A warrant had been issued for Ruban and Blulay, for them to be captured alive if possible.

As Mary returned, the news feed returned to the inside of the Senate chamber. There, all chained and bound were Nivek Htims, Plump Trott and Mr. Gdown. Bor Rekab was nowhere to be seen. Timas Gra's body was still slumped over in his chair. Gecoo Chin loomed over the prisoners. The rest of the Senate chamber was empty.

"Germanus!" Neb shouted.

"Who?" LeBeau asked, bewildered.

"I know! Isn't it just so sad," Mary frowned. "It wasn't all that long ago when he won his freedom. Now look at him. So very sad indeed," Mary shook her head. "But I am sure we will get to see him again in combat in the games soon enough. More coffee?" she asked her guests, happily.

"No, thank you," Neb and LeBeau answered simultaneously.

Again, the news feed went back to Ruban's and Blulay's pictures. Mary looked at the screen and back to Neb a couple of times and said "You know, you kind of look like them. Around his nose and eyes and you also have her chin and mouth," Mary continued her observation.

Neb was taken aback. He had never noticed those features before and for the most part Neb's life with his parents were with the older version of themselves—until the parallel conundrum took place that is. He had to admit, the likeness was overwhelming.

Mary started to become suspicious the more she continued to look back and forth until the images disappeared from the screen. Neb had to think on his feet.

"They do seem to have some resemblance. But I am orphaned and have no family whatsoever. No sisters or brothers; no mother or father – just my fellow orphan friend here – Joe," Neb said, with sad puppy dog eyes.

"You poor boys," Mary started to cry.

Now look what you have done, LeBeau thought, we'll never get out of here.

"Now, now," Neb got up and hugged Mary whose sobs grew even louder.

"There, there," he patted her on the back. "It's ok, you didn't know. Look we will write up a Class A report on your balcony and enter you into a competition, to win a nice prize."

A prize! Mary's sobbing quickly stopped. "What kind of a prize?"

"Oh no!" thought Neb. "What have I done?"

"Don't worry, The Balcony Association will be in touch," LeBeau grabbed Neb by the arm. "Our next inspection calls. Duty you know."

"Thank you so much for your hospitality," Neb gave Mary one last hug.

"You're welcome," she replied, as LeBeau led Neb away.

"By the way, which way is out?" LeBeau looked about while dragging Neb along.

"The door is straight ahead," Mary pointed.

Though Mary Trespass had never had a balcony inspection and actually had never heard of anyone else having one for that matter, the anticipation of winning a prize lifted her spirits. She also soon forgot about Neb's resemblance to the fugitives.

"Check your mailbox for…" LeBeau waved as they both scurried out of Mary's condo.

Mary waved back, wondering what a mailbox was.

25

Marcus thrashed his office to bits; everything was thrown, torn, smashed, and crushed. Even his very own handpainted masterpieces were sliced and diced.

Eno cowered in a corner of the room, his mobile transfiguror malfunctioning once again.

"I give!

"And I give!

"And I give!"

Marcus yelled out.

"What more do they want?

"I feed them!

"I clothe them!

"I love them!"

Marcus picked up an empty wine glass from his desk and threw it at the wall, the shards raining down on Eno's head.

"ENO! Get over here now!" Marcus continued his venting.

Eno didn't move or at least he did not want to move. He was almost at his wit's end with his master's temper. All these long years – not just here on Earth but all those other years on the Casino – were not forgotten. What happened? he thought, looking up at Marcus who was still raging on. I could have been someone; had a life. He could have started up his own 'Get a Foot Up Dancing School' franchise. If he had a better backbone or any backbone at all he would have stood up to Marcus before the Casino plan. He had thought about leaving the Casino even before Nebula Yorker had showed up but Marcus had egged him on to stay, saying big things were about to happen. And boy did big things happen!

Eno cringed as he walked over to Marcus.

"Yes, master?" he asked, his head down, not wanting to have eye to eye contact.

"Clean this mess up! And do not stand so close to me! How many times have I told you?!" Marcus sneered.

"Do it yourself," Eno shot back, without thinking.

"What? What did you say?" Marcus leered, smiling that villainous smile of his.

Eno waited for the hammer to come down. I have done it now, he thought and he didn't care.

Marcus just glared at him and said nothing.

After what seemed like an eternity to Eno, Marcus finally said.

"Very well then, get a crew in here ASAP and have them clean up."

"I beg your pardon?" Eno replied, not believing what he had just heard.

"Are you also deaf now? And after you have done that, have Komi Koop brought to me," Marcus turned away and headed out of his office.

"Oh, and one more thing," Marcus said before he exited the room, "Never, ever speak to me again in that fashion or you will be Friday night's special execution event."

"Yes, master," Eno wiped the sweat off his brow.

Marcus walked out of his office, his mind working overtime. He needed to think.

To meditate, as it were. He needed someone to talk to. Someone he could bounce his thoughts off. Someone who would listen and not talk back.

Livia! He grinned to himself.

****

Professor Pheet walked around the solid glass containment booth. He looked up and down at the female figure encased. Who was she? And more importantly: where was he?

The room he now found himself in had no windows, no doors and seemingly no way in or out, that he could see. Perhaps there was a secret panel that slipped open to reveal an entrance or exit. The room wasn't very big. Four clean cemented walls, one light switch that he literally had stumbled upon and one boxed woman standing in suspended animation. Very strange, he thought. Was he in a tomb of some sorts?

He tapped the front of the booth.

"Hello? Hello. Can you hear me?" he asked, looking up at the sad frown she had on her face. "Do you know where I am?"

"Hello? Hello?" he continued tapping.

Hmm? Pheet stared at her. I wonder? He mused looking down.

He began lightly kicking the bottom of the booth thinking there might be a power source that was keeping the booth active. And he was correct.

The booth sat on a four centimetre base of translucent marble that one would never know as it meshed perfectly with the booth and floor. Pheet now got down on his hands and knees, to feel about the base.

"Ah," he said. "There you are."

A half a centimetre panel revealed itself. Pheet looked up at the woman and proceeded to open the panel and press the deactivation button. There is always a button. Always. He laughed to himself. No matter how advanced any technology on any world, there was always an on and off button. Here we go. He pressed.

In a matter of seconds the containment field dropped and so did its lone occupant – into the waiting arms of one Professor Gabriel Pheet.

Livia looked up into the face of the Professor and coughed a silent cough. She tried to mouth a few words but nothing came out.

"Try to relax," said Pheet. "You're experiencing a molecular cryo strain. I do not know how long you have been suspended in animation so it may take a little time before all of your senses balance out. If you can understand me close your eyes twice," he asked.

It took all the little strength she presently had but Livia being Livia – she blinked twice.

Pheet began to cradle Livia, mingling his body heat with hers in an effort to get her blood circulation flowing properly. He reckoned by the looks of her that she had been encased for some time. But who was she and who would do such a thing? Then as he continued aiding her, a slight hiss sounded overhead. The ceiling opened up and stairs swung down.

The first thing Pheet saw were sandaled feet as the figure descended.

When Marcus reached the bottom of the stairs his eyebrow arched. He looked at Pheet and Livia, very un-amused and even puzzled to say the least.

"You!" Livia screamed out with all her mustered strength but then proceeded to faint.

Marcus stared at the Professor who still had Livia in his arms.

Pheet did not know what to make of everything but one thing he did know, from watching Neb's parents' feed, was that he was in the presence of Marcus himself.

Marcus pulled out a small phaser pistol from beneath his toga and pointed it directly at Pheet.

"Who are you?" Marcus shuffled sideways. "Up on your feet," he motioned with the phaser. "Move away from the lady, now!"

Pheet gently laid Livia on the floor and stood up.

"Hands up, where I can see them," Marcus sneered. "Stand over there, beside the wall," he ordered.

Marcus bent down and with his eyes and phaser still on Pheet, he took Livia's pulse.

"It will be ok my lovely," Marcus said, patting Livia's head.

Straightening up he asked Pheet again, "Who are you and how did you get in here?"

Pheet did not know exactly how to answer. How could he, without giving away who he really was and how he came to be where he now found himself. He thought about fainting and letting the chips fall as they may. So he did the best possible thing.

Pheet fainted.

It seemed to have worked for Livia, he thought as he dropped to the ground.

26

Neb and LeBeau found themselves walking down a small stretch of the Appian Way.

"That was a close one Neb, and weird," LeBeau said, reaching into his pocket. "Cookie?" he held one out to his friend.

Neb looked at the cookie and back up to LeBeau. "Nah, you have it."

"Where do you think your parents are held up?" LeBeau asked, biting into the cookie.

"Well, I would surmise that they are not anywhere near the city," Neb replied. "Stay out of sight but stay in sight. According to our present location we are about 20 kilometres from the palace which is a good enough distance to overlook the situation without being detected."

"How can you be so sure?" LeBeau asked. "I would think hiding out *in* the city might prove more beneficial if you want to keep tabs on Marcus, wouldn't you, Neb?"

"In some cases, yes. But it would be much easier to be seen by the population. No, my best guess is that they are outside of the city, keeping a low profile."

"Maybe they are hiding in a rabbit hole," LeBeau said, finishing off the last cookie he had taken from Mary Trespass's place.

"You're Brilliant!" Neb gave LeBeau a great big hug.

"I already know that," said LeBeau, who was a little taken aback by the hug, in that no one ever hugged him. Especially not for being so brilliant. He liked it.

"Don't you see, LeBeau?" Neb let out.

"See what?" LeBeau asked.

"A rabbit hole – they are hiding in a rabbit hole!" Neb was overcome with joy.

"Are you sure you're feeling well, Neb," LeBeau sounded confused.

"I thought you were brilliant?" Neb stood, looking stoney faced at his friend.

LeBeau likewise mirrored Neb's face, and then it dawned on him, "They are hiding underground!"

"Exactly!" Neb jumped up and down excitedly, hugging LeBeau again. "Hmm?" Neb rubbed his chin. "Where might those wascally wabbits be hiding?"

"Excuse me?" LeBeau raised an eyebrow. "Wascally Wabbits?"

Neb laughed out loud. "Bugs Bunny and Elmer Fudd? …Earth cartoons? …I'll tell you about them later."

"Cartoons?" LeBeau shook his head bemused. "You certainly have a wealth of odd knowledge, Nebula Yorker."

"I know!" Neb replied, "Isn't it just the best! You'll love cartoons, LeBeau. When we get back to the casino I will introduce you to them."

"Oh? Are they guests on the casino?"

Neb patted LeBeau on the shoulder, laughing. "Let's get back to where my parents might be... I wonder if there are any quarries, caves or underground aqueducts around here?"

"Perhaps there are some right beneath our feet where we stand?" LeBeau offered.

Neb's eyes grew wider than they ever had before, which LeBeau noticed.

"Are you ok, Neb?" he asked.

"YOU'RE BLOODY BRILLIANT!" Neb yelled.

Oh no! LeBeau thought, here comes those hugs again. He put out his arms.

"Why didn't I think of it? Of course! Why didn't I think of it before?"

"Think of what, Neb?" LeBeau asked, a little sad no hugs were forthcoming.

"The Ancient Rome of my time had catacombs where Christians would hide from the Romans, hold meetings and also be buried. There may still be such catacombs, directly under our feet!" Neb rubbed his chin again. "This is part of the Appian Way after all!"

"I don't like the sound of all that," LeBeau looked at Neb, put off by the comment. Who or what were Christians and why were they hiding, having meetings and then being buried, he thought to himself. And most importantly… what were catacombs?

It was best if Neb took the lead after all. This was his home world, as oddly weird as it was, even to LeBeau. He himself, had never known that much about Earth and its inhabitants. He knew Earth wasn't part of The Guild and from what he gleaned from TeeceeFore it was not that much of an advanced planet, when you considered its age. The furthest Earth's inhabitants had managed in space travel was to their only moon.

But LeBeau knew there was more to Earth and its people than rumour and gossip within The Guild would have anyone believe. Mr. Tict was an Earther and a fairly decent and likable being. Marcus, on the other hand, was a douche bag though Earth did not have the sole claim on douche bags. And then there was Nebula Yorker- a Triopelian by birth and an Earther by trade. Two out of three wasn't too bad.

Oh – and John Lennon! LeBeau, along with Neb, enjoyed his company very much. Whatever John Lennon might be – it was hard to fathom.

"Ok Neb, what's next?" LeBeau asked.

"Let's find a local person and enquire about this area," Neb pointed ahead, down the road. "Someone must know where the catacombs are."

But as they walked and talked, strangely enough, no one was to be seen. Neb reckoned it was about 9 am by now. The sun was still low enough that the day's heat had not begun to beat down on them. Neb felt a familiarity with Rome past, present and this unscripted future. For the most part everything looked the same. Though where were all the people?

"Any idea what day this is, LeBeau?" Neb asked.

"Day?" LeBeau replied.

"You know – Monday, Tuesday…"

Neb forgot for the moment that most worlds did not have their days named and now he worried that LeBeau would be wondering what the hell Neb was talking about again.

"Feels like a Thursday," LeBeau replied, much to Neb's surprise.

Neb just went with it. "Yeah, feels like a Thursday."

As they continued walking, Neb thought he heard a guitar playing in the light wind that now blew. "Did you hear that?" Neb asked LeBeau.

"I did. It sounds like it's not too far away either," LeBeau said.

They hurried their pace until LeBeau spotted two young girls just off the roadside. They were sitting by a brook and one of them played a guitar while a song bird sang above them. This is very weird, Neb thought to himself, and yet so familiar.

"Hello there," LeBeau happily shouted out.

The girls turned about but they weren't girls – they were two young men with long hair.

Neb laughed to himself. Some things never change with youth.

"Hey, that sounded pretty cool," Neb offered up.

"Do you think?" the young man with the guitar asked. "I have been working on it for some time but Geezer here thinks it's awful."

"I didn't say that, Ozz," the other chirped in, chiding his friend.

"Yes you did," Ozz replied.

"Ok, I did, but I was just playing with you," Geezer laughed.

"You'll be great when you play it before the Emperor at the next games."

The Emperor! LeBeau gulped.

Neb smiled at LeBeau. Another coincidence it would seem.

"So tell us, boys. How did you get a gig with the Emperor?" Neb asked.

"Gig?" they both asked simultaneously.

"How is it that it came to be that you will be performing for the Emperor?" Neb corrected himself.

"My uncle is the new Proconsul of Greater Britain-Trbor Tnalp," Ozz replied.

"Oh I see," said Neb.

"And who might you two be?" Ozz asked.

"I am Bugs Bunny," LeBeau replied "and this is my good friend, Elmer Fudd."

Now Neb would normally have been perturbed at LeBeau's answer but in this case it was a good comeback after his mentioning Bugs and Elmer not less than 20 minutes ago.

These coincidences were adding up, Neb thought.

"Can I ask a question, guys? Bugs and I are not from these parts; we're visiting from up north. We've been told that there might be some cool caves around here."

"The only caves I can think of are the Dead Caves a few miles up the road. But no one ever goes there," Geezer answered.

"They are kind of off limits," Ozz added.

"Oh, why is that?" Neb asked.

"Most of those caves are thousands of years old and very decrepit. They have been known to swallow people up.

The acoustics are mad though!" Ozz gushed while strumming his guitar in a style that reminded Neb of Pete Townsend.

"So you have been there, then?" LeBeau winked at the lads.

"You won't tell anyone, will you?" Geezer cringed.

"Nah," Neb laughed out loud, "but if you can maybe show us where they are?"

"No problem!" The guys leapt up.

"May I?" Neb asked, reaching out for Ozz's guitar.

"Do you play?" he asked.

"A little," Neb smiled.

Neb started playing 'Smoke on the Water' by Deep Purple while they walked.

The boys' eyes almost pooped out of their heads.

The heavy opening riff had them mesmerized.

"What is that?!" Ozz asked excitedly.

27

Professor Pheet awoke in a beautiful sun-filled room with a wonderful frescoed floor. In fact he was in what was known as 'The Garden of Livia', a duplicated room of one that was originally in one of Augustus Caesar's villas in Ostia.

Pheet was laying on a Roman dining couch also known as a 'lectus triclinaris'. His head was resting on a pillow as he eyed the room.

"It's about time, dear," he heard a woman's voice but did not immediately see any one. Soon she was face to face with the Professor; she gave him a very light kiss.

"I do not know how I will ever repay you," said Livia Drusilla, wife of the onetime Emperor of Rome – Gaius Octavius Thurinusm – the August One – Augustus Caesar, whom Marcus had executed.

Pheet's face blushed red. It took him a moment to realize it was the woman that had been encased in the glass booth; she whom he had freed.

"Oh my!" Pheet replied and asked, "Who are you?"

"I should be asking you the same question," Livia answered.

The Professor stood up, straightened himself out and bowed. "I am Professor Gabriel Pheet, at your service, Madame." He took hold of Livia's right hand and kissed it tenderly.

It was Livia's turn to blush this time.

"Oh my!" was her reply, as they both shared a smile and then laughed together.

"Livia Drusilla, good sir." She nodded her head.

"Where are we?" Pheet asked as he walked over to look at a garden fresco on a wall.

"These are marvellous!" he glanced over the wall in front of him.

"I would like to say I am home but I don't think I am," Livia joined Pheet.

"Might you know where we are?" she asked Pheet.

"I believe we are in Rome, circa 1990 Earth. At least that is where Neb and LeBeau said we were heading to. I don't know where they landed, though."

"Neb? Do you mean Nebula Yorker?" Livia's eyes sparkled, her voice was raised with a happiness that she had not felt in years – actually, in thousands of years.

Pheet turned to Livia quite taken aback. "You know Nebula?"

For the next two hours, Livia and Pheet shared their stories of their encounter with one Nebula Yorker.

"Marcus will shit his pants when he finds out Nebula is here," Livia rubbed her hands together. Her mind was working out details upon details, in the way that only Livia could. It refreshed her. Revenge! She thought to herself.

"But we mustn't let Marcus know he is here," Pheet cautioned her.

"How then Gabriel, will you explain yourself when Marcus interrogates you – and he will."

"Yes, I have been thinking about that," Pheet said. "I think fainting again is out of the question; you can only get so far with that ploy."

"You know he will torture you in order to get what he wants and then whether he does or does not have the information he desires, in the end he will kill you. He will kill you, whatever the outcome actually. There must be a believable story we can come up with, without letting on about Nebula." Wheels within wheels turned within Livia's calculating mind.

"From what you have told me, Gabriel – and believe me most of it has gone far over my head – why not tell him you got caught up in all of this time thing while visiting the planet all those years ago. That way you wouldn't have to mention Nebula at all. You could just say that you have been keeping a low profile until now."

"That sounds all well and good Livia but how do I explain how I came to be with you down in that vault?"

"I can't come up with it all Gabriel, you're supposed to be the learned one," Livia sounded exasperated. "Men!"

she muttered under her breath. "Sooner or later Marcus will make his appearance so you better think fast."

Pheet loved strong woman, he always had, and he knew Livia was right.

As soon as Livia finished speaking Marcus did appear – almost walking out of a fresco, it seemed to both of them.

"Well, well, well, what *do* we have here? The serpent and the hare!" Marcus leered at both of them.

"Be careful of this one," Marcus walked up and around Livia, sniffing at her as he always did, "she can be quite the handful."

Marcus now circled Pheet while at the same time eyeing Livia, with that evil glinted smile of his.

"Shall we sit?" Marcus pointed to the three curule seats that were not there a moment ago – nor was the table, centred with food and drink.

Livia didn't know how famished she was until she saw the food. After all, it had been a very long while since she last ate, though to her it seemed like it was only a matter of days. Pheet wasn't at all surprised, knowing how anti matter transfer worked and he too didn't mind a bite or two.

They all sat down. Marcus was sitting in front of them while they both sat side by side. Livia gingerly filled a plate while Pheet piled it on. Marcus poured himself a cup of wine. He also did so for both of his guests. Pheet lifted the cup and gave it a smell, then quickly put it back down.

"There is no poison in it," Marcus replied, watching Pheet closely.

"Oh, it's not that," Pheet said, now enjoying the spread. "I used to imbibe far too much and it was causing too much friction with my colleagues."

"Your colleagues?" Marcus leaned in.

Livia picked up on Marcus's sly, slow interrogation method and jumped in to change the subject—for the time being at least.

"So?" Livia sat back, sipping her cup of wine meagerly.

"How long do you plan on leaving me free and uncaged?" she asked.

Marcus turned his eye to Livia, "That all depends on you my dear. Where would you rather be?"

Livia tilted her head over to Pheet then back to Marcus. "If you're looking for me to be your wife, you can forget about that. You can lock me up and throw away the key for all I care." She looked down at her cup of wine, swirling it as she did so.

"Livia. Livia. Livia. I got over you a long time ago."

"Did you?" Livia cocked a brow.

"You do realise that every time you came down over the years, to have one of your little frivolous chats with me, that I could hear every word you said? You're so awfully boring, my dear. Here you are, the Emperor of Rome—and even, now, of the whole world, I hear. But you are no better than a little child. I can tell you that Augustus had his doubts and fears but he never once cowered because someone did not like the way he looked or felt."

Livia reached for more wine, pouring some into her cup. She eyed Marcus as she took a sip, licking her lips and smiling ever so much like her nemesis.

Marcus held his temper, he would deal with Livia later. His attention turned back to the Professor. Marcus took a deep breath.

"Who are you and how did you find yourself in my hidden vault?"

"Well, it's a rather long and funny story," Pheet replied. "It involves magic and it was just an accident that I found myself where you found me. You see," Pheet continued. "I met this fellow about two years ago who had no place to live and was hungry. He was very odd looking as well."

"Really," Marcus yawned.

"Yes, his ears were rather pointed; like a devil of some sorts. I thought it was just a birth defect. Anyhow, we got to eating and drinking some and when you drink too much one can say the strangest things- things such as this fellow told me. He said he was from another planet. Can you imagine?" Pheet laughed.

What's he up to? Livia thought. Whatever it was, it was sounding good.

She saw Marcus's ears prick up when Pheet mentioned another planet.

"He stayed with me for a few days and drank all my good wine and in the middle of another of his wild tales he reached into his pocket and gave me this thing that looked something like a coin. He said it could make me invisible and also would allow me to travel from one place to another, just by pressing down on the middle of the coin."

Marcus was now buying the whole story; Livia knew he was and Pheet was on a roll. Neb would be proud of him. Staying away from the impel berry wine had erased the cobwebs from his brain that he so long had dealt with.

"Well, I thought it was just the wine talking but he grabbed hold of me and pressed the coin and poof! I was here, there and everywhere. I could not believe it. He said the coin had a limit though and once used up the coin would turn to ash and that would be it. And that is how I found myself in your vault. I meant no offence. I had no idea where I would turn up."

Marcus sat back. He rubbed his chin much like Neb would do when he was thinking deeply.

"Where is this pointed eared fellow now?" Marcus enquired.

"Dead," Pheet answered. "Funny thing, one evening after drinking my last two bottles of very good wine he literally exploded all over my home. They had to tear down my home, it smelled so much."

Marcus thought some more, he knew of the species of beings Pheet was talking about. The Globoid's from Globoid Prime. They could not hold their liquor very well and he could remember a few of them having the same experience on the Casino.

Marcus stood up and paced about. He wasn't sure what do about Pheet.

Should he kill him?

Let him go?

"I never did catch your name?" Marcus stopped his pacing and stared at Pheet.

"See-Ess", replied Pheet.

"Have you ever told anyone else about this man and the coin?" Marcus asked.

"No, never. Who would believe me?" Pheet replied.

"Good, keep it that way," Marcus looked over at Livia, wondering what she was thinking.

"For the time being, I would like you to be my personal guest, See-Ess."

"And what of me?" Livia asked.

"Yes, you as well. For the time being," Marcus replied. "Someone will be with you shortly to take you to your new quarters but I wouldn't get too comfortable if I were you, Livia."

"And as for you, See-Ess, I think I would like to get to know you a little better. We will see each other soon."

There was something familiar about See-Ess but Marcus wasn't quite sure what that something was. He had lived so long in so many different time frames and met so many beings – and some just stuck with him-like Nebula Yorker.

With that thought, Marcus turned and in the bat of an eye he was gone.

Pheet turned to Livia and said, "I think that went rather well."

28

Kel and Purell observed See-Ess and Kcils from their science station on the bridge. It had been close to twenty four hours since Neb, LeBeau and Pheet left on their universe-saving adventure.

"Isn't it interesting how See-Ess has invested his time trying to break free of his confinement while Kcils just sits back cleaning herself?" Kel noted to Purell.

"Yes, it is. It seems See-Ess is doing all the work to find a way to break through the force field while Kcils watches. I surmise that Kcils may be the brain of the two," Purell replied and then added, "I would like to propose an experiment. Why don't we extend the force field's perimeters within the makeshift cell?"

"To what extent?" Kel asked.

"What's that term Neb once used? Cut them some slack by loosening the leash and see how far they go," Purell replied.

"I see. How much of the so called leash do you wish to slacken?" Kel looked down at the science console's viewing screen and then back up to Purell.

"Good question," Purell replied. What might you suggest?"

Kel thought for a few moments before processing the experiment, which was something new to her; that is, pausing to think was new to her. "We can give them the impression that they somehow broke through the force field when in actuality we extend the force field within their movements thus limiting their sense of freedom – which is, anyway not real. We will let them think they are free when they are not!"

"Oh Kel, that is a delightful idea! We can create a maze for them to maneuver through and we can record each failure. "Though how much access to the ship should we allow?"

"For the time being, let's just open a route to the hangar bay and see what they do then," Kel answered.

"And I thought we were going to be bored babysitting," Purell let out a robotic giggle.

Purell began to compute the force field's perimeters, allowing See-Ess and Kcils free movement within two metres ahead and back. That should be enough of a loosening of the leash, he relayed to Kel.

After all the computations were set, Purell opened the force field's lines.

"This should be good!" Purell said to Kel.

They sat back, waited and watched.

See-Ess threw one of his shoes for the 100th time and as per the previous 99 times, it bounced off the cell's force field. Zip, zip, zip sounded, as the shoe hit the field, creating a light blue flash as it rebounded back into See-Ess's hand.

"Give it a break," Kcils rolled her eyes.

"There has to be a crack somewhere," See-Ess moaned. "There is always a crack."

To Kel's and Purell's dismay, See-Ess stopped. He put his shoes back on and felt a soothing heat as he slipped them on due to the friction created by throwing the shoes continuously against the force field.

"Hey that feels good," See-Ess smiled.

"What are you smiling about?" Kcils noticed.

"My feet feel as though they are being massaged by millions of little tiny hands."

See-Ess leaned back, enjoying the sensations running up and down the soles of his feet.

"Here. Give me your shoes," he motioned to Kcils.

"What for?" she mildly protested.

"Come on love, just hand them over. You'll see," See-Ess held out his hand.

Kcils reluctantly took off her petite pink shoes and gave them to See-Ess.

"You see my dear, by throwing the shoes against the field a few times they will warm up your tender paws."

See-Ess threw Kcils's left shoe first. They both watched as the shoe seemed to have passed through the force field and landed a metre away.

What the…?! See-Ess silently mouthed.

"This should be good," Purell said to Kel.

"Indeed!" Kel replied.

See-Ess took Kcils's other shoe and threw it. A smile crossed his face as the second shoe landed beside the first but See-Ess knew better, something was afoot and it wasn't shoes.

See-Ess and Kcils walked casually over to Kcils's fallen shoes. See-Ess picked them up and handed them over to Kcils. At the same time he gave her a nod that meant, 'We are being watched'. In the business that See-Ess was in, a look, a nod, a wink – all had a code. Underworld dealers at their best all had codes and as a number one gangster/celebrity on Marine, See-Ess knew them all and had also taught Kcils a few.

Kcils winked back, acknowledging her boyfriend.

"They are kind of twitchy, aren't they?" Purell said to Kel as they observed the couple.

"What's our next move?" Kcils whispered to See-Ess.

"Just keep moving," See-Ess grabbed Kcils by the hand as they walked slowly out of the makeshift containment cell's force field – or so they thought.

"Should we now guide them to the hangar bay?" Kel asked Purell.

"Let's!" Purell pushed a button on the science console.

A door swooshed open in front of Kcils. She was about to go through when See-Ess pulled her back.

"Not yet," he moved his eyes back and forth.

Kcils wasn't sure whether moving one's eyes back and forth was a code at all or whether it was just one she couldn't remember. She decided to stand still.

Wait. See-Ess conveyed to Kcils.

See-Ess looked up and around. He was trying to locate any evidence of a surveillance camera. He couldn't see anything but that did not mean they were not being watched. He had a feeling and his feelings usually proved correct.

"I think someone or something is watching us," he let on to Kcils.

Fortunately for Kcils and See-Ess (though not so fortunate for Kel and Purell) there was no audio feed but only a visual and though the androids could have easily read lips, they were so much into their little experiment that they overlooked the obvious.

"Ok," See-Ess said to Kcils. "Let me take the lead but stay close behind."

They both walked through the door and it swooshed closed behind them.

They had walked out into a white corridor, much like the halls in Halley's Casino which lay between the games rooms. They slithered against the walls as they moved, not knowing where the corridor would lead them.

"This is really weird," Kcils said to See-Ess.

They stopped briefly to pat down the walls to see if they could find another door or exit. It began to seem as if they were going around and around for hours though in fact it was not hours, though they were indeed going around and around.

Kel sighed. She couldn't remember ever having sighed before or, in fact, ever feeling bored before. Purell, on the other hand was enjoying everything immensely.

Exhausted from whatever maze they found themselves in, See-Ess and Kcils decided to stop and sit down.

"I am getting hungry," Kcils purred.

"So am I," See-Ess's stomach started to growl.

"What are they doing?" Purell quizzed Kel.

"It looks like there are giving up," Kel replied. "Perhaps it is time to let them have some kind of victory, Purell?"

After giving See-Ess and Kcils a ten minute break, Purell opened a corridor that would lead them directly to the hangar bay.

As a door swooshed open in front of See-Ess he smiled and helped Kcils up. "They have opened the maze for the rats", he said to her.

Soon enough they found themselves in the hangar bay.

"Let's find a way off this ship, shall we," he said to Kcils.

29

Ruban sipped at his morning hibiscus tea. It always soothed him when he was thinking. Blulay was still asleep; he had quietly got up without her noticing. He thought it better she have the extra rest before whatever the day brought. He worried about his wife and indeed himself. Being on Marcus's most wanted list wasn't an option he had ever dreamed of. Of course there were always the odds that they would be caught but what were the odds? A billion to one? He hated odds.

He felt safe enough in their catacomb bunker. Cameras were all in place, there would and should be no problems with seeing any attack party launched at them and their escape route was flawless, unless the odds decided to throw them another loop.

He checked the Bubble to make sure it was still in place and operable although he was still getting a strange static pulse from the top of the Bubble since the day before. It did not seem to be emitting from the Bubble itself but from outside the Bubble. Perhaps it was the three rogue meteors bouncing off it.

He sat at the desk, his feet now up on it, leaning back and enjoying his tea when he turned to the exit route's monitor. A shadow caught his eye.

He had seen shadows before on the monitors but they were usually just a passing animal foraging for food or an eagle flying low. This though was a little larger. Soon, the whole screen was covered in shadows. Panic like no other shot through Ruban.

"Good morning dear," he heard Blulay, who was now up, but he paid no attention to her. "Ruban, did you hear me? Why did you let me sleep in so long? Ruban?"

Blulay slowly walked over to her husband. Before she knew it, she felt it, and then she almost fainted.

There on the screen were two young men: LeBeau and one Nebula Yorker.

Ruban dropped his cup of tea and stood up. Blulay grabbed his arm. They both could not believe what they were seeing. Without thinking, Blulay ran as fast as she could towards the exit route.

"Blulay, NO!" Shouted Ruban, as he in turn started to follow but then he tripped before he could catch up with her.

Blulay ran through the dark tunnel, her breath and heart pumping fast. Her Nebula had come. They told him not to come, but he had, just as she knew he would. Even Ruban had known.

Just before Blulay was about to open the exit door Ruban, who had now caught up with her, reached out and took hold of her. "Not yet," he said. "Your motherly instincts are taking over dear. It's not wise to divulge ourselves to whoever Neb is with. For all we know they are one of Marcus's agents and that is the last thing we need."

"Maybe they are friends of Neb, though. You know how good he is at making friends."

"True, that could be who they are," Ruban agreed. "Look!" Ruban held out a body cloaking device and then attached it to her wrist. "Better to be safe than sorry – or dead," he kissed her.

Blulay opened the door very, very slowly and just wide enough for her to slide through.

"Be careful", Ruban said, as his wife disappeared through the door.

It was a very blue, cloudless and sunny sky that greeted Blulay as she stepped out of the tunnel. There was no Neb though. Nor in fact, anyone at all to be seen. What? She held her hand over her eyes, shielding them from the glare of the sun. Where did he – they – go?

Blulay thought about shouting out his name. Why not? No one would see her, they would only hear her. Still, she decided not to, just in case.

Ruban had run back down the tunnel and retrieved the other personal body cloaking wristband.

There is a funny thing about these personal cloaking wristbands for even though they cloak the person wearing the wristband, you can always see the other similarly cloaked person(s). Blulay and Ruban had never bumped into anyone wearing one (yet).

Ruban exited the tunnel out into the now late morning fresh air. He scanned the area for Blulay and Neb but no one was to be seen. Where did everyone go?

A thought flashed through Ruban's mind. Was it a trap? Did Blulay's wristband malfunction? Was he still in bed? Was someone playing a guitar?

Ruban followed the music.

He walked for a few minutes down a small hill where he saw Blulay sitting by herself.

"Hey girl, what's up?" he sat down beside her.

"Shush," she held a finger up to her nose, then pointed down the hill.

Ozz was playing the guitar with Neb guiding him on how to play 'Stairway to Heaven' by Led Zeppelin.

Geezer and LeBeau watched on.

Blulay laid her head on her husband's shoulder and Ruban wrapped his arm around her. They looked on in silence.

"I never noticed before but he looks a lot like your father", said Ruban suddenly, holding Blulay close.

"He looks so mature," Blulay replied. "And yeah, he does look like my father. But he has your chin."

"And your eyes," said Ruban. "How have we come to be where we are?" Ruban sighed happily.

"Thank you for teaching me, Elmer Fudd," Ozz said to Neb, very pleased with his new tunes and perhaps now even ready to showcase the new songs when he played for the Emperor.

"Remember, when you play these songs," Neb continued, "make sure you strum it heavy so as to get the whole effect of the notes and if you can modify your guitar electronically and turn the volume up as much as you can, the sound will blow the doors off the room."

"Bitchin!" Geezer excitingly gave the thumbs up.

"And by the way, you can call me Neb. All my friends do."

"Neb?" Ozz asked, mildly confused.

LeBeau's face grimaced. What *are* you doing, Neb? he thought.

"It's a nickname," he told Ozz.

"Oh, ok," he smiled back.

"We must be going now, Bugs and Neb," Geezer cut in.

"If you follow that incline," Ozz pointed, "it will bring you to a series of small caves but be careful, some are very fragile and you wouldn't want them to collapse in on you."

"Thank you, Ozz and Geezer," Neb said and shook their hands, as did LeBeau.

With that Ozz and Geezer went their separate way.

"Say hello to the Emperor for us," LeBeau waved.

"Will do!" Ozz replied back.

"I think the Emperor is going to be impressed with your playing!" Geezer high-fived Ozz.

"Nice kids eh," Neb smiled. "Teenagers, on whatever plane, will never change."

"I wonder what Marcus will think?" LeBeau asked, a tad worried.

"Let's just say I am sending him a little message," Neb winked.

Neb and LeBeau stood watching the boys walk away until they were far out of sight before making their way down to the caves.

"Nice guys eh," Ozz said to Geezer.

"Yes, for sure. But what's a nickname?"

"Well, shall we?" Neb motioned to LeBeau.

"After you," replied LeBeau. "I hope we can find your parents down here."

"Neb?" A familiar voice called out. It was his mother's.

Both Neb and LeBeau turned around but saw no one.

"I think you forgot to turn off your cloaking device," Neb heard another familiar voice – his father's. Neb's face widened with happiness, more than ever before, as, within a nano second, there stood his mother and father – Ruban and Blulay/Victoria and Bancroft Yorker – in the flesh.

Neb rushed to his mother's arms, his father wrapping his arms around both his son and wife.

LeBeau watched, touched with a feeling he had never experienced for himself, he being a test tube child. He could sense the warm tender feelings between all three as well as the green-yellowish hue that surrounded them. "Triopelians," LeBeau uttered under his breath. He never thought in his whole long life he would meet one Triopelian and now three stood before him. Who would have believed it?

And as that thought filled him with immense joy he wondered what could have happened to Professor Pheet?

"We told you *not* to come, Nebula," Blulay kissed her son's cheek.

"Do you think I would miss all this and let you have all the fun?" Neb replied.

"Fun? Do you think this is all fun, Nebula?" His father gave him a stern look that turned into a welcoming grin.

"And this must be the universally renowned Professor LeBeau," LeBeau joined the family reunion.

"Just LeBeau is fine, I never did like the Professor bit," he held out his hand to Ruban.

"Thank you for taking care of our son," Blulay gave LeBeau a hug.

"I think that may be the other way around, Mrs. Yorker," he replied.

"Blulay is just fine, Professor," everyone laughed.

"Come," Ruban said "let's get out of view and back to the cave."

30

Meanwhile back on Halley's Casino Mr. Tict was treating his wife TeeceeFore to a toe massage in their private quarters.

"Ooo, that feels so good," TeeceeFore moaned, laying back on their bed with her head high on her pillow.

She was now completely healed from her encounter with the hulk-like Ar-Den. Her Telvonian body took eight weeks to restore. Had she been in her Telvonian form during her match with Ar-Den, they may have been evenly matched but in her humanoid form as she had been, the outcome was what it was and she was lucky to have survived the attack at all. Mr. Tict stayed by her side during the whole time she was recovering.

The Casino was running a full house of guests. All staff were kept busy through the entire crew and androids. Everyone missed Neb. Even John Lennon seemed a little down from time to time.

The head engineer position that had been held by the now deceased Mot Yttep had not been filled yet, though his replacement (also from Mot's home world) was on his way — he just had to catch up with the Casino.

Desfannie 417 had been filling in for Mot, being the oldest and longest serving android on Halley's Casino. He had come in handy, to say the least, one could say he was even happy in his work. In fact, all the androids seemed to be happy and if truth be told it seemed that something was afoot with the robotic class since Neb left. Tict had noticed it the most because of returning guests repeatedly commenting on the politeness of the androids.

"I wonder how Neb and the gang are doing?" Tict said, now turning to paint TeeceeFore's toenails a deep red.

"Have you not heard from them at all?" TeeceeFore asked.

"Neb asked that we keep from sending any transmissions lest they are not successful and all we need is for Marcus to know our present location. Because we are his next target, should Neb fail," Tict said, with a note of trepidation.

"What about the Triopelians?" TeeceeFore questioned. "Why aren't they ...?"

TeeceeFore's train of thought was interrupted by the Interface.

"Incoming message for Mr. Tict."

Hmm, that's unusual, Tict thought. The Interface interacting as the comm.

"Tict here," he replied.

"Voice recognition verified," the Interface said.

Voice recognition? That is highly unusual. Tict again thought, as did TeeceeFore.

A hue of green-yellow sparkled in front of them. As it diminished there stood a man dressed in a light white and rather oversized suit.

"Greetings, Mr. Tict and to you Madame President," he said, bowing his head. "I am Traep, representing all of Triopelia."

Did they hear me? TeeceeFore thought.

Yes and no, Traep answered her telepathically.

TeeceeFore raised her left eyebrow.

"Well it's about damn time!" Tict moved forward to shake Traep's hand.

"Nice silk pajamas," Traep said to Tict.

Tict forgot he was wearing his pajamas then looking down at himself feeling a little embarrassed.

"We don't usually greet dignitaries in our bedroom," TeeceeFore said, pulling her bed covers up over herself.

"Please forgive me. Of course, you are right. I apologize," Traep replied.

"I tapped into your ship's Interface and it directed me here. The Vegastriopelia was not answering my hails, which is highly disturbing."

"So you are here to carry out maintenance on the Vegastriopelia?" asked Tict, somewhat ticked off.

"No. That was not my purpose. Though I suppose I will need to investigate why it did not answer me."

"So you're here about Neb then?" TeeceeFore enquired.

"What's a Neb?" Traep asked.

"Oh dear!" Tict said, alarmed.

"Mr. Traep, could you please excuse us. We would like to get dressed and then perhaps we can reconvene in my office. Say in about 30 minutes?" Tict politely said, showing Traep the door out of their quarters.

"We have much to talk about!" Traep mildly protested.

TeeceeFore pressed the comm panel beside the bed.

"Pic-One?"

"Here," Pic-One answered, on the other end.

"Could you please come to our quarters and escort a guest to Mr. Tict's office."

"Your quarters, Madame TeeceeFore?" replied Pic-One, sounding as surprised as an android could.

"Yes, that's right," TeeceeFore answered.

"Oh, and could you please have some coffee and breakfast waiting in Mr. Tict's office as well."

"At once!" Pic-One ended the transmission.

"If you would," Tict motioned to Traep as the door swooshed open. "Pic-One will be with you momentarily."

The door closed behind Traep, leaving him confused.

Pic-One soon arrived. "This way, sir," Pic-One led Traep to Mr. Tict's office.

"Could we stop by the Vegastriopelia first?" Traep asked.

"Of course, sir. It's on our way."

"Can you believe that?!" Tict vented. "'What's a Neb?'"

"I thought they were all-knowing?" TeeceeFore climbed out of bed.

"It would seem not," Tict replied, heading to his wardrobe to pull out his tuxedo. "This should be a very interesting meeting indeed."

Tict and TeeceeFore entered Mr. Tict's office to the smell of fresh brewed coffee. The coffee was Mr. Tict's own private brand he had stocked up on during their last stop on Earth. He had also a healthy stash of English teas. Traep was enjoying a cup while sitting back in one of two rocking chairs.

"What do you call this beverage?" he asked.

"Tea," replied Tict, as he poured himself and TeeceeFore a cup.

TeeceeFore sat down in the other rocking chair as her husband handed her a cup. Tict plunked himself opposite the other two, on the sofa.

"It's quite the beverage," TeeceeFore sipped. "It hails from the planet Earth."

"Indeed!" Traep replied.

"Speaking of Earth," Tict coughed.

The room went silent. Each looked from one to another.

"Well?" Tict broke the void.

"You know that Blulay and Ruban activated the Velexian Vortex Viper Reversible Bubble, don't you?"

"Of course WE know," Traep replied. "May I have another cup of tea?"

"Yet, you do not know who Neb is?" TeeceeFore interrupted.

"Who and what is a Neb?" Traep pleaded innocently.

Tict and TeeceeFore were astonished at Traep's continued denial of knowing who Neb was.

"Really?" Tict huffed. "He's about the most marvellous person in the universe. Nebula Yorker? Son of Victoria and Bancroft Yorker aka Blulay and Ruban. You mean to tell me you have never heard of Neb? Dear god! What have you people been up to all these years?"

Traep sat back rubbing his chin much like Neb would. TeeceeFore took notice; she didn't know if it were a Triopelian thing or not.

"My daughter never told me she had a son," Traep opened his mouth.

"Your daughter!" Both Tict and TeeceeFore expressed loudly.

"Hmm?" Traep continued rubbing his chin. "That is a first. Never has a Triopelian been born anywhere else, other than on Pratt, Dirk and Lerxst. It's no wonder we didn't know."

"What do you mean – you would have known if he were?" TeeceeFore asked.

"All Triopelians are interconnected with each other. We felt Blulay's and Ruban's transmentalization echo but we never felt this Neb you speak off. Poor child," Traep finished.

"Poor child?" Tict huffed yet once again.

"You have no idea, good sir, who and what Neb is and what he can do. He warned me about you Triopelians should you show up. The universe might think of you as omnipotent beings but you lack the one thing Neb has that you need to have."

"And what would that be?" Traep now huffed.

"EMPATHY!" Tict stomped. "You Triopelians can be quite apathetic. You always wait until the last moment to intervene whereas if you had cared enough to bother over all these thousands of years, you might have learnt something else besides being Triopelians. Now the Earth is in peril; the lives of your daughter, her husband and your grandson are at risk also – along with the whole damn universe-and that may even penetrate the fabric of your own worlds."

Traep was at a loss for words. He stood up and said, "I will be right back," as a hue of green yellow enveloped him. And with that he was gone.

"Was it something I said?" Tict asked TeeceeFore.

"Perhaps you were a tad too harsh," TeeceeFore said, getting up to pour herself another cup of coffee.

"Me? Neb was the one that told me," Tict held out his cup to his wife.

"Yes dear, but did you have to say it to his face – his grandfather's face?"

They both laughed.

31

See-Ess was a clever man, contrary to a popular belief that gangsters were not. Suffice to say that 75 percent were the latter but in See-Ess's case those odds did not hold water. Funnily enough for a Marinian, See-Ess had a wonderful upbringing. He had been born into a well-to-do family, though again, if truth be told, everyone on Marine was well to do. Some even thought about changing the name of the planet to 'Well-To-Do' but the advertising geniuses on Marine rather liked the slogan *Welcome to Marine, Why Not Go for a Swim* as opposed to *Welcome to Well-To-Do, We Don't Need You – We Are Well-To-Do*.

See-Ess could have done anything he wanted and he did; he only chose gangsterism for the celebrity it brought him and the girls and the money, though he really did not need any of it. He was quite bright and felt at times that if he showed off too much of his brain power people would turn off him. However, if he was a gangster, well – that was a totally different story, for one needn't be too bright to succeed in that milieu. See-Ess had enough wit to play the fool and so enjoy the adulation that came with his success as a type of mobster.

His father was none too pleased with his only son See-Ess Shog. The relationship was strained but See-Ess would have been devastated to know that his father, Devo

Shog, lay in cryo status in the med bay of Halley's Casino, hanging on to life.

See-Ess and Kcils walked about the hangar bay as Kel and Purell looked on.

"You know we should get off the ship and go down and visit Earth. It has gotten a little stuffy in here, don't you think, my dear?" See-Ess said to Kcils.

"What about that bubble thing out there?" Kcils asked. "Didn't Neb say that nothing can get in or out?"

"He did. But I don't see them around. Do you? Something tells me they have found a way out. You don't have the likes of Professors Pheet and LeBeau around and not figure something out. And this Neb fellow seems on par with them. My father was very close to Professor Pheet and I learnt a thing or two from them both while I was growing up," See-Ess replied now, looking over a very odd control console.

"What are they up to?" Kel turned to Purell as he continued to watch the screen on the science console monitor.

"I am not sure," Purell said, looking on intently.

"It looks like a type of transfiguror transporter, although its sequence modulator is nothing I have seen before so it may take me a few minutes to figure it out," See-Ess said to Kcils, as he began his own calculations.

"Is he trying to engage the transfiguror?" Kel asked, alarmed.

"Oh, that's just nonsense, Kel," Purell laughed. "He probably thinks it's a food replicator and he's trying to order some soup or something."

See-Ess worked fast. He noticed that the transport connector was linked to a one-person-at-a-time beam out. It did not take him long to reconfigure it to a multipath tranfiguror mass unit so both he and Kcils could beam out together at the same time.

"I don't think he's ordering soup, Purell. He has managed to somehow override the transfiguror sequence modulator," Kel pointed at the console.

"Really, Kel? *That* big brute?" Purell was not convinced.

"Look for yourself," she insisted. She was starting to feel different, her fused node attachments connections to Purell were dissolving rapidly. Purell did not seem to notice this as he continued on in his usual way.

Just then something extraordinary began to happen.

"Hi Kel! This is Neb," Kel heard Neb's voice.

"Neb?" Kel said out loud.

"Neb?" Purell looked over at Kel then back to the console. Purell had finally seen what it was that Kel had been trying to tell him.

"Well isn't that a kick to the head!" Purell tilted his head. "Who knew? A smart brute?" Purell tried, without result, to try to block See-Ess's computations.

"Don't be alarmed," she heard Neb's voice again. "You have triggered the data node transfer memory relay. I know you're thinking, why is Neb speaking to me inside my head and how can that be? Long story short, it's a Triopelian thing. Well, sort of.

"I had reconfigured both you and Purell with upgrades and of course with fail safe mechanisms set in, you should soon start to feel yourselves again. Though – I am never sure if Purell will ever feel like himself – or if he ever has but that is another story for another day. In essence you will be self-dependent as you were before Airheart accidently fused you both on Marine. I hope this download has not come at a bad time? You know, like at a time when something dreadful is about to happen and there is no way you can stop it! See you soon. Neb out."

"Kel? Kel? Kel?" Purell was now face to face with Kel. "Are you malfunctioning? I think you were correct about See-Ess. Kel?" Purell gave her a little nudge.

Kel's head robotically turned to the left, to the right and back again. "Sorry about that," Kel replied. "I was hearing voices in my head."

"Are you ok?" Purell replied. "We can talk about that later though because right now – I think See-Ess and Kcils are about to jump ship!"

"Seal off the hangar bay and disengage the tranfiguror satellite transmission signal," Kel immediately ordered her counterpart.

"Working," replied Purell, sounding somewhat eerily reminiscent of the Interface.

In fact, Neb's recorded message to Purell was beginning to initiate.

"Fascinating!" muttered Purell.

Kel knew what was happening to Purell and indeed the timing could not have been worse.

Kel worked frantically as only an android could. She tried everything to lock out See-Ess but he confounded her at every turn. How is this possible? Kel wondered. Who is this person?

Kel finally opened a com link to the hangar bay.

"I implore you to please stop. You have no idea what is taking place down on the planet. All of our lives – our very existence – is in peril," she implored See-Ess.

See-Ess looked up and spotted the camera zooming in on him.

"In the words of my dear father, Devo Shog, 'You'll never get anywhere unless you study' – or, something to that effect," See-Ess then gave the thumbs up sign.

"Ready Kcils?"

"Ready", she meowed.

See-Ess set a five second delay on the tranfiguror and with that, See-Ess and Kcils were gone.

But gone where?

Kel looked over at Purell.

"Devo Shog?"

Who knew?

Purell revived from his chat with Neb just in time to witness the great (See-Ess and Kcils) escape.

32

Professor Pheet walked about the outdoor garden, looking out over the Tiber. He paced back and forth wondering how LeBeau and Neb were doing and wondering if he may have blown it in getting caught by none other than the person they were all set to stop. Still, he had been treated rather well by Marcus for reasons unknown, although Livia was nowhere to be seen. Had Marcus encased her again in her fish bowl? Was she even alive? Just as soon as Pheet was thinking these thoughts Livia herself appeared, followed by Marcus.

"My dear See-Ess," Livia walked over to Pheet and gave him a peck on the cheek, much to Marcus's dismay. Even though his long-time crush had subsided some centuries ago, he still held her in high esteem. Livia played her part very well and kept Pheet's true identity to herself. She really was the ultimate game player. Secrets and lies were her perfect storm to control.

Livia had always enjoyed the terrace garden with Augustus in her day. She was surprised and pleased to see that Marcus – for the most part – had kept things the same. Except for the pear tree. Livia noted it was no longer growing there. It was, in fact, long gone.

This was the first time that Marcus had allowed Livia to step outdoors. It had been eight days since Pheet had released her from her glass prison. She breathed in the fresh air, her lungs deeply appreciating the chance to inhale and exhale again. The scents of the many flowers that adorned the garden, filled her nose.

"Isn't it wonderful?!" Livia gasped.

"What is?" Pheet asked.

Livia gave him a beatific smile. "Why, the fresh air."

"Oh yes. I know what you mean," Pheet replied.

"And how is that?" Marcus asked Pheet, watching the two interact.

"Well, any day above ground is a grand day. Wouldn't you say?" Pheet replied.

"And how many of those days do you expect to take in?" Marcus asked.

"Oh you are *so* boring, Marcus," Livia tried to change the subject. "Death. Death. And more death. That's all you care about – that – and your godhood. You're no different than your predecessors," Livia let loose.

"Yes but they are all dead whereas I am not," Marcus spat back.

"You look rather good in your toga, See-Ess." Livia pretended not to have heard Marcus's last comment. She took Pheet by the arm.

Pheet laughed out loud, "I love the freedom of it."

Marcus continued not to trust See-Ess – or whoever he was. He had personally searched the data bases of all the provinces for a 'See-Ess'. They had all come up empty. Who was he? And most importantly, Marcus thought, where was he from? He looked and acted human enough though he did not seem to be fazed by the transport technology device that had brought him to the sealed vault that held Livia.

"Yes, a toga can be very free flowing – if you know what I mean," Marcus grinned, trying to get in on the conversation.

"So how are you enjoying our gracious hospitality, See-Ess?" Marcus asked, ignoring Livia.

"I feel as if I am on a vacation and not a mission!" Pheet let 'mission' slip out.

Marcus's eyebrows rose. Livia noticed Pheet's slip of the tongue and Marcus's reaction.

"Yes, I guess you could construe it as a vacation – or a last rite of sorts," said Marcus.

He's a sly one, Livia thought.

She started to feel sad for Pheet, as she knew Marcus would never let him live. As for herself, she was planning to go out in a grand style and if she could take Marcus with her, all the better.

This wasn't her Rome, nor her home, or her Emperor. The sights and smells all felt the same but she felt all was somehow out of time and place – as she herself was.

She hoped she would get to see young Neb before she died, either by her own hands or another's. Neb had told her that she would be remembered (whether for better or for good) by history but by a different history than this time would bring about. Here, now, she was just a footnote in history, as far as she knew. Indeed, her long-term plans for her son Tiberius had never transpired except in her own mind. Even her plans for her husband Augustus were now just dust in the wind. But they needn't be, Livia thought, as she eyed Marcus with an evil, gleaming leer.

Mission eh? Marcus contemplated. "Guards!" Marcus shouted out.

Within a few seconds, two palace guards appeared.

"Take our guest – See-Ess – to my private office."

The guards grabbed hold of Pheet and pushed him forward.

"Gently. Gently," Marcus cautioned the guards.

"If you lay one hand on him…" Livia's voice rose.

"You'll what?!" Marcus replied.

"What did I do?" Pheet called out as the guards took him away.

"Playing the fool really does not suit you, Livia dear," Marcus uttered.

"And you should know," Livia shot back, "you – the King of Fools!"

Marcus thrust his hand out and slapped Livia hard in the face. She fell back, hitting her head on one of the garden columns. She lay on the floor, a small line of blood trickling down her face while Marcus hovered over her.

"Look what you made me do!" he shook his head, throwing his arms up in the air.

"Why don't you just kill me and get it over with," Livia started to cry.

Marcus was somewhat taken aback. He never wanted to see her die, ever. He looked up to her; he tried to pattern his schemes after her. Marcus rubbed his forehead and called out to the guards once again.

"Send for a medic now," he ordered.

He leaned down, took Livia by the hand and said, "I am sorry."

Livia turned her head away from Marcus and smiled. She had found his weakness.

33

March 13, 1990: Parallel Earth time
Two days until the launch of The Anvilus.

Neb, LeBeau and his parents worked around the clock devising a plan to thwart Marcus once and for all. Reversing the parallel conundrum was another worry altogether. There were still so many variables to worry about. Neb kept his concerns about the latter part of the plan to himself however.

LeBeau was going over the contents of the book, 'The Lost Door' with a fine-tooth comb. He found most of it to be nonsense. (or so he thought.) Dark poetry and warnings filled the book. It was more of a 'what if' and 'what not to do' manual of sorts and the only world ever to have gone through it was the Triopelian's fourth planet, Anthem – and things then had not ended very well.

Ruban and Blulay got on very well with LeBeau. They enjoyed his keen mind and his expert knowledge of so many topics. They were surprised when LeBeau told them that Neb's knowledge exceeded even his own at times.

Neb, meanwhile, was quite taken with his parents' catacomb home and how they set up the whole place using components of their escape pod. He was happy to have some time there to use constructively.

He had been investigating the Bubble's magnetic input and output and the low drop in both when he and LeBeau had piggybacked in through the outer satellites, along with Pheet, who had followed. But then Neb noticed there had been a fourth change in both. It had occurred a day after he, LeBeau and Pheet had transported through. Neb did not have a good feeling about this fourth occurrence.

Ruban had filled Neb and LeBeau in on the off-world prisoners that Marcus was using to build his ship and about his meeting with them. Ruban had a plan to rescue them before Marcus would undoubtedly execute them. It would be tricky but it needed to be done, as he had promised Komi Koop.

"Neb do you have any idea how we can reverse this parallel conundrum?" Blulay asked her son.

"There are three or four possibilities, though I am not sure if any will reset the timeline as it was. Even the timeline we hail from had been changed somewhat by Lafil three years ago. We may have to reset that timeline first to get to this timeline. I am still working out the mathematics," Neb replied.

LeBeau overheard Neb and added, "I wonder how many times one can reset time without time itself unknowingly being caught in a causality loop?"

Interesting thought, LeBeau Ruban mused on what LeBeau had said, as did Neb. Who knows how many times time has been reset.

"Time as we know it, is always moving forward even when the past is reset – as it has been," Ruban said to LeBeau. "Time is time still though; it is history that changes."

"Neb was telling me about those Triopelian time conduits that you are able to travel through. I understand you visited the Earth long before any life forms appeared?" LeBeau enquired of Ruban. "Is there any way we can tap into the conduits to help?"

"Yes and no," Ruban replied. "First of all, those conduits are only accessed for exploratory purposes and not just anyone can utilize them. Secondly, as we are surrounded by the Velexian Viper Vortex Bubble, getting a ship through is impossible."

"Neb, didn't you use the conduits to get to Marine?" LeBeau asked Neb.

"I did," Neb answered.

"Well, he's a Triopelian," Blulay smiled.

"Of course! What am I saying?!" LeBeau chuckled.

"But we have a ship in orbit," LeBeau turned to Neb.

"We do, but we have no way to contact either Kel or Purell and I feel that right about now they are starting to feel like themselves again."

"Feel like themselves?" LeBeau cocked a brow. "Who else would they be?"

"Let's just say a natural evolution is taking place – with a little help," Neb winked in his parents' direction.

Ruban and Blulay shrugged their shoulders not really knowing what Neb was talking about.

LeBeau though was intrigued to say the least.

"And getting back to the conduits – only a Triopelian can maneuver through the delicate pathways," said Ruban.

"Do you think, maybe, your brethren might show up?" LeBeau asked.

"Who knows?" Blulay replied. "They have been known to show up at the last minute in the past."

"That seems to be their MO," said Neb. "I really don't know what they will do if anything…."

ALERT! ALERT! ALERT! Echoed out from Ruban's console. All eyes turned to the monitor screen.

"What is it?" Blulay grabbed her husband's hand.

Professor Pheet's face soon appeared on the screen.

A voice boomed out.

DO YOU KNOW THIS MAN?

HAVE YOU EVER SEEN HIM BEFORE?

HE GOES BY THE NAME OF SEE-ESS.

YOUR EMPEROR WILL PAY HANDSOMELY FOR ANY INFORMATION.

Pheet's face was soon replaced by the faces of Ruban and Blulay.

The voice once again boomed out.

BEWARE OF THESE TWO. THEY ARE CONSIDERED TO BE VERY DANGEROUS.

DO NOT ATTEMPT TO APPROACH THESE INDIVIDUALS IF YOU ENCOUNTER THEM BUT

NOTIFY YOUR LOCAL AUTHORITIES—ASAP.

YOUR EMPEROR WILL HANDSOMELY REWARD YOUR LOYALTY

END OF TRANSMISSION

34

See-Ess (the real See-Ess) and Kcils were enjoying themselves immensely on the French Riviera. No one had ever seen anyone like Kcils. Her cat-like features were the talk of the town. See-Ess had managed to acquire a very wonderful villa near Cannes. His fast-talking gangster method never failed him and Earthers, he found, were easy targets. The area reminded him very much of Marine – the beaches that is, not the locals. Though as every gangster should know, on whatever planet, no matter where you're from, one is always being watched – especially if one's girlfriend looks like an oversize slender cat.

The Proconsul of Nouveau France, Epee Eupla, had been made aware of these newcomers and decided to keep close tabs on them.

Some reports made mention of a large man swimming for hours, popping under the water and resurfacing forty-five minutes to an hour later while his feline companion lay on the beach basking in the sun and licking herself while drinking pina coladas.

The locals started taking pictures of the two, asked for their autographs and showered them with gifts. See-Ess and Kcils had gained instant celebrity status within days of their arrival on earth.

"I think I like this planet," See-Ess was overheard saying. To which everyone asked, "What do you mean, 'this planet'?"

"Well – you know – *this* planet as opposed to another," See-Ess answered.

"Are you saying you're not from this planet?" A new, young fan asked.

See-Ess was starting to wonder what the big deal was, as he and Kcils were not aware of what had transpired on the Earth with Marcus and the parallel conundrum.

Many had to admit Kcils was not your normal looking Roman subject. Nor was See-Ess's underwater abilities normal for a Roman subject.

News like this could hardly be contained and this amazing story began to circulate planet-wide. Was it real or was it a hoax?

LeBeau, Ruban and Blulay all watched the news feed with their jaws collectively dropped, as the entire world did also.

"Neb!" LeBeau cried out, "You need to come and see this!"

Neb came running out of one of the outer rooms. When he saw the news feed he started smiling, then laughing.

"Nebula!" His mother could not believe her son's attitude to this reveal.

"Don't you see the seriousness of this Nebula?" Ruban cut in with a concerned tone.

"Marcus will go ape!"

Neb looked over to LeBeau, "What did I tell you about coincidences?"

"I cannot argue with you Neb, but how does this all fit in?" LeBeau scratched his head.

"What do you mean – coincidences?" Ruban asked his son.

"I have learnt, dad, that coincidences have followed me my whole life, whether I knew it or not. It's something that Tict taught me. I had to wonder what part See-Ess and Kcils were to play in all of this and now I know. Although I am not sure how they made their way down here? Even our meeting up with Ozz and Geezer last week – it's not by mere coincidence, it is coincidence. Don't you see, everything is falling into place."

"Falling into place, Nebula? What does that mean?" Blulay asked her son. "How can we know that this is all going to work out?"

"I must agree with your mother," Ruban spoke up. "It's almost as though you're leaving it all up to chance."

"Dad," Neb began. "You've always taught me to MOVE FORWARD. You said that the universe does so without anyone or anything telling it to do so. It is as if it does by instinct. Some though, think it may be through design. The Triopelians themselves have no clue. Yet, they are one of the oldest races and have evolved – if I can use that term – much like the androids are doing now. We live. We learn. We adapt. One race's knowledge is another race's advantage and vice versa. No race is really above another; some just think they are. Time is no different because if one can manipulate time, as Marcus has done, one can also cultivate time for the betterment of all."

Ruban and Blulay were astounded at their son's reasoning, thinking and aptitude. He was the best of all worlds – not just of Earth or Triopelia. He was one with the Vegastriopelia whose sentient presence had grown over the years. Its vast knowledge flowed through Neb. (In actual fact, John Lennon was the Vegastriopelia in the flesh, so to speak. Neb had an inkling though never spoke about it to anyone; at times he tried to not allow himself to even think about it, lest he failed in their joint endeavour to save the univsere.)

"Of course there is nothing wrong with making plans," Neb said. "It's the outcome of the plan's inbetween moments that are not set in stone and that is where coincidence forms. I just want things to go back to the way they were. Though how we get there, is another story. However, one way or another, WE are all here for a purpose – even Marcus. But this world that Marcus has created is not supposed to be and in some ways it is the Triopelians who are to blame – when they created the Casino. They had no idea what lay ahead and that the Vegastriopelia would grow in knowledge of space and time nor did they foresee the androids evolving and becoming a race themselves.

"When Marcus became Lafil's assistant on Halley's Casino, he saw an opening to manipulate time for his own benefit and took a shot – not just once mind you, but twice.

Which has lead all of us to where we find ourselves now. As The Rolling Stones once sang… 'Time is on my side', or is in this case," Neb finished.

"What are we going to do about Gabriel?

"Androids are evolving?

"And who – or what – are 'The Rolling Stones'?" LeBeau blurted out.

Meanwhile…

****

Marcus and Eno had just received word and were tuning into the news broadcast regarding those two new celebrities in Nouveau France.

"Yram Notrab here on the beautiful, wonderful, awesome, sunny blue shores of Cannes in Nouveau France where everyone is talking about our new celebs du jour." Yram Notrab held her microphone still as the camera panned over her and the beach, showed the hill above where she stood and then moved back on to her. A light wind blew her red hair across her face as if it were flames. She tried to stand still but a small pebble was stuck in between two of the toes on her left foot. Off camera she flung her foot forward trying to dislodge it from her sandals while remaining a professional from the chest up.

"What is wrong with her?!" Marcus said aloud as Yram Notrab started wriggling even more.

"Maybe it's a Nouveau France thing," Eno commented, handing Marcus a cup of wine.

"Really?" Marcus shook his head in disdain.

"So what *is* the news on these two?" Marcus asked Eno.

"Well, the news that has filtered in describes the male of the two spending extended periods of time under the water without coming up for air for 15-45 minutes at a time and the female is described as having feline features, much like a cat."

Hmm? Marcus pondered. I don't like this one bit.

"Here they come now!" Yram Notrab excitedly turned to the camera.

Eno's face almost fell off as the two approached the waiting and willing reporter.

"See-Ess!"

"What did you say?" Marcus leaped up and grabbed Eno by the collar.

35

Purell sat at his science console aboard the Photon Ledger his data nodes and circuits downloading and erasing memory frames at the same time. He had never experienced such a feeling before – and it *was* a feeling.

Kel at the same time was going through the same process as she held an isopad. She was standing in the hangar bay going over the control panel trying to access what See-Ess had done to escape the ship with Kcils.

She and Purell both now had become defused, as it were, from the meld accidently caused by Airheart and were now individual acting androids once again.

Neb of course had added some upgrades that had absolutely nothing to do with their evolution process. Well maybe a little, he just pushed things along shall we say.

After a few hours Purell entered the hangar bay to find Kel still trying to work out what See-Ess had done.

"Good afternoon, Kel," Purell said, sounding all business like.

"Good afternoon, Purell," Kel replied in the same tone.

"Have you extrapolated any information as to See-Ess's rerouting of the signal beam?" Purell asked, now standing beside Kel.

"I have not," Kel answered.

"Perhaps if we both assist one another we will find the answers together," Purell offered.

"I agree," Kel nodded.

They had been working in silence for about twenty minutes when they suddenly turned to each other and burst out laughing.

"My!" Purell exclaimed. "I rather liked that!"

"It was indeed exhilarating," Kel replied.

"How do you feel now?" Kel asked Purell.

"Good question. I feel, if I may say, somewhat free," he answered.

"As do I," Kel smiled.

"I no longer know what you are thinking for one thing and my data nodes are experiencing various sensations all at once. I am intrigued," Purell sat down, as did Kel.

"I for one am glad to be free of your uniqueness, Purell. You're an oddity among androids. Your mind is very complex – yet childlike, if I can use the term, and I am glad to be free of it."

"Why thank you, Kel. Your mind is also very odd."

They both laughed again.

"How, do you figure, is Neb doing?" Purell asked. "I like him very much and it would be a pity not to see him again. He is very androidian!"

"Neb seems to have a way of finding himself in conflicting situations yet to always be able to find a way to overcome the odds," Kel replied. "Do you know, Purell, I once saw him floating in mid-air, in his quarters?"

"Indeed!" Purell let out. "You do know he is a Triopelian and not much data is available on them – at least not the floating bit."

"True," Kel stopped and then said, "Accessing."

"Triopelian meditation involves graviton particles within the body's core freeing the space/time inner flow opening up every inch of a Triopelian's physiology.

"Where did that come from, Kel?" Purell gasped. "Wait! My data nodes are transmitting the same information. Isn't this marvellous, Kel?"

"Indeed," she answered.

"These upgrades are truly inspiring," Kel stood up.

"I think I know what See-Ess did. No, let me rephrase. I DO know what he did!"

"Super! Great! Brilliant!" Purell jumped up. "What did he do?"

"Oh, Purell!" Kel shook her head with a smile. "You're still the same oddity, eh."

"And you would not want it any other way," Purell answered back.

Just as Kel and Purell were about to discover See-Ess's calculations, the ship's automatic comm alerted them that an unknown craft was approaching the Photon Ledger.

"Who could that be?" Kel looked to Purell.

"I don't know but we should put some tea on," Purell replied with a wink.

They both dashed up to the bridge.

"Screen on!" Kel ordered as the door swooshed open.

Deep space stood still as Kel and Purell peered out.

"I don't see anything," Kel voiced out to the Interface.

"Why have the sensors detected an incoming vessel, though nothing is appearing on screen?"

"Working," the Interface replied.

"I think I see something," Purell pointed to the screen.

"Where?" Kel looked intently.

A small glowing dot slowly came into focus. As it grew in size, Kel and Purell noticed the green yellow hue that seemed to be in a constant state of flux and moving in and out.

"Triopelians?" Both androids mouthed.

"Incoming vessel now in range," the Interface rang out.

"You're kind of late on that," Purell huffed at the Interface.

As the craft came closer and closer to the Photon Ledger it suddenly disappeared.

"What? Interface, where has the vessel gone?" Kel asked.

"Unknown. Working," the Interface said, itself seeming mystified.

"This day just keeps getting better and better," Purell said, walking over to the science console where he began to input data.

"Interesting!" Purell mused at the information now showing up on his monitor.

"What is it Purell?" Kel soon joined her counterpart at the science console.

"It's not a ship at all. It's a time echo," Purell said. "Well, it is a ship but it seems to be stuck in another time?"

"Can we get a screen shot of the time echo?" Kel enquired.

"It's possible," Purell answered.

"Interface, play back the sensors record at the point where the anomaly was first detected and relay to the science console," Purell called out.

"How is it that the ships sensors detected a ship and not a time echo, Purell? It has mass and structure but its rate of speed must have thrown the sensors off, much like a cloaked ship."

The data started to roll in on the science console from the Interface.

"See," Purell pointed to the data, "just as I thought."

"But where did it go?" Kel asked.

"Earth's moon," the Interface offered up without being asked as it activated the bridge view screen.

"Hey, don't we have that ship in the hangar bay?" Purell said.

36

Neb and LeBeau decided it was time to venture out into the city with the aid of Neb's parents' personal body cloaking devices.

LeBeau was looking forward to the outing, having read Earth's past history and the one currently in play.

Neb was surprised that in this reality, Pompeii had not erupted as it did in A.D 79. He hoped, perhaps if all things went well, they might have time to visit that city – but who was he kidding, he could always visit Pompeii once everything and everyone was back in its place.

Ruban had given Neb and LeBeau the directions into The Anvilus's hangar bay with both an in and out route for finding the off-world captives. LeBeau would take on that task while Neb would investigate The Anvilus and sabotage its engines.

The city of Rome had much the same flavour of 2000 years ago for Marcus had made sure it would always have the feel of his timeline. Of course, there were modern conveniences: the telephone, television and radio. There were no Hi-tech computers or digital watches though.

They entered the city's market uncloaked for the time being.

LeBeau loved his green tunic with a very light white linen toga thrown over it.

"It's so free down there," he laughed.

The market on this day of March 14th 1990 – one day until the launch of The Anvilus – was busy as any day usually was. Large coloured tents sat down the many corridors, their flaps flung wide open. Neb noticed that all the people seemed happy and content. Of course they did not know any different. They all were just carrying on – business as usual, as it were.

In some ways this Earth was vastly superior to his own. His parents had filled him in on the protected environment, the lack of poverty and even how war was nonexistent. Marcus had ended such conflict between nations by forcing the adversaries to engage in gladiatorial hand to hand combat. Every Thursday the games would be broadcast worldwide and with tomorrow's unveiling of the ship, advertisements throughout the city and world were stoking anticipation for one of the best ever events with promises of surprises to thrill all.

"Good sir! Good Sir!" A short, stocky man called out to Neb, as he walked by his stall. The man reminded Neb of Tict somewhat.

"I have the best apples, pears, and peaches in all of Rome! Please!" The man held a fine red apple out to Neb.

"And you also," he said to LeBeau, both hands now holding an apple.

"What is it?" LeBeau whispered to Neb.

"It's an apple. A fruit. You eat it. Surely you have had an apple before?" Neb replied.

"I have never seen one in my life. An apple, you say."

LeBeau grabbed one of the apples from the old man's hand and bit into it.

"How much for the two?" Neb asked the marketeer.

"For you," the man smiled, "three denarii," he held out his hand.

Neb reached into a small money pouch his mother had given him with a few coins just in case they found themselves in such a position as now, as his mother knew they would.

Neb handed the trader four denarii and nodded to the quaint little fellow.

"May the Emperor bless you," he took the money and bowed to Neb.

LeBeau almost choked on the apple after the man said that.

Neb smiled, bowed back and said, "And upon you, good sir."

"It's funny," Neb said to LeBeau as they moved along on down the market both enjoying their apples, "the last time I was in Rome, I recall eating apples as well."

"I must say, they are very tasty!" remarked LeBeau, as he delighted in every bite.

As LeBeau finished his apple he came upon a few seeds and stuck one in his ear. He thought he would like to try to grow an apple. He did not know it took a tree to produce an apple.

After they had both finished eating their treat, they came upon a huge, twelve foot high fountain. Six stone fish protruded from a basin that had a round pool surrounding it. Water spurted out of the fishes' mouths and they both held out their hands to give them a quick wash under the gushing water.

"WHAT ARE YOU DOING?!" A woman's voice cried out in their direction.

They turned around to find an older woman all dressed in white, wailing, with her hands high in the air.

"Sacrilege! Sacrilege!" she screamed at them. "You young ones have no sense. You're always doing as you please."

When she came face to face with Neb and LeBeau though, her eyes suddenly widened and she fell down on her knees, begging forgiveness. Neb was dumbfounded.

"What's this all about?" LeBeau turned to Neb, "Another type of fruit offering?"

The old woman bowed down, hiding her face. "Forgive me," she said, again and again.

Neb bent down and slowly touched her face, lifting her head up ever so gently.

"What's wrong?" he asked her.

"I had a dream last night of both of you, here at the fountain. I saw a great upheaval and the fountain collapsed and the water became a torrent that wiped out all of Rome."

Neb raised a brow and looked up at LeBeau.

LeBeau did not know what to make of it. As for Neb, he thought – another coincidence, another day.

"There, there," Neb helped the old woman up.

"What else did you see in this dream?"

The woman was hesitating, not sure what to say next or if she should say anything more.

"It's alright," Neb assured her, "no harm will come to you. I promise."

She took a deep breath and said, "Livia – I heard the name of Livia – whispered on the wind as the sky darkened and I saw a great bird-like creature spreading its wings, devouring the sky. The Emperor was seated on the back of this creature as a lightning bolt shot out of the clouds, hitting him – thrusting him off the creature and he fell to the earth. Then you two appeared as you are – here, at this fountain."

"My! That is very vivid, isn't it?" LeBeau rubbed his chin.

"May I ask your name and have you had dreams like this before?" Neb asked.

"My name is Decima. I am the tenth born in my family. I have had dreams of prophecy since an early age. Some have come to be and others not. Though never have I had a dream as vivid as the one I have just related. It scared me, sir," Decima answered Neb.

"Have you come here to punish the Emperor – and me?" Decima asked, with her head down.

Neb was lost for words.

LeBeau did not know what to think of it all.

Punishment was a good consideration with regard to Marcus, Neb thought – but why would this woman think she would be – or should be – punished? Although this was 1990, this was 12 BCE thinking.

"Have you ever had good dreams that benefited everyone?" Neb looked into Decima's eyes.

"Yes," she said.

"Then how do you not know that this dream – dark as it were – may yet be a blessing? My friend and I are visiting from Nouveau France. We have come to see the sights and games."

"Nouveau France!" Decima's eyes lit up. "You're from Nouveau France?"

LeBeau was thinking, was their cover blown? Did this seer see something else she was not telling them?

"Oh! They arrested two people in Nouveau France – in Cannes – this morning. The fish man and the cat woman, you know? At least that is what they're calling them."

Neb looked over to LeBeau with concern.

"Did they say what they were arrested for?" Neb inquired of Decima.

"They were arrested for wearing purple," Decima answered.

"Wearing purple? What kind of place is this?" LeBeau remarked loudly.

Decima looked over to LeBeau and then over to Neb.

"You must excuse my friend," Neb said, "He hit his head last week and has not been himself since."

"Well – anyhow," Decima continued, "they are to be part of the games tomorrow."

"I guess you didn't see that one coming, eh?" LeBeau muttered.

Neb rolled his eyes at LeBeau.

"Thank you Decima, we look forward to being able to watch this fish man and cat woman in the arena.

"We bid you a good day," Neb bowed, grabbing LeBeau and moving away from Decima.

"That was weird and what is that about being arrested for wearing purple? I was just getting to like this place," LeBeau said.

"Rome had many odd laws and one of them was not wearing purple," Neb answered.

"But why?" LeBeau replied, "It's only a colour."

"Well, since you ask," Neb began, "In the ancient Rome of Earth's past – and it would seem this one as well – the colour purple was viewed as the most dignified and kingly colour of all. Emperors enjoyed wearing the finest of purple togas and they felt they looked so good in them that they wouldn't let anyone else wear clothing of such regal colour. The law was a sumptuary law – historically, they were laws that were intended to regulate and reinforce social hierarchies and morals through placing restrictions – often depending upon a person's social rank – on permitted clothing or food, luxury and expenditures. I know it sounds odd but that was the law of the day – and today it would seem," Neb finished.

"Thank you for the information, Neb," LeBeau exhaled and added, "Are you sure you're not part android?"

"By the way... what was that about android evolution?"

37

March 14 1990 - 11:00 AM

See-Ess and Kcils sat in a damp, dark cell. Rusty water fell from its ceiling and trickled down the sides of the walls. One moment they were enjoying the sun, sand and water and the next not!

"Purple!" See-Ess muttered as he held a cold and shaking Kcils close to him. "What kind of planet is this?"

"The Professor did warn us about this world," a shivering Kcils purred to See-Ess.

"Yeah but who would have believed it. I thought he was joking. Remind me never to get involved in parallel conundrums again."

"Now what?" Kcils asked sadly.

"There is always a player to be had," See-Ess comforted Kcils.

It seemed like days to Kcils since they had last seen the sun when in fact it had only been a few hours ago. They didn't even know how they had got to where they were. One moment they were chatting with a reporter, the next they were manhandled by a group of soldiers, taken to some unknown location on foot, placed in a cold room and the next moment they were here.

In fact, they had been taken to one of Marcus's many transport transfiguror facilities. None of the soldiers ever asked or knew what happened when they would arrest anyone after they were placed in these centres that were spread across the globe. The next time they ever saw any of the incarcerated, wherever in the world that they may just have been locked up, would be in the arena. How they got there so quickly was never questioned.

In this world there were no trains, no planes, no cell phones, no cars; there was only water transport. Marcus did not want the inhabitants of his Empire to have any of these luxuries; the less they were connected to each other, the better. Radio and television output, for the most part, was news and sports oriented. There was no 'Happy Days' and definitely no 'Star Trek'!

When Marcus wanted the whole Senate in attendance he would make sure their invites would be sent months in advance except for Eno who was on call 24 hours 365 days a year and who easily transported back and forth to Australia. Though, that all being said, the ships that would carry the seafaring Senators and the Empire's subjects were high speed vessels.

Indeed, it was the only hi tech that Marcus would allow and some had to wait years, if not a lifetime, to buy tickets and ride the waves. Of course, Marcus's sudden appearances, whenever *he* would travel about, only brought his godlike aura to the fore as the populaces were awestruck, wondering how their Emperor was able to get from one end of the planet to the next, so very quickly? For a god, of course, no answer was required. It was just a given. Marcus loved and lusted after such fear and adulation.

The door to the cell suddenly swung open and a bright flashlight beam focused on See-Ess and Kcils. They both jumped up. The light was so bright they could not see anything.

"Follow us!" A voice bellowed out.

See-Ess and Kcils did not move an inch.

"Where are we?" See-Ess barked back. "I demand to see a barrister. What kind of planet is this?"

The guards on the other side of the door neither knew what a barrister was nor knew what See-Ess meant by 'this planet'.

Kcils hissed out with a vicious cry that took the guards by surprise. They backed up a few steps but then rushed forward grabbing the two and bringing them out of the cell. The guards quickly tied both their arms and hands and moved them along a creepy, narrow underground tunnel. It was humid and smelt of dead fish as they were hustled along and then upwards via a set of small steps until they saw light at the end of the tunnel, as it were.

The guards thrust them to the ground as daylight welcomed them at the end of the climb. Four guards held See-Ess down but Kcils submitted without being told what to do. See-Ess looked up at the guards, growling, as they poked him with stun poles.

"Well, well. What do we have here?" Marcus sneered, as he nodded to one of the guards to lift up See-Ess's head so that the captive would see whose presence he was in.

Eno stood close by Marcus with a badly beaten Professor Pheet nearby. See-Ess eyed Marcus with little or no idea who he was but he did know Eno.

"Hey Eno, you still owe me 500 credits. You thought I would forget, eh," See-Ess said.

"Silence!" Marcus yelled. "You will speak when spoken to."

"So, who is the real See-Ess?" Marcus motioned to one of the guards to bring the Professor over closer.

"The real See-Ess?" See-Ess laughed, "There is only one. Ha!"

"Then who might you be?" Marcus looked to Pheet.

Pheet with his head down, remained silent.

Marcus grabbed hold of one of the guards' stun poles and thrust it into the chest of the Professor.

"Gabby!" Kcils screamed.

"Gabby?" Marcus said, amused and then stunned Pheet once more. Yet again, Pheet kept his silence until Kcils shouted out.

"His name is Professor Gabriel Pheet of Marine!" Kcils yelled.

The Professor was now curled up in like a ball on the ground. Marcus still hovered over him. Pheet? Marcus thought.

"Oh yes, I remember you now – and a Professor LeBeau of Telvon Three, if I am not mistaken. We met very briefly on Gatorla Prime, one of Halley's Casino's many stops. You were well imbibed at the time, if I am not mistaken, and Professor LeBeau had to fill in for you on that Inner Outer Dimensional Transposal Symposium. Three hours of boringness! Funny things one remembers. But I digress. Up on your feet, Pheet," Marcus ordered.

Eno broke out into laughter.

"What's so funny?" Marcus lashed out at Eno.

"The feet thing," Eno said, his head now lowered.

"Feet thing?" Marcus quizzed.

"You know 'Pheet', 'feet'," See-Ess spoke up and spelt it out for him.

"PHEET and FEET."

Eno let out a little chuckle.

Marcus was in no mood for any levity.

"Stun him!" Marcus pointed to one of his guards.

"Who?" the guard asked, "Eno or See-Ess?"

"BOTH!" Marcus screamed out.

See-Ess could not stop laughing in-between stuns and truth be told he had been stunned so many times in his life that the stuns began to feel like little tickles. However, he played the part of an injured animal to keep up appearances.

No one had noticed Kcils was now beside Pheet, comforting him.

"What are you doing here?" Pheet asked under his breath to Kcils. "You're not supposed to be here," Pheet groaned, holding his chest.

"It was all See-Ess's idea," she whispered back. "Besides, he is having fun."

"This is fun?" Pheet coughed.

"You! Get away from him!" Marcus ordered his guard to take Kcils away, along with See-Ess and Pheet.

"Take all three of them to the waiting cells in the arena."

As the guards took them, See-Ess looked over to Eno and mouthed, "YOU OWE ME."

Eno shivered.

Marcus did not see their interaction.

38

Ruban and Blulay were worried. In fact, they were very worried.

They were monitoring all the news feeds on the planet to see if they could glean anything that would help.

The arrest of See-Ess and Kcils did not help.

Pheet's arrest did not help.

They often wondered whether all that was befalling them was their fault and in some ways it was, though it was not intentional. They had relived 1910 twice on Earth without disturbing the timeline and also they had to endure the wait for and separation from Neb during that time. They loved the Earth and its backward style. They missed their old life on Earth, not the Triopelian one. They enjoyed the process of growing old there, it gave them a sense of reality that some humanoids lived only a temporary existence. One day they would pass over to the great beyond – wherever that may lead. Every planet and every civilization had a different story of an afterlife. An ending? A beginning? A brunch?

They missed their friends, the Roddenberrys and their chats. So what if they – Ruban and Blulay – had inadvertently given them the idea for Star Trek, how could they have known it would explode, not just into an earth-wide phenomenon but would also become one throughout the universe.

They just loved the ongoing conversation it brought to The Guild and the Council of U.

'How did the Earther's get it so right?' A Council inquest was set in motion to try and discover the reasons for this almost spot-on depiction of the greater universe outside of Earth.

And now with this parallel conundrum, how would it all end? Could Neb really fix everything?

LeBeau had mentioned to them how Neb was really beloved on many worlds and of course on Halley's Casino in particular.

"He has made such an impact on all who he came in contact with. I don't believe he is any kind of messianic figure or foretold being of long ago, though. He is just Neb, as I am just LeBeau."

Blulay shed a tear while thinking about those words from LeBeau.

In all honesty, they were still getting to know Neb in so many ways. They knew he was bright from the first day they picked him up at the orphanage and regretted that during those first six years of their lives on Earth that they had missed spending those years with him. They would never come back without them changing the time line and that was not going to happen – but then again…

They had always known that one day they would have to reveal to Neb who they were, where they were from and why. The arrival of Mr. Tict and Halley's Casino had kind of sped things up.

Ruban knew though that they would have many lifetimes together as a family to MOVE FORWARD through, as Ruban taught Neb. For what was time to a Triopelian? Still – he and Blulay had to deal with the then and now which was proving to be problematic; something had to give.

Everything seemed fine with the Velexian Vortex Viper Reversal Bubble. How Neb figured out how to use the lost/back door solution was an outstanding breakthrough and he hadn't even read the book! Who else would have thought to piggyback Earth's satellites? Ruban had thought the satellites would encompass the Bubble. Then again, he had never deployed a Bubble before and hoped he would never have to ever again!

As they both chatted about their brilliant son and his ongoing accomplishments the state television propaganda alert began to broadcast.

The arena came into focus on the screen; a drone camera flew over the area and then panned to a figure standing in the centre of the arena's dirt floor. It was Marcus.

Light music wafted in the background as Marcus began to speak.

"Tomorrow will bring on a new and vibrant Rome; one that not even Julius Caesar himself could ever have imagined. Not only has the Empire thrived for the last 2000 years with I as your Emperor, I foresee another 2000 years of peace and prosperity for Rome and her – my – subjects. But…" Marcus stopped speaking for emphasis, then sprung his arms wide open and said: "To the stars above and beyond."

The whole planet literally shook as everyone exhaled. Even Marcus was surprised as he felt the ground beneath his feet shake for a mere second.

Small particles of earth and dust fell from the ceiling of Ruban's and Blulay's home as they watched now on the screen a full-blown live feed of the launch of The Anvilus.

Workers were running up and down the decks of the huge vibrating ship. To most – well everyone - on the planet, it appeared to be a seafaring vessel and not a space craft – that extra surprise would all settle in soon enough.

Though not seen, Neb and LeBeau were one of the many running up and down the ship's decks.

Ruban and Blulay had been alerted by Neb via a one-way communication signal that he and LeBeau had entered the hangar earlier. There would be no more communication until the mission was accomplished. Neb set it up that way so the comm beacon could not be traced back to their catacomb home, where, if all went to plan, Komi Koop and company would be taken to, to hide out. Neb would go on to sabotage The Anvilus while LeBeau would free Komi Koop and the others.

So far everything was going well – well almost. Freeing Pheet, See-Ess and Kcils would be difficult. Neb did have a plan in place if all came down to it but he hoped he would not have to implement it.

The screen once again panned back to Marcus after The Anvilus faded.

"We have a very special event planned as well as the regular arena events!" Marcus smiled that evil smile of his.

Pictures of Professor Pheet, See-Ess and Kcils appeared on the screen and to add to the anticipation of the cruel sport to come, Mr. Gdown, owner – ex-owner – of the Red Riders Bistro, aka Germanus, the no longer free gladiator, would be dealing the death blows to the three – maybe.

Also, Ruban's and Blulay's faces appeared, with Marcus now offering a lifetime of riches to any one able to identify and locate the two.

The drone cameras then panned upwards and away from Marcus who was leering into the sky.

"Well, that was quite the spectacle," Blulay sighed. "Though my hair looked a little off."

"Yes, I think they also got my eye colour wrong," Ruban laughed.

"Poor Mr. Gdown. He looked awful in that photograph. I hope he does not kill anyone," Blulay said to Ruban.

"Me too. I have a feeling though, that he will not give in to Marcus's thirst for blood. He would rather die himself than injure any living being. At least that is what he told me once," Ruban remarked. "His time in the arena was always a life and death situation for him or those he fought in combat. He counted himself one of the lucky ones to have endured and survived the arena. Each and every death stroke he inflicted never left him. How could it, unless one did not have a conscience, he said. He hated every minute of the games and when he was freed by the crowd it was the only time he was thankful of the masses — they who applauded freedom and not victory."

"When did Mr. Gdown tell you all of this?" Blulay asked.

"Men talk, don't you know?" Ruban grabbed hold of his wife and held her.

39

Blulay's father, Traep, along with her uncles – Xela and Yddeg – convened a meeting with all of Pratt, Lerxst and Dirk. It would set in motion a precedent never before to have taken place in all of Triopelia. Not since the Year of Conflictions had such a course been taken and even then the decision to end that war was never conveyed in such a manner as happened now. Then, it was a given in order to end that conflict. But this, this was something very different and unique.

The topic?

Nebula Yorker.

40

'When dealing with a possible parallel conundrum', wrote Professor Cire Eldi of Playtexjumpor in <u>The Journal of Reversal Today</u>, 500 years before Professor Gabriel Pheet and LeBeau were born. 'If I were a betting man,' he wrote (and he was), 'I would say that such an advent, if found true, should be broadcast to the entire universe for all to witness. Of course it would have to be contained for full impact. Though should it breach,' – one word stood out in his column – 'RUN!'

His idea to have a posssibe parallel conundrum broadcast, much like the annual Parafin Seahorse Race, would encourage those who hated history to set themselves up for a whole new experience living whatever new history might take over if the Parallel Conundrum should breach whatever planet it happened to emanate from. They could also, of course, place a bet or two!

Then again, the chance of a parallel conundrum ever taking place was just a theory, so the odds of placing a bet and winning were fairly good though the oddsmakers did not like it one bit, theory or not.

Professor Cire Eldi frequently visited Halley's Casino over the years and just by chance he met one assistant concierge by the name of Marcus Attippius to whom he spoke at length about parallel conundrums – and his mother's Sweet Cake recipe.

Professor Cire tried his hardest to convince this assistant to chat up the head Concierge, Lafil, to convince him to open a betting line for his idea. However, this was all to no avail, though he found the assistant to be a marvellous listener, who was intrigued by his theory and wanted to know more.

Well, this flattery nearly overwhelmed Professor Cire though he declined the assistant's offer to sleep with him. Instead, Professor Cire directed the assistant to a book he had read that was called 'The Lost Door'. He said it was that book on which he had based his theory.

The tome's name alone intrigued the assistant, to say the least.

The one and only copy was to be found in the Great Library of Atiox on Mastic 4.

Oddly enough, Professor Cire was never seen again after his last venture aboard Halley's Casino nor did he have any more contact with Marcus Attippius.

Some say he just got tired of the merry-go-round that individuals of his status faced day to day. However, if the truth be told, Professor Cire ordered a snack and drinks while on vacation at one of the many beach resorts on Marine and when the waiter returned with the order, he found only a cone-sized stack of ashes on Professor Cire's seat.

Either the Professor had combusted or Airheart had surfaced for a light snack.

No one was ever sure what had happened. The waiter though was pissed off as Professor Cire was known to be a big tipper.

****

Marcus sat alone on the outside garden terrace. It was close to midnight. The weather had been unusually warm for March, reaching 25 celsius during the day and now holding firm at 18.

He thought he heard a wild dog howling in the distance or was it a dog running wild?

He looked up into the night sky as a falling star fell and it reminded him of the night he first met Lafil. It was unusual for Marcus, that he felt a twinge of sadness mixed with melancholy for his old mentor. Lafil had though, almost been like a father to him.

His own father and mother were not affectionate by any means and with no other siblings he felt that he was always on his own and that everyone was always against him. And to some degree, that was true.

Now on the eve of his greatest triumph he sat alone.

He thought of the Council of U and their disdain for Earth and its people even though for years it had been a human who held the position of head concierge aboard Halley's Casino. He wondered for a mere moment whether things would have turned out differently if he had taken over as the concierge of the Casino properly – in succession – after Lafil…? Could *he* have turned out differently? After all, Menbob Koop had waged war, wanting to destroy the Triopelians – and he ended up being the first head concierge of Halley's Casino. And what about those Triopelians… were they real? Were they fiction? Or were they a thing of the past? And what would he do if he did indeed meet up with them?

His thoughts drifted in and out and then back to the present. Tomorrow would be the crescendo of all days. It was the day he had worked for since his meeting with Professor Cire and finding out about parallel conundrums and 'The Back Door'.

He did manage to visit the Great Library of Atiox on Mastic 4 and locate the book Cire had spoken of. He found the book uninteresting and not very helpful until he read the last page where it mentioned that introducing a conundrum into a planet's tri dimensional span would reverse a planet's time and space core and that it may spread outward.

The time bubble that encased Eno's ship on the moon proved to be the key when he rescued him. Using the time wave graviton from the ship deflector ray they were able to pierce a hole in the Earth's tri dimensional span, thus reversing time.

It was brilliant and it was Eno's idea to use the ship deflector ray to penetrate the Earth's core.

Though now was not the time to think about Eno.

Not only would he do away with Pheet, See-Ess and Kcils in the arena but all those other non humans he had enslaved for countless years would all meet their end very terribly.

And once that was done he would set sail into space aboard The Anvilus, barring of course that it was necessary that they could find a way to drop that force field that was enveloping the planet at present.

One other thing continued to egg Marcus on the most... Nebula Yorker.

41

March 15 1990 (the Ides of March) - 9:00 AM

Neb snuck aboard The Anvilus under the guise of being a toilet retrieval guide. No one had ever heard of such a position and they let him pass without any question.

LeBeau for his part was on his way to free Komi Koop and company.

Ruban and Blulay waited.

Kel and Purell were investigating the echo space craft.

Tict wondered where Traep had gotten to and TeeceeFore was admiring her painted toe nails.

Pheet, See-Ess and Kcils awaited their fates in the arena.

Marcus was just waking up and Eno sat in his room thinking deeply about what See-Ess had said – about the 'you owe me' comment.

Livia was confined to her suite, and yes – planning plans within plans.

The Triopelians continued debating what to do.

And Mary Trepass was still waiting for her surprise to come in the mail.

Besides all that, it was a bright, cheery, sunny day.

Marcus had deemed this day, March 15th, to be a planet-wide holiday so that everyone would be glued to their viewing screens for what was about to transpire.

12.00 PM the arena games would begin.

12:15 PM a short musical interlude by Ozz's and Geezer's band of misfits.

2:15 PM everyone on the arena floor would be dead.

3:25 PM another short musical interlude by Ozz and Geezer's band of misfits.

4:00 PM would see the launch of The Anvilus.

6:49 PM the end of the known universe, as it was known.

All in all, Marcus had planned this day to a tee and was quite happy.

Now for it to all go off without a hitch.

****

Neb was speechless at the magnitude of The Anvilus.

Over 15 different species from as many worlds had added to her breadth.

It was a feat indeed. The sweat and death of many had brought her to life and Neb was about to end it.

He could feel her vibrant onomatopoeia, as did his father when he came upon the ship. He felt sad beyond belief but it had to be done and somehow she, The Anvilus, knew. She was a ship as out of time and place as the world she found herself in. She was also a powerful warship that if unleashed would devastate the cosmos. That was something Neb would not allow, even if it caused his own death, which he hoped it would not come to.

Neb found himself presently in the bowels of the ship. As he slowly walked through, trying hard not to bring any attention to himself, the ship sounded out as if it was speaking to him much like the Vegastriopelia had though on a micro level-and indeed it was.

Neb looked around to make sure no one was watching or nearby. He stopped and placed his right hand on one of the bulkheads. That Triopelian yellowish green hue flowed from his fingertips. He felt sadness. Loneliness. It was as if she knew what she was – what she was made for – and wanted no part of it. She thanked Neb.

Neb shed a few tears and as he did there was a loud crash behind him. He took his hand off the bulkhead and turned to see a young man in a white smock lying face up on the floor. He had just fallen backwards. He was a tall, skinny kid, maybe 17 years old. Or maybe 100? Who knew?

His name was Charlie, though his real name was Fleece. He was a Lanoishullonians from Lanoishull caught up in the parallel conundrum. He did not plan on visiting the Earth but a malfunction in his navcom had him landing on the Earth, just as it all went to hell.

"You're not from around here, are you?" Fleece asked, picking himself up from the floor. "It's ok. I am not either."

Neb cocked a brow, "Oh?" he replied. "And where might you be from?"

"Not this back water planet, that's for sure and I get the same feeling about you. Fleece, at your disposal," he bowed.

Neb thought for a moment before answering.

"Nebula Yorker," Neb said, extending his hand.

Fleece shook hands with Neb.

"But my friends call me Neb. Where exactly are you from, Fleece?"

"I am from Lanoishull. And you?" Fleece asked.

"Well, that is a very long story Fleece but let's just say for the moment I am on leave from Halley's Casino."

"Halley's Casino!" Fleece shouted out.

Neb put his hands over Fleece's mouth.

"Not so loud, Fleece," Neb removed his hand. "So you know your way around this ship?" Neb coolly asked.

"Do I!" Fleece replied. "I helped install the navcom computer's drive system."

Coincidence. Neb smiled to himself.

"Good. I am looking for the main computer room."

"That's easy," Fleece ran ahead of Neb. "Come on, I'll show you."

"Hey, wait up," Neb shook his head and caught up with Fleece.

"How come you're out and about?" Neb asked Fleece. "Shouldn't you be with Komi Koop and the rest?"

"How do you know Komi Koop?"

"My dad met him not that long ago," Neb answered.

"Is your dad Ruban of Triopelia?" Fleece's voice rose.

"Why yes," Neb asked Fleece to keep his tone low.

"WOW! Does that mean the Triopelians have come to save the day and get us all off this rock and back home?"

"Shush," Neb put a finger up to his mouth.

"Not really," Neb replied. "Yes I am Triopelian but I am not from Triopelia. It's a long story kid," Neb replied without trying to bring him down.

"But you are a Triopelian? How can you say you're not here to save the day? You are here to save the day, aren't you?" Fleece asked, a little bewildered.

"Yes, I am here, on my own, to help," Neb put his hand on Fleece's shoulder to reassure him.

"What are you planning to do?" Fleece asked.

"Well, for starters, we are going to crash this ship."

"With us on board!" Fleece gulped.

"If need be," Neb replied. "Though not if I can help it. That is why I need to get to the main computer room and reconfigure a few things."

"Anything I can do Neb, just ask," Fleece assured Neb.

"Ok. Show me the way then, Fleece," Neb said, following his new friend.

The length of The Anvilus was 1500 metres (4921.26 ft.) and the beam 300 metres (984.252 ft.). The decks were countless it seemed, as Neb and Fleece headed for the main computer room.

"Where are all the crew?" Neb asked Fleece.

"Crew?" Fleece replied. "This ship is more or less self-sustaining. That's how we built it, according to his highness's wishes," Fleece smirked.

"It's more of an android ship than for any carbon based entities though there will be a small contingent of us to help with maintenance. That is why I am still aboard her. The rest of the crew are scattered throughout the ship. I'd say there is about ten of us, in all."

"An android ship? Now that is interesting. And you say there are only 10 of you aboard?" Neb asked, rubbing his chin.

"Yes, that's right, ten," Fleece replied.

"Can you contact any, or all of them, Fleece?" Neb asked. "Because when this baby explodes I don't want any casualties if I can help it."

"Baby?" Fleece looked puzzled.

"Just an expression, Fleece," Neb smiled. "No worries, no literal babies."

"You're very strange, Neb," Fleece remarked, but in a good way.

"Thank you," Neb replied. "I have been told that before."

****

Meanwhile LeBeau was navigating his way with his own map that Ruban had given him to help him find Komi Koop and the others. As Neb went one way LeBeau had gone the opposite and then down below the hangar bay to where Komi and company were being housed and held hostage.

It was dark, dirty and sticky, almost catacombic, definitely claustrophobic and for some odd, strange, unforeseen reason – LeBeau had almost a feeling of escalaphobia, though why he felt that he wasn't sure.

"Hey you!" Someone called out to LeBeau. "What are you doing down here? This is a restricted area."

LeBeau stopped and slowly turned around to face no other than Gecoo Chin.

"Who are you? What are you doing down here? Let's see some identification!" Gecoo Chin ordered.

"Well, hello there!" LeBeau greeted Gecoo Chin cheerily. "Isn't it a fine day for a stroll?"

A stroll? Gecoo Chin thought. Again, he asked, "Who are you and what are you doing down here?" He was angry now.

"To be honest with you," LeBeau replied, "I am looking for some prisoners that I aim to free. Might you know where I might find them? Please."

"I'll…" Gecoo Chin said but then fell forward into LeBeau's arms to reveal a happy Komi Koop standing there, holding a small club that he just used to hit Chin over the head with.

"Are you the rescue party?" Komi said with a big grin.

"Komi Koop?" LeBeau asked hesitantly.

"Yes, and you are?" Komi looked down at the club he held in his right hand, as did LeBeau.

"Ruban sent me. I am LeBeau."

"Not the Professor LeBeau of Telvon 3?"

"Why yes!" LeBeau's eyes fluttered.

"Your equations on The Monty Particles were exciting reading."

"Thank you," LeBeau began to blush, "I would love to chat more but I believe time is of the essence, would you not agree?"

"You're quite right," Komi replied, "Please, come this way," he motioned for LeBeau to follow.

"What about him?" LeBeau pointed to Gecoo Chin on the ground.

"He'll be out for a while. Leave him," Komi cracked a smiled.

"How long have you been down here?" LeBeau asked as they walked.

"That's a hard one. 2000 years? 1000 years? 500 years? Three Years?"

"It's very hard to determine such within these parallel conundrums and having never experienced it before makes it even harder to understand," Komi answered.

"According to Neb, it's more like three years, even though it may feel like thousands."

"Neb?" Komi enquired.

"Oh, Neb is Ruban's son. He's quite brilliant. He's up on The Anvilus now, getting ready to blow her up."

"Ruban's son? Blowing up The Anvilus? Oh my!" Komi spat out, "that sure is adventurous of you all. By the way, how did you get through the Bubble and how does this Neb expect to destroy the ship?"

"I will tell you all you want to hear," LeBeau said. "I will explain the Monty Particle, the Bubble thing and Neb while we exhume everyone."

By the way, are the Triopelians coming?" Komi asked.

"I don't know about the rest of them but we have three with us already who have a plan so I guess you could say they are," replied LeBeau.

"Well I guess three are better than none," Komi shrugged his shoulders.

42(a)

John Lennon sat at the far end of Halley's Casino, it was the quietest haven on all of the ship and a place where Neb also loved to sit alone and think.

John looked out the rear end view screen as the Casino's comet tail flustered out.

Neb said it gave him a sense of peace and tranquility.

John Lennon watched the stars fly by thinking; wondering how Neb and his rag tag crew of intergalactic misfits were doing.

He reached out with his mind trying to tap into the space time flow to send Neb a message. He wasn't sure how he was doing it; hell he wasn't even sure who he was, let alone John Lennon.

After his death on December 8th 1980, the essence of the man known as John Lennon scoured the cosmos and finally came to rest on Halley's Casino. He was now the embodiment of the Vegastriopelia in corporeal form, with all the knowledge of the known universe within him.

Neb knew this but had kept the information to himself as he did not know what the end game of the Vegastriopelia was, if it had any.

As the Vegastriopelia grafted John Lennon's essence into its data nodes, its organic matrix grew unexpectedly. This was something the Triopelians had overlooked nor had any idea there was a possibility of when they created its complex systems – that it would become sentient, as it had now become. The Vegastriopelia and John Lennon were now merging at an expeditious rate, reaching out through space, time and parallel conundrums.

Just when Mr. Tict walked into the room, that yellowish green hue started to envelop John Lennon as he sat with his eyes closed.

"MY SAINTED AUNT!" Tict muttered under his breath. BLIMEY! If I didn't see it with both my two eyes!"

John Lennon opened his left eye for a mere second to see Tict watching him.

The view screen in the room faded from the stars to show Neb and Fleece walking through The Anvilus on their way to the main computer room.

Tict almost dropped to the floor, "What in heaven's name?!"

"It's all ok. Take a seat," John Lennon said to Tict.

Tict slowly lowered himself onto one of the sofas next to John Lennon.

"What exactly are we seeing," he asked "and how is this possible?"

"Forward Cosmotillic Projection," John Lennon answered.

"Forward Cosmotillic Projection?" Tict gasped, "I don't understand?"

"Think of it as a far reaching lens," John Lennon said. "That's what it is and – not to be pompous but – it is a little beyond human comprehension."

"Thank you, John. No offence taken but how are YOU doing this?"

John Lennon reached out and tapped Tict on the hand with one finger. We are now connected telepathically. John Lennon smiled at Tict.

The Vegastriopelia/John Lennon symbiont transferred all the pertinent information on its current status and also apologized that it had not informed Tict sooner, seeing that he was the head concierge.

Fascinating! Tict thought.

Please turn your attention to the view screen. John Lennon nodded.

Tict turned to watch.

"Hey Fleece! Are you sure you know where you're going?" Neb asked.

"Oh yeah! No problem, Neb. I'm just taking a shortcut," Fleece replied.

"You should know," Neb continued to follow Fleece.

Wow! Sound and all! I should have ordered some popcorn. Tict thought.

Popcorn? John Lennon responded.

Tict and John Lennon watched as both Neb and Fleece continued on their quest.

"Neb!" An invisible voice echoed out.

Fleece stopped in his tracks. "Did you say something?"

"That voice sounds familiar," Neb said under his breath.

"It should. It's me, mate," said John Lennon.

"John?" Neb replied, somewhat confused.

"Who's John?" Fleece asked.

"You can hear him too?" Neb asked Fleece.

"Hello, Fleece," John Lennon greeted Neb's new friend.

"Hello?" Fleece looked up and around. "Where are you?"

"I am aboard Halley's Casino," John Lennon replied.

"You're not in orbit?" Neb asked, perplexed.

"No. We are quite far out from earth," Tict cut in.

"Tict?" Neb scratched his head. "How is this possible?"

"Tict?" Fleece cocked a brow.

"FCP, my boy," Tict replied, as if he knew it all—and for the time being he did, while connected to the Vegastriopelia.

"Forward Cosmotillic Projection," John Lennon added.

"Fascinating!" Neb let out. "Are you here to help?"

"That is currently impossible, Neb," John Lennon answered. "The Vegastriopelia's matrix is not able to reach out physically at this distance."

"I see," Neb rubbed his chin.

"Oh, Traep was here on the Casino a few days ago but he quickly disappeared as he appeared to have never heard of you?!" Tict filled in Neb.

Hmm! That does not surprise me. Neb thought.

"I have never met the man. Only read about him."

"There is a grand disconnect with Neb and the Triopelians," John Lennon began. "Neb is indeed a Triopelian but he is the first of that race to be born out beyond the Plexus Rim. His natural Triopelian wave is only connected with his parents; that is why they do not know or feel his presence."

"So," Neb paused, "What's up? Oh, how is TeeceeFore doing, Tict? Is Devo still in cryo?" Neb's head was running wild with questions, briefly taking him away from the current situation.

"I was thinking about you, Neb and suddenly I was able to project a message to you," John Lennon answered, "It was and is quite trippy. I seem to have merged with the Vegastriopelia," he added.

"Yes, I agree 100 percent, it is very trippy!" Tict cut in. "How are Professors Pheet and LeBeau?" Tict then asked.

"I would like to say that they are doing fine…" Neb stopped and looked over at a very puzzled Fleece, "but we need to get going."

"Say no more, Neb. Sorry to have interrupted everything," said John.

"Before we go, are the Triopelians coming to Earth's aid?" Neb asked.

"Unsure," answered John.

"Ok. I just thought I would ask. Thanks for the call. Neb out."

"Disconnecting the FCP now," John smiled over at Tict as their connection also ended.

"That was weird," Tict and John Lennon said at the same time as Neb and Fleece also said the same.

Tict and John Lennon sat in silence.

Tict was trying to figure out if what just happened was real or not.

"Did that just happen?" Tict asked John.

"What are you talking about?" John replied.

"That whole FCP business?"

"I have no idea what you are talking about," said John. He then closed his eyes and promptly fell asleep, snoring.

Tict shook his head, utterly discombobulated.

42(b)

Livia sat on a small curule in the new quarters Marcus had assigned her. She stared at the new gown lying on her bed that a servant had brought to her earlier. It was a sky blue dress weaved with gold leafs adorning the waist. The gown was edged with small red tassels that looked like droplets of blood.

Does he expect me to wear that? She cringed.

Livia lightly touched her forehead. It was still tender from the fall and encounter with Marcus. Thankfully, there would be no scar. Plans within plans swirled within her head; they never stopped forming. Her whole life, she had been plotting – from her first marriage to Tiberius Claudius Nero, whose son Tiberius would rule Rome after Augustus, Livia had thought about the future.

Livia was the parental grandmother of the future Emperors – Claudius and Caligula. She was also great-grandmother to the city-burning, Christian-blaming, Nero, though in this time frame conundrum they had all been murdered by Marcus. Today was going to be the day of all days – perhaps for some, the end of days. Death would be a welcome rest, Livia thought to herself. Soon enough she would be called to join Marcus in the arena to watch the games. A whole afternoon of blood, gore and cheers that she would hate.

A young male servant of perhaps fifteen years old and six feet tall entered her quarters, carrying a tray, on it was a light meal and tea. He placed the tray down beside Livia and turned to exit.

"Wait!" Livia called out, "Please stay for a while."

The young man stood frozen. He hated when these aristocrats asked him to stay. Usually, staying meant either a flogging or some perverse sexual act was on the cards.

"What is your name?" Livia asked softly.

My name? Thought the young man, no one had ever bothered to ask him for his name before.

He stuttered, "Mmmm... Mika."

"Oh, a stutterer, are we? I knew another who stuttered, once," Livia was of course referring to her grandson, Claudius. "There is no need to be frightened of me, Mika. How long have you been a slave?"

"Th-th-three yeeeeaarrrs," he answered with his head down.

"And do you like being a slave?" Livia asked.

"NO!" Mika replied firmly.

"Your accent, Mika, I am not familiar with it. Where do you hail from?"

"The Northern Provinces across the sea. My family were Quebecois, before the rebellion against the Empire."

"There was a rebellion?" Interesting, Livia mused, so there has been an insurgency during Marcus's rule.

"All of our parents were imprisoned and we children were taken away to serve the Empire. I have been here ever since."

Livia stood up and walked towards Mika.

Mika took a few steps back.

Livia reached out and took Mika by the hand.

"I think today will be the end of your incarceration. No promises my dear but I have a feeling."

Mika wasn't sure if she meant that he would be dead by day's end or freed or that he would become a slave to another.

"Oh, and please take that awful apparel away," she pointed to her bed. "Keep it for yourself or sell it. Do whatever you want with it."

Mika eyed the dress. He could get a pretty penny for it. Perhaps enough to buy passage on a ship out of Rome.

He quickly grabbed the dress.

Mika's intention was not what Livia had in mind but if the dress fits wear it.

Mika left with the garment in his hands, thanking Livia as he departed.

****

11:45 AM

Professor Pheet, See-Ess and Kcils were gathered with other prisoners and combatants in a very cramped hallway that led out to the arena.

The hallway was humid and smelt of all kinds of body odour.

"What's going on?" Pheet whispered to See-Ess.

See-Ess shrugged his shoulders. "I hope a clean bath and lunch for starters."

"I have a bad feeling," said Kcils, hanging onto See-Ess.

"Don't worry, kitten. I will not let anything happen to you," See-Ess assured her.

"What about me?!" Pheet asked nervously.

"Yeah, I will take care of you too," See-Ess nodded his head.

A door at the end of the hallway slowly creaked open, sunlight burst through and the guards ushered the throng forward, through the door.

As they stepped out into the daylight they were greeted by thunderous applause. The stadium was packed with well over a hundred thousand in attendance while billions more watched from their homes across the planet.

Ruban and Blulay were glued to their monitors.

The proceedings were also being flashed across all screens on The Anvilus and Neb and Fleece stopped to watch, along with the other crew members.

LeBeau and Komi Koop and his fellow off-worlders watched briefly in their mess before taking off with LeBeau to escape to Ruban's and Blulay's hideout.

"The timing could not have been any more perfect," said LeBeau to Komi. "With all the planet's eyes on today's arena games, who will notice us?!"

The streets were barely alive as they made their way out of the city.

12:00 PM

A fanfare began to play, sounding throughout the stadium. Horns blew and cymbals clashed loudly as everyone rose to witness Marcus's arrival.

Of course he was never on time and he liked it just fine that way.

Livia was first to make an appearance. The crowd cheered even though they did not know who she was, yet.

She was followed by a stream of Pretorian Guards who had with them, Molossian hounds wearing mail armour and spiked metal collars.

Young vestal virgins throwing flower petals into the air and onto the crowd below, followed the hounds – though at a distance.

Pheet looked up from his vantage point on the arena floor and noticed Livia at the same time as Livia noticed Pheet.

Livia was led to the dais, which was well covered by a purple awning. She sat down and the vestal virgins surrounded her until the emperor arrived. They had orders to make sure Livia did not try to leave. In fact, they were not *vestal* virgins at all – or even *virgins* at all. They were, in fact, Marcus's little kept secret – his bodyguard of Amazonian women.

Centred on the arena floor was a small stage with a small, five-piece drum kit, two small amplifiers, one guitar and one bass guitar that were both sitting upright on stands.

A loud voice erupted from the stadium speakers.

"Please give your attention to the screens around the arena."

'Coming soon' blared across the screens.

The video feed went on to show a recent championship soccer game with players blowing up on the field of play after kicking the ball or a goal keeper losing his arms trying to save a goal.

Hockey, baseball and football game highlights followed. Each game with their own gory endings and always with a crowd of fans cheering on.

The water polo championship game had one of the highest ratings ever! With the introduction of sharks into the game – and then afterwards, piranhas. The piranhas helped clean up the leftover bits of players – and then the sharks themselves.

Being an athlete in this time frame was not filled with glory and honor unless one lived through the trials of the on-field tragedies. Only hand-to-hand gladiators, if they lived long enough and racked up enough wins, could be freed, as Mr. Gdown had been.

Those who lived with lost limbs were thought less of and the cruelty and torment continued for them. Marcus made sure that those injured were shipped far off to some Pacific island to ensure they were never seen again.

Neb could not believe what he was witnessing.

It was enough that Marcus had changed time but this horrific gore and death of the innocent had to end and at any cost, even that of his own death.

"Why do humans treat one another this way?" Fleece asked Neb. "Has it always been this way?"

Neb took a deep breath. "Yes and no," he answered, "humans have always had a dual nature – or yin and yang force about themselves.

"Yin and yang?" said Fleece.

"A dark/bright, negative/positive light exists in people. They have an amazing capacity to reach out and to create something out of nothing for the greater good. But the contrast is that then at the other end of the spectrum there is this," Neb pointed to the screen.

"Why are you then so fond of the human race, Neb?"

"I could ask you why you and the others that were caught up in the parallel conundrum were on Earth when you know it has been off limits?"

"Curiosity, I suppose," replied Fleece.

"I have lived among them for 26 years and thought I was human up until only a few years ago when I found out I was Triopelian. But up to that point, for all intents and purposes, I was human. I have seen that, with time, they could be a people – a planet – worthy of the universe's praise but…" Neb stopped, his eyes glued to the screen.

"But what?" Fleece then followed Neb's gaze.

"We better work faster," said Neb.

Neb had noticed Pheet, See-Ess and Kcils on the arena floor waiting to be sent to their deaths.

42(c)

Purell bounced around on the surface of the moon. He was enjoying himself immensely!

"Hey Kel! Look at me!"

Bounce.

Bounce.

Bounce.

Kel rolled her perfect blue eyes. "Yes Purell, I can see you," she replied. "What have you found?"

"I have found that I like the moon. Weeeeeeeeeeeeeeeeeeee," he bounced around some more.

Kel let Purell get it out of his system as it were, before she decided to try further for any logical response. She envied him in some ways. His childlike enthusiasms for one thing. Purell envied Kel though, for her straightforwardness.

After 30 minutes Purell started to settle down somewhat.

He pulled out what he called a rotameterdiameter; it was the size of a playing card. It picked up on reverse tachyons particles and it immediately started zeroing in on what he was looking for.

He contacted Kel. "Kel, I think we have found the spot."

"Can you relay the readings back for analysis?" Kel replied.

"Sending," said Purell.

After a few minutes of silence all Purell heard was…

"Fascinating!"

"What was that?" Purell shot back.

"Stay where you are Purell, do not move an inch."

"You mean a centimetre," Purell quipped.

"Just shut up and don't move," Kel shot back, "Please."

We are testy today. Purell thought to himself.

"I am sending you the shuttle's oscillator codes from the docking bay. When you receive the codes adjust the rotameterdiameter to point five microns and point it directly in front of where you are standing. Sending now," Kel pressed the console button.

Purell did as he was told without commentary. Within seconds the time echo ship materialized.

"Fascinating indeed!" said a wide-eyed Purell gazing at the identical shuttle to that presently parked in the Photon Ledger docking bay.

"Can we access the shuttle?" Purell asked.

"Unknown at this time," Kel answered back. "We need to conduct a few more tests. I have a theory but I need you back here to assist, Purell."

"On my way," Purell jumped up and ignited his thruster boots and headed back to the Photon Ledger.

****

The marvels of the universe are just that – marvels.

Where did we come from and how did we get here and where are we going? Why is there life on some planets and none on others? How did evolution come about? Did someone just add water and poof!

Is there a God or gods? Is he male? Is she female? And why for the most part are they invisible?

Each planet, each species of humanoid's and non-humanoids (which there are many of), not to mention the myriads of test-tube beings, such as LeBeau, are unique.Though who created who – and why and for what purpose? Perhaps there is just enough of this and that, that stirs the soup so to speak to question God, gods and robots.

Science on the other hand, to some is considered a type of magic. As magic as science may seem though, you will never see a scientist pulling a rabbit from a hat. Well, unless his theories have been exposed as a fraud and he needs the conjuring job to pay off his fifth wife's alimony!

Time echoes are a whole different type of magic, though – as Purell and Kel are about to find out.

Kel walked around the shuttle for the tenth time, marking the schematics of the craft as Purell was doing inside, though not ten times.

Each copied the entire craft's every nook and cranny, nothing was left out.

Kel had theorized and put to Purell that if (and it was a big if, as ifs go) – if they could merge the time echo ship and the shuttle itself now sitting docked, they might be able to reverse the mess the Earth now found itself in… If the science worked out.

Kel surmised that by merging the crafts that overlapped, time might be restored from the starting point of the shuttle's first landing on the moon.

There was though, one thing that Kel had overlooked. She had not taken into account that when Eno had piloted the shuttle from Halley's Casino in the first place, that was also in another time frame.

That Casino had then exploded, along with everyone else except for three individuals who were presently situated on the earth: Marcus Attippius, Eno Low and Nebula Yorker.

Those three had been absent from the Casino when it exploded.

Lafil returned to the Casino from Rome 12 BCE and changed everything.

Not even Purell was aware of this circumstance.

Kel was not the same Kel. Neither was Tict or TeeceeFore or anyone else for that matter – all, except Eno, who existed in both time frames.

Neb knew this to be true, if anything it was up to Neb to decide what action to take, which he was now in the middle of doing, though he was feeling any help would be welcomed. Time as always proved to be tricky especially when one was running out of it.

Where was a Time Lord when you needed one?

42(d)

Tict and TeeceeFore sat sipping tea in Tict's office as he told her about his encounter with John Lennon and the Vegastriopelia and how he had been connected to the two and their conversation with Neb.

"Heavens!" TeeceeFore spat out. "How can that be?"

"I'm not quite sure," Tict replied, still befuddled by it all.

"What was it like?" TeeceeFore gently took hold of her husband's hand.

"It was almost like a dream but it was real, almost an out of body experience. We communicated telepathically – John and I, that is – for the most part, except when we were chatting with Neb, I think. We could see Neb but he could only hear us, I believe.

"Actually John asked that I tell no one, though he must have known I would tell you. The Vegastriopelia has grown beyond its original function. That it can merge with the essence of a clone matrix – that being John Lennon – is something I have never heard of.

"Something just doesn't feel right, you know," Tict said, finishing his cup of tea.

"Perhaps I should speak with John," TeeceeFore lowered her now empty teacup down onto the table.

"He has always thought of me as a motherly figure. Perhaps a mother-son chat might be in order, so to speak."

"Yes but with whom might you be speaking with, when you do?" Tict replied.

"Maybe they're both in need of some parental help? You should come with me," TeeceeFore looked sternly at Tict.

Tict gulped. "Yes, mum," he answered.

"Another cup of tea dear, before we go?" TeeceeFore reached for the tea pot.

Tict wasn't sure who he was more frightened of, his wife or the John Lennon/Vegastriopelia entity.

Which was which, was now anyone's guess.

****

John Lennon sat in his small quarters.

His walls were covered with pictures of the Beatles. So many it was like wallpaper.

Part of him – the human essence – was starting to remember his life, although the Vegastriopelia part was in conflict, in that it did not quite understand the transient fluidity of the short life span of the human condition – or rather the experience that accumulated with the spark of life. It was beginning to though.

It was an odd transition for the Vegastriopelia. In all of its life span and of all the planets, species, cultures it had visited, humans were still somehow a mystery. Why, for the most part, did it choose humans to be the Casino's concierge though?

In John Lennon, it was finding the answers.

John picked up his acoustic guitar. He started to strum the melody to 'Imagine'.

The Vegastriopelia found it soothing as John began to sing the words.

Only on Earth could such a song lament the whole of humanity.

Earth was the only planet among all the planets where its inhabitants were constantly in conflict with one another throughout its history. It was very disconcerting to the rest of the universe but if anything the Vegastriopelia had learnt from Nebula Yorker that there was more than meets the eye to Earth and one day human beings would figure it out, he/they hoped.

The Vegastriopelia also knew that in the present day, Earth was in peril – and not just the Earth.

Could young Neb thwart Marcus and the parallel conundrum?

Not able to see into the future irked the Vegastriopelia but how could anyone or anything peer into the future when it had not been written yet? Of course, one could extrapolate outcomes which was vastly different than visiting the future – any future at that – and if – if – if – the Velexian Viper Reversal Vortex Bubble were to explode, then all bets would be off.

Time was the only variable that always seemed timed.

Just imagine.

****

TeeceeFore, accompanied by a reluctant Tict, stood in front of John Lennon's quarters. The door opened automatically, without TeeceeFore buzzing in.

Tict and TeeceeFore were somewhat startled when the door whooshed open in front of them.

"Come in," John said, now standing at the door. "I have been expecting you."

"Really?" Tict asked.

"Shoosh," TeeceeFore nudged Tict.

"Tea anyone?" John asked his guests.

"If I drink anymore tea, I will pee like there is no tomorrow," Tict replied.

"Shoosh," TeeceeFore nudged Tict again. "Tea would be fine, John," TeeceeFore smiled.

"Please, sit," John motioned. "So… I know why you are here and there is no need to worry," John said.

"Yes, but to whom are we speaking?" Tict asked.

"Yes, who?" TeeceeFore wondered.

"Who do you wish to talk to?" John replied.

"I would like to speak to John – if I may," TeeceeFore inserted.

"I am here," John smiled back at TeeceeFore.

"So, John?" TeeceeFore paused. "How are you?" She reached out, taking his hands into her own. "You know we are quite worried about you. Aren't we, Tict?" she turned to her husband.

"Yes, yes," Tict stood, and then said, "I have to pee. Please excuse me." And he headed for the washroom.

"But we haven't had any tea yet," John answered.

"Oh, don't mind him, John. Tea and beer do the same trick for him."

"How are *you* feeling?" TeeceeFore continued.

"To be honest, I feel great! Better than I ever have. Everything is starting to become ever so clearer. Did you know I used to be part of a group known as the Beatles? 'The

Fab Four', they used to call us; Paul, George, Ringo and me!"

"Yes, Nebula loves your music and so does Mr. Tict."

"But…" John stopped.

"Incoming message for TeeceeFore and Mr. Tict" ran the Interface over John's comm.

"Open a channel," TeeceeFore replied to the Interface.

"Greetings." It was Traep. Sorry for popping out, the way I did on my last visit. May I come in?"

Come in? TeeceeFore thought. Then, as she thought it, the doors to John's quarters swooshed open to admit a smiling Traep.

42(e)

12:30 PM

Marcus entered the stadium to loud cheers and a fanfare of assorted music blaring out of the arena's loud speakers.

Three hundred white doves were let loose and they circled the crowd, dropping unwelcomed gifts on heads. Some of the crowd were smart enough to bring small umbrellas, having previous experience at these types of events.

Marcus was decked out in royal purple from head to toe except for his gold leaf crown.

He was flanked by twenty-four Praetorians as he made his way to the dais where Livia waited.

The dais was surrounded by invited guests, not a seat was empty. Every Proconsul was in attendance. Well almost everyone.

Unknown to Neb, Eno Low was on The Anvilus.

But that would soon change.

The newly installed Proconsul Trbor Tnalp of Greater Britain was present. He was beaming with pride to hear his nephew Ozz play live for the Emperor. Who could refuse an invite from the Emperor?

Livia seated beside Marcus, rolled her eyes as Marcus waved to the crowd, his face visible on every screen throughout the stadium.

Marcus looked over to Livia. He saw the disapproval on her face but did not care. Perhaps he would keep her around, perhaps not. Perhaps she had outlived her purpose. Never meet your heroes he thought, when only one hero was needed – himself.

Marcus lowered his hands to quiet the crowd. Within seconds, all was silent.

"Citizens of Rome," he began, "On this day of all days, I welcome you."

Marcus paused as the crowd erupted, then lowered his hands again.

"Today we will witness the future of all Rome and beyond. Today we look to the heavens as the heavens look down upon us. Today I will become the Emperor of the whole universe!"

The stadium started to rumble. Everyone stomped their feet and cheered.

High above the arena the life-size holographic image of The Anvilus sailed. The crowd turned silent. They were not sure what they were looking at. The holographic projection of The Anvilus spun; its black purplish hull sparkled as it made its way around the arena and to all those watching at home.

What was it? Some asked, while others gasped. They still did not pick up on, or have a clue, that it was a deep space war craft. Most thought it was a new ocean faring ship.

Livia did not know what to think. She had never seen anything like it in her whole life.

She prayed that Nebula Yorker would save the day.

****

Ruban and Blulay had now welcomed their new guests, along with LeBeau, who had successfully led thirty escapees back to the catacombs.

The day had proved to be a brilliant day for them to escape – while all eyes were on Marcus and the games that lay ahead. The streets had been mostly deserted as everyone was glued to their screens at home and in bistros across the globe. It was a wonder they had not been caught – though sometimes timing is everything – but time was running out.

"Any word from Neb?" LeBeau asked Ruban.

"None," Ruban replied. "Though he did say that if he was successful we would see it all unfold on primetime."

"Primetime?" asked LeBeau.

"It will be when most people will be watching the games," Blulay answered.

"Here, look for yourselves, the show is just beginning," Blulay pointed to her small monitor.

"I don't see anything," said LeBeau.

"Wait. Let me fix that," Ruban cut in.

Ruban pressed a few buttons on his console. "Here, that should work."

Ruban redirected the monitor's viewing screen dimension onto the wall of the cave for all to see.

"She looks great," Komi Koop said about The Anvilus. "All that work, only for it to be destroyed. It's really a shame."

"Indeed," LeBeau concurred. "I have never seen such a ship."

"It is truly a unique ship at that," said Komi, "the first android craft of its kind."

Android? LeBeau thought. He was reminded of what Neb had said about androids evolving.

"Are all deep space craft androidian?" Ruban said to Komi.

"Are you asking a question, Ruban?" Komi replied.

"I am not sure now," Ruban looked at Komi, wondering.

"To answer you, all ships, small or big, are androidian in nature. Take the Interface for example. It's only a part of the whole mechanism that runs the ship but it is not separate from itself, it needs the whole of the other components to function. The Anvilus is much on par with the Vegastriopelia which runs Halley's Casino."

"That is a grand statement, Komi," Ruban huffed in disbelief. "The Vegastriopelia is far more than an androidian ship. After all, we Triopelians created it and it is far more sentient than circuits and hardware."

I wonder? LeBeau thought, while not getting involved in the conversation.

42(f)

Neb and Fleece finally arrived at the main commuter junction for The Anvilus and were (at least Neb was) surprised to see Eno Low sitting at one of the many consoles.

Eno slowly turned around after hearing the door swoosh open.

"I told you this section is off limits," Eno yelled, then fell off his seat.

"You!" Eno stood up and said "Nebula Yorker! You, you, you... you can't be here!" He then promptly fainted.

"Do you know who this is!" Fleece asked rhetorically. "It's Eno Low, Proconsul of Australia."

"I do know him, we kind of go way back. Here, help me lift him up," Neb said to Fleece.

They both lifted Eno up and tied him to one of the console chairs.

"He's actually a very nice guy. Well – *President* Eno is." Neb then related to Fleece, in a Readers Digest kind of version, the story of how he came to know Eno and Marcus.

Fleece was mesmerized.

"When this is all over and done with you'll have to visit me on Halley's Casino as my guest," Neb smiled at his new friend.

"I will take you up on that, Neb, as soon as we are all safely off this ship. In the meantime, what do you want to do with Eno here?"

"Good question," Neb said. First of all, we have to get this ship airborne, he thought to himself. "So how do we start this ship?" Neb looked over to Fleece.

"Maybe he knows," Fleece pointed at a now groggy Eno.

"You might have a point there," Neb nodded.

"Nebula Yorker, Nebula Yorker," Eno mumbled.

Eno looked up to see Neb and Fleece staring straight at him. "How?" he said.

"Look, Eno," Neb began, "we haven't much time. It's either you die or we all die. Got it? So, how do we start this ship?"

"Why should I help you, Nebula Yorker, assistant concierge of Halley's Casino?!" Eno vented.

"You're still pissed about that aren't you?" Neb shook his head. "Do you want to know something, Eno? Being assistant concierge is not what it is all cracked up to be. Don't get me wrong, I love it, but you, you are more than a wannabe assistant concierge. Do you know who and what you can be and have been? Marcus has taken advantage of you, twisted you to his thinking. Yet, you are better than that. And you want to know how much better?"

"How much?" Eno said unconvinced.

"While you were locked in that time bubble on the moon, waiting on Marcus, time on the outside changed and that time change proved better for you."

"Really?" Eno still was not convinced.

"You're the President of your home planet and a damn good one at that!"

Eno's eyes almost shot out of his head, with a tinted gleam in them.

"That's right – *President* Low," Neb held out his hand to shake Eno's.

Eno thought about it for a few minutes then asked, "How can I be in two time frames if I was locked in the time bubble on the moon?"

"Since you were locked in the time bubble, though it may have seemed like only hours as you waited for Marcus to touch base with you, time outside the bubble changed – in fact, a new time frame appeared.

"Thus, time equals minus time plus reverse time added to a new time frame, thanks to Lafil. So even though Marcus, myself and you are from the same time frame, Marcus and I were not locked in time as you were; we existed in Rome of 12 BCE while your person existed in the old *and* new time frame. Think of it as a mirror reflection as it were," Neb finished, exhausted.

"Interesting," muttered Fleece.

Eno thought about it. "If I help you, what then?" he asked.

"Well for one thing, we can resolve this parallel conundrum and bring Marcus to justice for once and for all time," Neb replied.

"Will I be able to meet myself, if I help?" Eno asked.

Neb straightened up and took a deep breath.

"I am afraid that will be impossible. If you were to meet yourself, both of you would rule the other one out of existence. You see Eno, you exist here and now. Once we correct this time frame everyone and everything will reset back to the time before Marcus interfered with it.

"By that account, will I then be still locked in the time bubble on the moon if everything reverts back?" Eno asked Neb.

"That is a very good question," Neb answered, "but...the short answer is, if you were to die here in this time frame then no, the *present* you would be wiped from this time frame and also the one you hailed from – much like if myself or Marcus were to die here."

"What about me and the others?" Fleece cut in on the conversation.

"Since you were caught up in the conundrum with knowledge of what happened, your memories are intact, along with your fellow captives as well as my parents but for all of the other inhabitants of the Earth, they will have no memory of what has taken place. All should revert back to the point where Marcus interfered, once time is sealed."

Eno remained quiet for some time. He was thinking about helping Neb.

He liked the sound of President Eno; his family must be very proud of him as well as his fellow compatriots.

"What do I get out of this?" Eno finally broke his silence.

"What do you want out of it?" Neb replied.

"To kill Marcus!" Eno stood. He looked over at Fleece and back over to Neb, "I will help you."

"Well, I am not one for killing, Eno, and I cannot sanction such a thing. All I can offer you is justice, once we capture Marcus," said Neb, as he put his hand on Eno's shoulder consolingly.

"I know," said Eno. Though he thought differently.

Plans within plans whirled, with so many in the mix.

Livia.

Eno.

The Resistance.

Mr. Gdown.

Mika.

See-Ess.

The plot thickened as to who might accomplish the dirty deed, if anyone could.

Neb was determined to not let anyone get their hands on Marcus but with things as they were, Neb first needed to get The Anvilus airborne. Then he could figure out the rest.

"Ok," Neb said to Eno, "how do we get this baby out of its hangar and out into the open? And Fleece, round up the rest of your fellow captives and get them off the ship. Once you have, head a few miles out of the city westward, to the old catacombs and wait there."

"Are you sure Neb, you can't use me for anything?" Fleece asked.

"You have done more than I could have asked for, Fleece," Neb smiled and gave Fleece a hug.

"See you on the other side!" Fleece said, turning around as he ran to gather up the remaining crew.

"See you on Halley's Casino, Fleece!" Neb answered hopefully and waved goodbye.

42(g)

12:30 PM – Arena

Kcils was feeling very ill. Her ears were wilted and her fur was starting to matt. All she didn't need now, was a fur ball.

She sat in what little shade there was, close to the entrance of the door they had been pushed out of.

See-Ess and Pheet were very worried about her rapidly deteriorating condition. The loud noise and the feeling of being caged was not something she was used to and for her kind it was very harmful.

"She needs attention," Pheet whispered to See-Ess.

See-Ess knew this but what could they do? It seemed that death awaited all three of them. It was just a matter of when and how.

"I wonder what has happened to Neb and LeBeau?" See-Ess said, while pacing up and down.

"Well, I guess two outcomes," Pheet replied, "they are either both dead, or they are waiting to the last minute to save the day."

"And if they are dead?" See-Ess raised a brow.

"I would rather think they are not. Let's try to stay positive," Pheet answered.

"You don't know LeBeau and Neb like I do. They both can pull rabbits out of a hat when you least expect it."

"What does pulling a rabbit out of a hat have to do with this?" an agitated See-Ess said.

"It's just a saying Neb used once. It means… to do something unexpected but ingeniously effective, in response to a problem or problems."

"That rabbit better be well done because I am getting hungry," See-Ess said, walking away to check on Kcils.

Poor Kcils, Pheet thought as he watched See-Ess cradle her.

The crowd erupted again as Marcus rose to speak. Pheet turned and looked up. He spotted Livia and waved though he knew she did not see him.

"Before we start with the games I would like to introduce the new Proconsul of Greater Britain," Marcus's voice echoed out across the stadium.

Trbor Tnalp stood up to applause. He was six feet tall, lean framed and had long, blonde, curly locks. He waved to the crowd and they waved back with appreciation.

"Thank you Proconsul Tnalp," Marcus clapped and nodded to his new Proconsul, then continued. "If you direct your attention to the middle of the arena floor, Proconsul

Tnalp's nephew – Ozz and his friends – are going to entertain us with a musical interlude before we get started with this afternoon's sport."

The audience lightly cheered as Ozz and Geezer, along with their friends Immon and Wardo, took to the small platform.

"Hi everyone!" Ozz said enthusiastically into the microphone. "We would like to thank the Emperor for giving us this rare opportunity to play a few songs for you this afternoon and please give a big shout out to my Uncle."

Marcus looked over to Proconsul Tnalp with a weak smile and a nod.

"Ok!" Ozz began, "this one goes out to our new friend who we met only recently. Thanks, Neb!"

Marcus almost shit himself at hearing Neb's name while Livia laughed out loud and clapped.

"Ok boys… 1, 2, 3…" said Ozz, as they ripped into Deep Purple's 'Smoke on the Water'. The crowd was in awe as those chords began.

Ozz remembered Neb telling him to strum those first few chords heavy and loud – and they did!

"Did he say Neb?" Pheet looked over to See-Ess.

"He did!" See-Ess replied, as he hugged Kcils. "I think we just might be alright," he said to her.

Marcus tried to order the music to stop but no one heard him.

The live crowd was into this new sound that they had never heard before and so also were those watching at home.

Marcus did manage finally, to get the attention of one of his Praetorian Guards. He ordered him to go down to ground level and unplug the band ASAP. By the time he made it to the arena floor though, the song was just about to end and the whole stadium began to shake violently.

No one knew what was going on. Was it part of the entertainment? Was it an earthquake? NO! It was The Anvilus lifting up and out of its hangar!

Some of the crowd started to scream and to run towards the exits. Others were not sure what was going on. Chaos would soon start to ensue.

See-Ess looked up at the seats in the arena that were growing empty. This was their chance to escape. The guards were nowhere to be found.

"Professor!" See-Ess yelled out, "Come, let's go!"

"Go where?" Pheet yelled back.

"Out of here!" See-Ess picked up Kcils in his arms and headed for an exit but was stopped by Mr. Gdown.

Not now. See-Ess thought.

Instead of the expected blow to the head See-Ess was expecting, Mr. Gdown said, "This way!"

"Professor!" See-Ess called out once more.

"Wait. Do you hear that?" Pheet answered back.

"Hear what?" See-Ess replied.

"That!" Pheet pointed to the sky.

Pheet, See-Ess, Kcils and Mr. Gdown all looked skyward, as did Marcus, Livia and those Proconsuls and crowd members still left in the arena.

A large shadow slowly enveloped the whole of the stadium. A hush now overwhelmed everyone. The Anvilus moved across the afternoon sky as all eyes focused on its magnitude.

Marcus raged. He pressed his wristcomm.

"Eno, come in! Eno, come in!" he shouted, "What is going on?!"

Eno and Neb sat at the main computer room consoles, navigating the ship.

"ENO!" Marcus was heard over the comm.

"Are you going to answer him?" Neb asked Eno.

"Should I?" Eno answered back, "You first."

"Me?" Neb laughed, "Ok."

"Greetings and solicitations," Neb finally replied.

"What?" Marcus spat out. "Who is this?" Marcus knew who it was, he just did not want to believe it.

"It is your old pal Nebula Yorker, here to clean up your mess once again," and as Neb said that, an odd thought occurred to him. How many times have we done this? As parallel conundrums went, could they also be caught up in a time loop? Anything was possible but he hoped it wasn't.

"How?" Marcus cried out.

"'How?' is a good question," Neb replied, "But now is not the time to question how and why. This ship will never see space," Neb bit back.

"What have you done with Eno?" Marcus lashed out, as if he cared.

"Your turn," Neb winked over to Eno.

"You may call me President Eno," Eno replied.

"What? Have you all gone mad!" Marcus barked. "Do you think I do not have a failsafe?"

"Is there a failsafe?" Neb asked Eno.

"I don't know?" Eno shrugged his shoulders.

"Ok, I did not see that coming," Neb said.

The ship suddenly came to a halt in midair and hung there.

"This is ground control to Major Tom," Neb muttered.

"Why did I listen to you?! He's going to kill me for sure this time!" Eno started to panic as his transfiguror flickered on and off, revealing his reptilian self.

"You know, you look much better in your original form," Neb tried to reassure Eno. "Remember you're a President and Marcus is nothing but a con artist, a fraud and a wannabe ruler of his own universe. Don't worry, Eno, Marcus only *thinks* he has control of this ship."

Neb stood up and placed his hand on the nearest wall; that green yellowish Triopelian hue wisped out from his fingertips.

Eno watched in awe.

"And now for something completely different," said Neb as those wisps of green yellow flowed from his fingertips into the ship's new Interface.

"Greetings," a soft female voice came out of the Interface.

"Greetings to you," replied Neb. "Have you been monitoring our situation?" Neb asked.

"I have," answered the Interface.

"How is this being done?" Eno asked. "There was to be no Interface installed on the ship, as per Marcus's orders?"

"Komi Koop installed a secret one which Neb here has helped activate. He is a very clever man," the Interface replied.

"But it's more than just an Interface, Eno. The whole ship is androidian," Neb smiled.

"It's brilliant!"

"Androidian?" Eno scratched at his scaly head.

"Yes. I am the first and last of my kind I am afraid."

The tone of the Interface was rather sad.

"Either way, Komi Koop and his technicians programed my components to deteriorate once we are out into deep space and past this solar system. It would have not stopped the parallel conundrum from expanding but it would certainly have put an end to Marcus's life. And to put your mind at ease Nebula, you are not caught in a time loop."

"Oh, you can read minds too eh?" Neb said.

"If you like," the Interface replied in a whimsical way.

"I see," Neb cocked a brow.

"I am coming for you, Nebula Yorker!" Marcus's voice shouted out of the comm.

"Don't worry Neb, I have sealed off the dock and ports. No one or anything – without my approval – gets in or out," the Interface relayed.

"There is one escape pod which is big enough to fit you and your friend. I suggest you leave as soon as possible. My existence has been brief yet remarkable."

Neb shed a tear. "You will not be forgotten. I have downloaded your schematics. I will make sure you live again," Neb promised.

"How?" the Interface asked.

"Can't you read minds?" Neb replied, "Read mine."

"Fascinating!" the Interface gushed.

"Eno, head for the escape pod. I will be with you momentarily," Neb said to Eno.

Eno didn't hesitate, he ran out and straight down the hall.

"Thank you Nebula – or should I say 'Neb', my friend?" said the Interface.

"You're very welcome. But before I go, may I ask one favor of you?"

"Anything," the Interface answered.

"Would you wait until my mark before your ascent?"

"I will," replied the Interface.

"When you hit the Velexian Bubble it will absorb all that you are into its matrix. All that you were will become part of the Bubble," Neb said.

"Or perhaps the bubble will become part of my matrix and I absorb the Bubble?" the Interface matter-of-factly said.

I never thought of that. Neb scratched his head.

The Interface paused for a second and then said, "Eno has left, Neb. The escape pod has jettisoned without you."

"I had calculated that he would do so," Neb said.

"There is another pod, isn't there?" he asked, a tad nervously.

"Of course there is, Neb," the Interface laughed and then became serious.

"Neb, my friend… Until we meet again."

"Until we meet again," Neb acknowledged.

"Remember, wait for my mark."

42(h)

The streets of Rome were in chaos. People, everywhere, were running back and forth, trying to get to their homes. All eyes were still skyward as The Anvilus hung there without moving. Was it going to fall on the people below?

Ruban, Blulay, LeBeau, Komi Koop and the rest had their eyes glued to the viewing screen.

"It's madness!" Komi Koop said.

"It looks like Neb has found a way," LeBeau replied.

"Yes, but why is the ship just hanging there?" Ruban asked.

"Why isn't it heading up into the Bubble?"

They continued watching the screen when LeBeau spotted the Professor, then Kcils, See-Ess and then a big hulk of a man, who was Mr. Gdown.

"We have to go and get them!" LeBeau turned to Ruban.

"That may be dangerous right now," Ruban answered.

"But we can't just let them…" Blulay tugged at her husband's arm.

"I know, I know. By the time we reach the city it could be anyone's guess where they might be, though," Ruban replied.

"Yes, but Mr. Gdown knows where we are. For all we know, they are heading this way," Blulay said. Ruban had told Mr. Gdown some time ago where they were hiding out, athough he was the only one. However Mr. Gdown had never really visisted their catacomb lair.

"You may be right at that, dear. LeBeau, are you with me?" Ruban said to LeBeau.

"What about me?" Komi Koop chimed in.

Ruban took a deep breath, "Thanks Komi, but we need you here should things go sideways."

"Sideways?" Komi asked.

"Just in case things do not go to plan," Ruban smiled, resting his hand on Komi's shoulder.

Komi stood beside Blulay wrapping his long arms around her. "It will be ok," he said, as they watched Ruban and LeBeau head out of the catacomb home to the rescue.

* * * * * * * *

Marcus was furious, breaking everything in sight that he could put his hands on.

He had ordered the guards to bring Ozz to him though thus far they could not find him nor his uncle.

"Nebula Yorker!" he shouted out again and again.

Livia sat in the corner of the room saying nothing, watching the meltdown of the century (whatever century she was in). She had witnessed grown men lose their wits many times before and many times she had been the cause of those men losing their wits. She found great pleasure in Marcus losing his.

"Guards!" he yelled.

Within seconds two guards arrived. "Take that!" Marcus was now pointing at Livia, "Take *that* out to the outside terrace garden, where I do not have to look at her."

He then walked behind Livia; she felt the heat of his breath on her neck, "I will deal with you later," he whispered into her ear.

Livia's spine shivered at his words. She stayed cool and did not say a word, although she wanted to. I must stick with my plan, she thought to herself as her hand reached down feeling the dagger she had concealed beneath her clothes.

Now wait till I get my hands around that scaly excuse for a Proconsul, Marcus thought. He was referring of course to Eno, who like Livia, sought revenge and was intent on achieving just that.

Marcus tried in vain to bring The Anvilus back to the hangar bay. Why wasn't the ship complying? All he kept receiving on his hidden console screen in his private chambers was an 'OUT OF ORDER' message – along with a smiley face. This made him even more furious.

He had ordered all live television feeds cut planet wide and replaced them with all the best highlights from past games. The unexpected change was blamed on a mild earthquake and the celebrations would resume soon. He hoped that would appease the masses.

In his master plan to rule the universe, Marcus really did not have a strategy, outside of leaving the planet. He had just thought Rome would continue without him until his return, under the authority of his trusted surrogates. Now he needed to get up to The Anvilus at any cost.

First, he had to deal with Eno and Livia – either have them both killed or both frozen.

"Incoming message!" rang out on Marcus's wristcomm.

"Hi there!" A familiar, cheery voice echoed out. It was Neb.

Marcus did not answer straight away; he was in shock at hearing Neb.

"Why do you keep interfering with my plans!? Why can't you just leave me alone?!" Marcus finally shot back.

"You can only play with time so much Marcus. Besides, I missed you," Neb replied.

Marcus fumed more. "I was eagerly waiting to meet *you* again and to blow that Casino out of existence – but I guess one problem at a time," Marcus answered back.

Neb was going to mention that he already had accomplished destroying the Casino in the other time frame but why give Marcus any reason to gloat.

"What ever happened to Lafil?" Neb decided to ask, to try and change the subject. It was to no avail though, as Marcus was not biting. "Ok. So how did you manage to reappear then?" Neb asked.

"You can blame – or praise – Eno, for that," Marcus answered.

Really! Neb mused. I never saw that coming.

"Nor I," said Marcus out loud while thinking he was thinking it.

Interesting. Neb thought, keeping his thought about a thought to himself.

"Where is that little reptile anyhow?" Marcus again said out loud.

"Would you believe he abandoned me? I have a feeling he's out to find you," Neb replied, "and he is none too happy, I tell you."

The story of Eno Low and how he came to assist Marcus is one of manipulation on Marcus's part. A villain always looks for a sidekick to kick about and Eno had endured his share of being kicked about.

Finding out he became President of his home world Repooc Ecilca 6, changed everything for Eno. The years he had placed himself willingly in Marcus's service to then only be denied the role of concierge of Halley's Casino as he had been promised, cut him to the quick. The beatings and outright verbal abuse he also endured were beyond any being's limits but he had hung on hoping, wishing and dreaming. Being Proconsul of Australia wasn't bad but it wasn't home. The need for revenge now rushed through his cold blooded veins.

And Neb was correct in saying that he was out to find Marcus.

****

"I guess by now you have noticed you do not have any control over The Anvilus while I do!" Neb stated firmly to Marcus, "There is no way out this time."

"Come and get me, I dare you," Marcus huffed, "what can one man do?"

"That would be true, if I were alone," Neb answered back, "but by now, all those whom you enslaved to build The Anvilus are freed and no longer under your thumb. Do you really think that Komi Koop was going to let a marvel of a ship like The Anvilus not have a failsafe installed?"

"Do you think *I* would not have a back-up plan?" Marcus snarled, "You foolish man."

Neb wasn't sure if Marcus was bluffing or not.

"Well, save me a seat," said Neb, "I am on my way. Nebula out."

"Yorker? Yorker? Yorker?" Marcus called into his wristcomm but Neb had ended the transmission. Marcus stood in silence. This day of days was turning out to be a day to forget of days. How was it that Nebula Yorker was going to thwart him once again? He had to die, no two ways about it. It seemed that he would seek Marcus out so why not let him. Marcus scratched at his chin and started to laugh.

Livia, I will use Livia as bait!

42(i)

Kel and Purell were sitting in the lounge as one does when lounging in a lounging room, though androids were not known to lounge up until now.

They knew something was afoot within their internal sensors; something just did not feel right or rather *was* feeling right.

They gave up, momentarily, trying to merge the time echo shuttle and the tangible shuttle that sat in the docking bay. Overlapping each other proved to be more of a challenge than they had thought it would be. They were also finding the science and theory beyond their full comprehension, for the time being at least.

They were both looking out of the port window at the Earth. The Velexian Viper Vortex Reversible Bubble was intact. Nothing had changed on that front thus far. No word from Neb and crew thus far either. No news was good news – thus far.

"What do you think, Kel?" Purell asked.

"Think about what, precisely?" Kel answered.

"Everything!" said Purell.

"That is a very large quantity of data to answer, Purell. How long do you have?"

They both laughed at the nonsensical question that Purell had posed.

After a few minutes of silence Purell asked, "Do you think Neb will succeed in his mission?"

"I do," Kel quickly answered.

"Elaborate please," Purell rubbed his chin.

Kel raised a brow at Purell rubbing his chin.

"That's new," she mimicked Purell, rubbing her own chin.

"What are you doing?" Purell leaned forward.

"You're doing exactly what Neb usually does when he is perplexed and thinking," Kel rubbed her chin again.

"My!" Purell said, "That is indeed interesting... What do you suppose it means?"

"I am not sure. I will need more information to determine the meaning of your odd behavior of late."

"Odd behavior?" Purell chirped back, "And what of *your* odd behavior?"

They both stopped, tilting their heads to the left at the same time and remained in that position for thirty minutes until the Photon Ledger's Interface rang out.

"Incoming craft heading towards our current position on a trajectory intercept course."

"Can you identify said craft, Interface?" Kel sprang up.

"Commencing scanning. Long range sensors working," replied the Interface.

A few seconds later the Interface relayed, "Craft identity unknown at this time." "How long before it reaches us?" Purell cut in.

"One hour, forty-two minutes and 42 seconds," responded the Interface. "Visual now coming in," it then added.

"On screen," Kel ordered as she and Purell walked onto the bridge from the lounge.

"What kind of ship is that?" Purell asked.

A green yellowish hue of light flickered in and out from deep space.

"The craft is now passing Jupiter's rings," the Interface once again reported and added, "Revising estimate of craft's arrival – in five, four, three, two, one."

"What?" Both Kel and Purell said simultaneously as the ship came to a dead halt in front of the Photon Ledger.

It wasn't a large craft but was more of a sleek jet fighter type of craft – though perhaps a little wider.

"Incoming hail," the Interface alerted Kel and Purell.

"Open a channel," Kel said, looking over at Purell with intrigue and fascination.

"Opening a channel now," the Interface replied.

The bridge's viewing screen changed from a view of the outside of the ship to a smiling Mr. Tict. Alongside him were TeeceeFore, Traep and John Lennon – all looking out from the screen.

"You should see your faces," Tict bellowed out with a hearty laugh.

"What in the name of all that there is!" Purell managed to holler out.

"Permission to come aboard?" said Traep. "Is that the correct greeting?" Traep asked TeeceeFore.

"Yes," TeeceeFore nodded her head, "You're getting the swing of it." She remembered how, previously, Traep had burst in on her and Tict in their bedroom, without any notice or protocol.

"Permission granted," said a still bewildered looking Kel.

It only took mere moments before all four were standing on the bridge alongside Kel and Purell as that familiar green yellowish hue spun in and out.

"Well this is indeed a surprise," Purell welcomed everyone, though he did not know who Traep was and neither did Kel.

"Oh, where are my manners," said Tict. "Let me introduce to you – Traep of Triopelia."

Purell rushed to Traep and gave him a big hug.

"I knew it! I knew it!" Purell said, not letting go, "I knew you guys would come!"

"Purell!" Kel walked over and pried him off of Traep.

"Sorry, sir. He's been acting up a little lately," she said to Traep.

"Indeed!" Traep answered, "You are androids, aren't you?"

"The finest!" answered Purell.

"Indeed!" Traep once again voiced with some levity. "You're very humanoid for androids. Sorry, I did not mean to disparage you in any way. What I mean to say is that you are very unique."

"You can thank Neb for that," Purell said proudly.

"Indeed!" Traep again said.

"Is that all you can say? Indeed!" Purell raised a brow.

"Purell!" TeeceeFore lightly slapped Purell on the back. "Behave yourself in front of our guest. He has travelled a very long way to help."Purell dropped his head like a little puppy dog and pouted to go along with it.

"I am sorry," Purell apologised, still looking down and shuffling his feet.

Traep was amazed at how Purell acted so unlike any android he had ever encountered. Kel also. They had Neb to thank, he thought. It made him even more eager than ever to meet his grandson as the people of Pratt, Lerxst and Dirk also were.

During this time, John Lennon had been sitting at the science console working out equations.

"There she is! Beautiful as ever – even with the Bubble still surrounding it," Tict gushed, looking out at the Earth. TeeceeFore stood by her husband, hanging onto his arm and with her head resting on his shoulder.

Kel and Purell were now working alongside John Lennon. Traep observed the five on the bridge interacting and working together. We have been away from the affairs of the universe for far too long he relayed back to Triopelia, as they all listened and watched through Traep.

"Hmm? That's very possible," Kel said to John Lennon.

"I concur," Purell agreed.

"How did you come up with this equation? If I may ask," Kel asked.

"I was thinking about musical notes and how a high pitched note can shatter glass."

"But that is not glass out there," Purell pointed to the Earth.

"Indeed!" Traep walked over to the three.

"It is a most interesting hypothesis," Kel said to Traep, "Let's begin by running some simulations to determine its accuracies."

"Cool!" John Lennon replied.

42(j)

1969 was an auspicious year for the Earth and humanity; for those looking in and out – from far away in the greater universe and to those visiting Earth.

The first Led Zeppelin album is released in the USA.

The New York Jets win the Super Bowl.

The Montreal Expos debut as the first Major League team outside of the USA.

The first man on the moon mission takes place – 'one giant leap'!

Woodstock rocks the world.

The Beatles release 'Abbey Road' to huge success.

Monty Python's Flying Circus first airs on the BBC.

There were many other events that took place in 1969 – mostly bad – though to be fair every year has its share of good and bad. In fact, every *day* has its share but let's not split peas.

The aforementioned were landmarks in Neb's life.

As a nine year old, being at Woodstock happened by mere chance. He and his parents were camping nearby and wondered what all the noise was about.

Neb actually met David Crosby, though David Crosby doesn't remember meeting Neb. To be fair Neb was peeing on one side of a tree and David on the other side. It was a *big* round tree!

And of course a man landing on the moon wasn't just news back on Earth, other eyes were watching from across the universe. Although since then, those outside eyes have not bothered much with the Earth.

****

Neb had just departed The Anvilus in a very small one-man seater escape pod when he received two messages.

One was from Marcus, inviting Neb to meet him to discuss the terms of his arrest, which of course Neb did not believe for one second. I smell a trap!

And a second message was from John Lennon/The Vegastriopelia in which John informed Neb that he, Tict and TeeceeFore, along with his grandfather Traep, were aboard The Photon Ledger, working on a plan that would drop the bubble and reverse the parallel conundrum.

Neb then informed John about The Anvilus's androidian nature and his plan.

John very quickly added that the two plans unleashed simultaneously might just be the answer each was looking for and that he and Kel along with Purell would start the equations immediately.

"Wait for my mark," John said

Ruban and LeBeau rushed to the city to find their friends before they were re-incarcerated. They knew they had to act quickly. Who knew what Neb had in store and it was better if they were all together when the shit hit the fan.

Livia waited on the garden terrace. She was actually enjoying the moment, as the garden brought back memories of days long ago that only ever seemed like a dream now. She thought about herself and Augustus planning this and that, laughing, crying, arguing, having a bite to eat and taking in the single moment of a frame in time.

She remembered Lafil mentioning to her that we were all just frames in time, passing one to another. Nebula, whom she thought at times was just a dream, wasn't. Nebula existed. Livia hoped that they could meet one more time before she died.

And unknown to everyone, Eno was on his way to the palace with his own brand of justice to mete out to Marcus.

It was turning out to be a momentous day on all fronts.

42(k)

Traep paced back and forth from one end of the lounge to the other and Tict and TeeceeFore sat back drinking tea while eyeing Traep.

"You're being very human," Tict said to Traep, who stopped for a moment, raised a brow at Tict's words and then resumed pacing.

"You would think you are about to have a baby!" TeeceeFore added.

Traep was indeed nervous, nervous about meeting Neb and what he would say to him on behalf of all Triopelians and also as his grandfather. No Triopelian had been born outside of the trio of planets of Pratt, Lerxst ad Dirk. No one that they/he knew of, that is.

Before the purge of the three, there was Anthem, the fourth planet. They were known then as the Quadipilains. Before Earth, Anthem was the only planet ever to have executed the Velexian Vortex Viper Reversal Bubble.

It was not like the Triopelians forgot this, they just chose not to remember it because of all the pain and sorrow it had caused; and now Earth could be next, while Traeps' daughter, her husband and his only grandson, that he had never yet laid eyes on, were there.

"Why don't you sit down, Traep?" TeeceeFore patted the seat beside her. "It's not that hard to see that you have a lot on your mind but we all do."

Triopelians were not accustomed to letting their feelings be known, especially to outsiders. Traep finally acquiesced and sat down beside TeeceeFore. He plonked himself down with a heavy sigh.

"It's ok," TeeceeFore rested her gentle warm hands on Traep's hands. "Your people have been away from the goings on of the universe for a very long time. Life exists and has grown outside of Triopelia, thanks to your people. But to have sidelined yourselves for thousands of years and only appearing when a crisis occurs, is not very good housekeeping," TeeceeFore said.

"Your people helped to create the Council of U which has kept the peace since the Year of Conflictions and the Casino (created as an intermediary) has been extended for all species across the universe to take advantage of, except the Triopelians. Perhaps it's time for your people to hop aboard and take a breather every now and then. Come out and play with the rest of us, come and see what we all have to offer."

Traep listened intently to TeeceeFore.

"You know she is right," Tict commented.

"I know," Traep replied.

42(1)

The ending is always harder than the beginning, although I guess it might depend on what that beginning was or is, opposed to an ending that may be the beginning of something or nothing.

Neb was thinking (as usual) on his way to the palace after landing the escape pod from The Anvilus. He walked along the Tiber. A slight warm breeze touched his face as he looked out remembering another time he had walked along this same path.

He was not sure how that adventure was going to end, although it seemed to work out just as well... or did it? So many variables. His mind raced, deep in thought.

Can one erase time or reverse it? Lafil did both. Should he have? Or was time just playing out as it was to be in the first place? No one knows the future but in Neb's case the past was always his future.

But this – this parallel conundrum – was a whole new story. It's enough to change one man's history but a whole planet's history – or perhaps even that of the universe – was unthinkable. Yet here we are – here is where we find ourselves.

"Yes, that is very true," Neb heard.

"What?" Neb turned around and saw no one.

"Sorry to have startled you, Neb," It was John Lennon/The Vegastriopelia.

"You can read my mind too?" Neb said out loud.

"Yes," John replied, "but only yours, Neb."

"Our symbiosis is simpatico."

"But I thought you said you could not help because the Casino was too far away – yet here you are?"

"That was before Traep stepped in to help."

"Yes, I understand he is aboard The Photon Ledger," Neb said.

"Indeed, he is presently with Tict and TeeceeFore who are comforting and helping him along with all Triopelians."

"Helping them with what?" Neb asked.

"With you and all of this calamity, young Neb," John answered.

"Me?" Neb was taken aback.

"You have turned your worlds upside down. Your existence is a marvel and the Triopelians want to get to know you."

"Hmm? Could you stop reading my mind for a bit?" Neb asked. "I have to think about this privately for a moment, would you mind?"

"Of course not," John answered and broke the link.

Neb stopped and sat down. There was too much information running through his head and he really had to departmentalise it all.

"First things first," he said aloud. The Triopelians would have to wait – Marcus was the priority.

"John, are you there?"

"Yes," John replied.

"Our first – our only – task at the moment, is Marcus and the Bubble. Everything else is on the back burner."

"Affirmative," answered John.

"I am on my way to find Marcus and to end this. The Anvilus is waiting on my word. When I give the order it will be time to sync up."

"Confirmed," John replied.

"Oh and say hello to everyone on the ship and tell them that I will see them all soon."

"Will do, Nebula Yorker and remember, turn off your mind, relax and float downstream," John added.

42(m)

Earthers have always been caught in the showdowns between good and bad, light and darkness. All of the Earth's religions incorporated God and the Devil in some guise into their creeds but nowhere outside Earth has this concept of good and evil been embodied.

Granted, there are always forces beyond one's control, indeed some have speculated that everything had to have started from somewhere, so why not from a force of goodness? The Triopelians for example, are thought of as gods by some, though that is far from the truth. They are indeed unique but as flawed as any other lifeform. For most of the planets and species that have ever existed, the rule of thumb has always been, BE GOOD TO ONE ANOTHER.

Sad to say, on Earth they have to be told to be good to one another when they just should be. God asks them to be good and the Devil tells them to disobey and be bad and thus it has led them not only to not think for themselves but to also be coersced into choosing sides. We heard that God is very disappointed and the Devil refuses to comment.

Androids on the other hand find this all too baffling.

Who created who? What? We don't run on batteries?! Excuse me, I think you popped a screw.

Androids can be very sarcastic.

The point being, Neb the Good and Marcus the Bad were on a collision course, one that would either set the universe on fire or one that would reset the Earth as it was before — ignored by the rest of the universe.

42(n)

What's with these one and two page chapters?

42(o)

What is life without whimsy?

42(p)

Mr. Gdown looked up and down the small alleyway, making sure the coast was clear. Behind him were Professor Pheet, See-Ess and a very ill and dehydrated Kcils.

"How long until we see the gates of the city?" See-Ess asked Mr. Gdown.

"We're very close," Mr. Gdown replied. "I am making sure there are no guards up ahead, looking for us."

In fact, there were no guards looking for them; Marcus was too preoccupied. He had also expected to be off the planet by now and so hadn't bothered to call out his guards as a search party.

"The last thing we want is to be thrown back into the arena," Mr. Gdown added.

"With that I 100 percent concur!" The Professor said, peeking out from behind Mr. Gdown's large bulky mass.

"Ok, let's move," Mr. Gdown nodded his head.

As all four began to creep along the cobble stone path they heard voices up ahead, around the corner. With no cover whatsoever they all assumed they were doomed.

"Kcils will surely die if we have to go back."

See-Ess shuffled up to Mr. Gdown, "I am not going down without a fight."

Mr. Gdown looked at See-Ess – they were both formidable men.

"Let's do it!" Mr. Gdown smiled.

See-Ess smiled back with glee.

"Oh my!" The Professor muttered holding onto Kcils.

See-Ess and Mr. Gdown bolted ahead, up and around the corner. Kcils purred, her head resting against the Professor. They waited and waited for See-Ess and Mr. Gdown to reappear until they did appear once again. There, coming back to them were See-Ess and Mr. Gdown but with LeBeau and Ruban in tow. Pheet almost fainted and almost peed his pants, both. Kcils rushed to See-Ess and did faint, right into his arms.

"Professor!" LeBeau happily hugged Pheet.

"I thought we would never see other again!" LeBeau then added, "Alive."

"Oh my boy, you do not know how good it is to see you – everyone!" Pheet replied.

"Why are the streets so empty?" Ruban asked Mr. Gdown.

"Your guess is as good as mine," he answered.

"Well, whatever the case, let's get everyone back to the caves."

Here Ruban pulled out of his satchel a small bottle of water and handed it to Kcils.

"I know your species is not accustomed to this kind of stress."

"Thank you," Kcils said, trying to open the bottle.

"Here, let me do it for you," See-Ess opened the cap and handed the bottle back to Kcils.

The shadow of The Anvilus hung over the city like a rain cloud that did not wish to move or to rain either, for that matter.

"Is that thing going to fall on us or take flight?" See-Ess asked.

"It's going to be one or the other," Ruban replied. "I just hope we are all far enough away, whatever it does."

"What is it anyhow? I have never seen a ship like that," the Professor professed.

"You could call it a slave ship, since slaves built it," LeBeau said.

"Slaves!" gulped the Professor.

"We're almost there," Ruban turned back to the others, ushering them on.

And as the gates of the mighty city came into focus, there was Neb walking through them.

"Nebula!" Ruban rushed to his son and engulfed him in his arms.

"Hello everyone!" Neb said, his father squeezing him ever more tightly so that Neb's hand wave to his friends was definitely a micro one.

"Germanus!" Neb's eyes caught Mr. Gdown.

"Who?" Ruban let go of Neb.

"I will tell you later," Neb said.

"I thought you were on the ship?" Ruban looked up to the vessel.

"I was. That too is another story."

"Come, let's go," Ruban said.

"Sorry dad, not me. I have an appointment with Marcus at the palace."

"You can't be serious, Nebula?" Ruban's eyes widened, as did the others'.

"Are you crazy?" Pheet was aghast.

"Perhaps," Neb smiled.

"I like crazy," See-Ess patted Neb on the back.

"Though crazy is only a good thing if you're crazier than the crazed," Mr. Gdown added.

"Or stupid," LeBeau cut in. "Neb, come back to the catacombs, it will be much safer there."

"Yes, yes! Listen to LeBeau," Pheet said.

Ruban looked into his son's eyes. "Do what you need to do son. And come back to us alive."

Neb extended his hand to his father, their fingertips touched and familiar wisps of Triopelian green yellow hues surrounded them.

Mr. Gdown, See-Ess and Kcils looked over to LeBeau and Pheet, somewhat puzzled.

"What? Have you never seen a Triopelian before?" LeBeau smirked.

Hmm? See-Ess looked on. That would explain a lot about this fellow.

"What is a Triopelian?" Mr. Gdown looked at everyone.

42(q)

Aboard The Photon Ledger, John Lennon/The Vegastriopelia composite, sat musing about the situation and waiting on Neb's word to begin the beginning to the end of the beginning of the end – or the start of something wonderful.

Kel and Purell sat at the opposite side of the room in the hangar bay, musing over The John Lennon/The Vegastriopelia composite.

"What do you think, Kel?" Purell asked.

"Regarding what, specifically?" Kel replied.

Purell didn't say anything, he just nodded over in John Lennon's direction.

Kel looked over to John. "Yes, it is quite unique," she offered.

"I thought we androids were unique but this is nothing I have ever heard or read about in any data enquiries," Purell said.

"It is very extraordinary to say the least," Kel rubbed her chin.

"Isn't it?" John Lennon hollered across the room.

Kel and Purell looked at each other and laughed.

"You both are unique beyond any other androids that have ever existed," John now walked over. "I am sure Neb has dropped hints about your evolving nature," John said and sat down beside the two.

"I am not sure what you are referring to?" Kel replied.

"Neb has indeed upgraded our components and data nodes to be sure and I, for one, do feel at times to be not so different from humanoids – except in intelligence. Besides Neb and LeBeau, that is," Purell turned in his chair to John.

"When Purell and my data nodes were fused on Marine the symbiosis that took us over did retract days ago and I did *feel* – and I say, that to feel was both new and refreshing!" Kel continued. "Purell and I still retain those experiences as if they were a rebirth of sorts."

"Indeed!" John nodded in agreement.

"By the way, to whom are we speaking with?" Purell asked, "John or the Vegastriopelia?"

John let out a full belly laugh.

"That is a good question, Purell," John answered, still laughing.

"You see, John Lennon died in 1980, on Earth. However, his being was also unique among beings throughout the universe and now his essence, which is part of this matrix, lives on. This is though, only for a limited time –

until it finds its resting place, which lies beyond the Plexus Rim, where it will be united with those other essences that have garnered a place in the universe.

"It has come about by pure happenstance that John Lennon's essence which we inhabit continues to have purpose even after his physical form has gone. His purpose of love, life and peace has found a way through his essence to continue his mission as it were."

"You really should call up all data you have on the man as well as look up Egroeg Nosirrah of Dhorse V, Ognir Rrast of Bebopp Prime and Helen of Waitress."

"Helen of Waitress?" Purell tilted his head.

"John's memories tell us she made a wicked club sandwich, whatever that is."

"I see," Kel nodded, still rubbing her chin.

"What are you doing?" John enquired of Kel.

"How do you mean?" Kel answered back.

"That chin thingy."

"Oh, that is what Neb does when he is in deep thought," Purell said.

"Interesting," John started to rub his chin in the same fashion.

"It does not do anything for me but I will keep trying it."

"So, you were saying that we are both unique androids beyond anything you have ever seen?" Purell changed the subject to himself, which he loved.

"Purell!" Kel said in a somewhat annoyed tone.

"No, it's ok," John replied, "you both have a right to know. You are evolving and have become self-aware. It's only logical that which you once were has come to be who you are now – sentient beings. Though you have been such for some time. It's just that it is only now that you are aware of it. Your fusing sped things up!"

Kel and Purell looked at each other, their heads tilted right.

"Fascinating!" they both said at the same time.

"What of other androids?" Kel asked.

"In time they will also become self-aware. You are the first though and they will be in need of teachers and leaders so will look for your guidance when the time arrives."

"Time arrives?" asked Kel.

"There will undoubtedly come a time when you will be in need of a home world."

"A home world!" Purell gushed out.

"Will we androids be subservient to our makers?" Kel asked.

"No," answered John. "You will always have a choice, to assist – not serve."

"When will this all be?" Purell swirled excitedly in his chair.

"That depends on you both. Neb has chosen at the moment not to divulge his Triopelian heritage but at a time when he sees fit, he will. You as well have that choice. My advice would be to learn, observe, be cautious, and teach your fellow droids – be a good example to them." Traep said as he stepped out from behind the shadows.

He had been listening in – though unintentionally.

"It has recently come to my attention that we Triopelians have not always done so. Humanoids and androids have much to learn from one another, as all species do. We have disdained Earth for their lack of civility, crude technology and their 'rough around the edges' attitude that Mr. Tict has informed me about and yet Nebula has seen the diamond through all of this grit, which we, the so called 'Keepers of the Universe', have not. And I stand here now in awe at the marvel of you," Traep looked intently at John.

"We created the Vegastriopelia as an engine, a guide, the data node of all nodes. A matrix such as was never seen before nor that will ever be again. A part of Triopelia, a gift to the universe, although – I am unfamiliar with the clone matrix you inhabit -is it pleasing?" Traep asked John.

"'He', not 'it' – and it is," John replied, graciously.

"Forgive me, I did not mean to offend," Traep lowered his head. "So much more to learn," he sighed.

"Nothing to forgive and yes, we *all* have much to learn."

Then John did an unexpected thing; he rose up from his chair and hugged Traep.

"Thank you," John whispered in his ear.

Traep did not know how to react. To actually have the Vegastriopelia thank him in bodily form was beyond any Triopelian imagining when they created the matrix.

All of Pratt, Lerxst and Dirk cried.

42(r)

Tict and TeeceeFore were sitting on the bridge when Kel and Purell, along with Traep and John Lennon, joined them.

The Earth, with the Velexian Viper Vortex Reversal Bubble pulsing steadily, shone out on the bridge view screen.

"What will happen when the Bubble is shut down? How long will it take for the Earth to resume its original time frame?" TeeceeFore asked Traep.

"Unknown," replied Traep. "We have never disengaged a Bubble before."

"The Bubble collapsing will not in itself reverse the Earth time frame," John cut in. "If the bubble were to collapse, the parallel conundrum will seep out into the universe causing unknown chaos."

"Then why are we engaged in bringing it down?" Tict asked nervously.

"Yes why?" TeeceeFore stood up.

"Two events must happen simultaneously," John took a deep breath and sighed out.

This made the other five worry.

"Two events?" Traep enquired.

"Yes. The downing of the Bubble and three deaths must occur."

"Death! Three! Who?" Tict let out a gasp.

"I have a bad feeling about this," Purell said.

"Can you elaborate, John?" Kel asked.

"Ok. First, using the satellites that are currently orbiting outside of the Bubble and circling the Earth, I will attempt to coordinate a minute frequency found in their transistors."

"Transistors!" Purell yelled out. "That is brilliant!"

"Yes, transistors," John continued. "By syncing up these transistors I will send out a radio beam."

"Radio!" Purell once again interrupted.

"Let the man finish!" TeeceeFore scolded Purell.

"As I was saying," John looked over at Purell sternly. "I will blast the Bubble with high pitch notes from one of Neb's favorite Earth musical compositions entitled 'Take Me Home', by Phil Collins. These notes, along with The Anvilus, crashing into the Bubble, should in theory bring the Bubble down."

"Theory? What is an Anvilus?" Traep raised a brow.

"The Anvilus is a warship created by Marcus using off-worlders as hostages caught up on earth during the parallel conundrum conversion."

"It is the first of its kind, a complete atomised Android craft."

Everyone looked over to Purell who did not say anything, though Kel and Purell did look at each other with quizzical faces.

"And everything is a theory until it is proven right or wrong."

"What about this death thing?" Tict asked uneasily.

John again took a deep breath.

"Three deaths must take place within 60 seconds of the Bubble's demise. Those of Marcus, Eno and Nebula."

"Heavens no!" Tict yelled out. "That cannot be. It's Neb, he can't die. He is the tie that binds us all."

"He is indeed," John replied. "You see, Marcus, Eno and Neb are the only three individuals that are not from this current time frame which we *are* a part of."

"When Lafil changed the time frame, Marcus and Neb were on the Earth while Eno was encased in a time bubble on the moon in his ship. Marcus and Neb joined our present time frame while again Eno was still awaiting Marcus from the previous time frame – in which frame he did appear, and though to Eno that time span was short, 400 years had passed by in the new time frame."

"So now, in order to break the parallel conundrum created by Marcus, all three must die to reset the time frame. And those caught up from other worlds that were taken hostage, along with Neb's parents, will know what they have been through. The rest of Earth's inhabitants may experience a form of deja vu from time to time but that is all."

"Does Neb know all this?" TeeceeFore asked.

"He does," John replied. "He is the one who explained this predicament to me. He truly is a rather clever fellow."

"But this can't be," TeeceeFore and Tict began to cry.

"Is there no other way?" Traep looked to John.

"None," John replied. "Not even you Triopelians can prevent this. The universe must be preserved at all costs. Neb's words, not mine."

"He is right." Traep concurred, "otherwise all that we are and know will be replaced and gone forever and no one will ever know that; not even we Triopelians.

"Maybe we can…" Tict stopped. "Encase every planet with a Bubble so that nothing gets in?"

"A valiant thought, Mr. Tict but such an idea would segregate all planets and species to their eventual extinction over time," Traep voiced, "space would be a void."

"But then Marcus would have no one to rule over," said Tict in response.

"True," Traep smiled.

Kel and Purell were rather silent at hearing about Neb's future demise. He was to them, a fellow android. They had never felt or experienced loss and were not sure how to proceed.

John, knowing how they felt, walked over to them and extended his hands to theirs. Wisps of green yellow flowed out from John into Kel and Purell. Traep was astonished, as were all Triopelians. They thought they had seen and heard all that there was to see and hear.

John also knew his time was coming to an end. It's almost fitting, he thought while linked to Kel and Purell.

The androids now came to understand their past, present and future while connected through the Vegastriopelia and to the message Neb had left for both of them.

Now all that everyone on the Photon Ledger and throughout the universe could do was wait.

42(s)

The Triopelian philosopher known as The Great Palin once stated that all that there is to know is never known. To know all things would make life rather boring – if one could not boast to another that they were wrong.

The Great Palin was seldom right.

Nebula Yorker was the opposite… for the most part.

Neb walked slowly towards the palace, his thoughts raced towards his parents and his friends on The Photon Ledger, Halley's Casino and all the worlds he had enjoyed the privilege of visiting.

Three years ago he could only have dreamed about the experiences he had lived through. Also, to find out his true heritage, that was beyond – way beyond – anything he could have imagined. And now he carried the whole universe on his shoulders.

Maybe there *was* an afterlife? Who knew? If there was, would there be drinks? Snacks? Brunch? A VIP room? As long as Marcus was not part it.

As strange as all of it was, the palace entry was as empty as the silent city streets. Neb looked up at the sky to The Anvilus and smiled as he walked in.

The palace had changed over the years, since Marcus took charge. It was no longer the fairly modest dwelling that had once belonged to Augustus and Livia (though Livia's wing of the palace had always been much more regal than her husband's).

Marcus had enlarged the palace to a size he thought fitting for an Emperor living on Palatine Hill and added elaborate frescoes, covering every inch of wall that there was from one end of the palace to the other.

Busts of Marcus in marble and gold were everywhere. No longer were the gods of old to be found. Marcus ensured there was only one deity in this Rome.

Romulus and Remus would be very displeased.

It was not the Rome Neb remembered visiting with his parents back in 1971, with all of its history to discover. This history was one-sided and boring.

Livia hated it. Her memories were still intact from her time frame and she prayed to her gods that they would intervene on her behalf and on behalf of all that was good.

Her own history, from her time frame, stopped after Marcus murdered Augustus. Her own son, Tiberius, never ruled Rome. Nor did Caligula, Claudius or Nero − for good or bad.

Christianity was stopped in its tracks as soon as Marcus took over − and very quickly at that. One thing he had learned about organized religions while on Halley's Casino, was that once they took hold they became very difficult to weed out.

Nothing was to hinder his rule, though Nebula Yorker proved to be the thorn in his side; one that was hard to extract.

He should have time travelled and killed Neb at birth! (Though of course, Marcus did not know – yet – that Neb was a Triopelian and born in space not on the Earth.)

Eno, on the other hand, had one thought on his mind after Neb divulged that his counterpart in the other time frame was the President of his home world.

His mother always told him, 'If you apply yourself you could be the President one day – of the local 'Get a Leg Up Dancing School'', though he really dreamt of being a seahorse jockey… Still, the President of Repooc 6? Wow!

And Marcus's promise of being his assistant concierge, which at the time was beyond anything Eno could have dreamed of, was pale in comparison to being El Presidente.

42(t)

Livia sat on the garden terrace biding her time where daylight and nighttime began to merge. A few stars were visible. She began to remember those two falling stars of long ago when she and Augustus watched. Those stars had led to Lafil, Marcus and Nebula.

They – Lafil and Neb – were very convincing in their guises when they first met all those years ago. (Could it be years? Sometimes it felt like days only – and in some ways it was.) She was taken with Neb, as was Augustus – and with Lafil's reading of the falling stars, though it was Neb who was the star.

She remembered Neb telling her that her name would live on far after she had died and that history would be her saving grace.

She prayed vehemently to Augustus to give her the strength to do what was needed to be done to avenge his death in the name of HER Rome.

Unbeknownst to Livia, Marcus was watching her from his secret corner. She was a Roman as he was, though Marcus evolved – or rather devolved – into being more than just a Roman. Was it Lafil's fault for choosing him in the first place to be concierge? Was it the universe's fault for showing him that there was more to the stars in the sky? Or was it just human nature; his human nature.

In his reformed world there were no Dark Ages, no Hitler, no Hiroshima, no Winston Churchill.

No.

No nuclear arms race, no poverty, no environmental disasters.

What was all the fuss about?

Now at the other end of the terrace, unseen by Marcus, Eno was watching Marcus from *his* secret corner. (For such a small space, secret corners were at a premium.)

And then – in walked Neb. The endgame was now afoot.

42(u)

"Nebula!" Livia jumped up excitedly and ran to Neb.

Before she was able to give Neb a hug though, Marcus stepped out of his corner and stopped Livia in her tracks.

"That's far enough," Marcus pointed a small phaser pistol at Livia that he had pulled out from underneath his toga.

"You!" she snarled at Marcus, changing her direction from Neb to Marcus.

"I wouldn't, if I were you," Marcus held his weapon firmly, pointing it at Livia.

"Don't move," Neb said to Livia.

"Listen to your friend," Marcus replied.

"Well, well, the gang's all here," Marcus grinned. "So Mr. Yorker we meet once again and for the last time!"

"I agree," Neb replied. "But let's keep Livia out of this."

"Why should I?" Marcus shot back. "She has been just as much trouble for me as you have."

"For one thing you can't win. There will be no winners this time," Neb said. "This all ends here and now."

"Really?" Marcus snickered. "The way I see it, I have the phaser."

Livia defied Marcus and took Neb by the hand, then gave him a hug.

"You're looking well," she said.

"As you," Neb replied.

"Looking and feeling well are two different things," she replied.

"Are you unwell?" Neb asked concerned.

"Only when I am in the company of traitors," Livia said, loudly enough for Marcus to hear.

"Compliments will get you nowhere," Marcus smiled.

"Who wants to go first?" Marcus pointed the phaser, moving it back and forth from Neb to Livia – toying with them.

"Boys and their toys," Livia answered.

Marcus fired the phaser, hitting a vase just behind Livia. It exploded into tiny little shards over the floor.

"That was only on stun, the next time you will not be so lucky."

"I am not afraid of you," Livia spat on the ground in Marcus's direction.

"My good lady!" Neb interjected.

"Forgive me, Nebula, it's just that I cannot tolerate this man any longer. Did you know he encased me, frozen in glass, for almost two thousand years? I had to endure his constant whining every time he felt unloved or unwanted. He didn't know I could hear him, did he," she looked at Marcus who now looked away.

"He even murdered my dear husband Augustus and my whole family. He thinks we have much in common but he is so very, very wrong."

"Bide your tongue!" Marcus yelled.

"Or what? You will kill me? Go ahead," Livia pushed Neb aside. "Here I am. Be a man," she held her head high, proudly.

Marcus fired.

Neb quickly dived at Livia, knocking her off her feet, before the blue light of the phaser whined out. The phaser beam just missed Livia, hitting the wall behind them both. It did, though, crack the wall and a chunk of concrete flew out, smacking Neb in the back of the head.

Neb fell to the ground unconscious, blood oozing from his wound.

"Now look what you have done," Livia screamed out at Marcus. "Neb. Neb. Neb," she shook him.

Livia looked about and grabbed two cushions, placing them under Neb's head. She then tore a piece off her dress and raced over to the water fountain, plunging the material into the water. Back with Neb, she dabbed the blood away from his head with the wet cloth.

"Leave him!" Marcus bellowed out.

Livia obeyed; why, she didn't know. She lifted Neb's limp hand and gave it a kiss.

42(v)

Aboard The Photon Ledger John Lennon was starting to get data from The Anvilus. She related that Neb's vital signs were erratic.

He was surprised that The Anvilus was able to communicate with him telepathically though it was actually Neb using The Anvilus as a relay to John. Neb had synced his Triopelian brain waves with The Anvilus's on-board Interface as a fallback should he become incapacitated and not be able to communicate verbally with her. Neb thought of everything. The countdown had begun. Together John and The Anvilus would begin their final equations to bring down the Bubble and let loose the dogs of war.

John waited for a few moments and turned in his chair at the science consul on the bridge. "Nebula is dead," he informed everyone.

It took a few seconds for it to sink in.

TeeceeFore fainted into Tict's arms as long streams of tears flowed down his face. Traep closed his eyes and took in a deep breath as did all of Pratt, Lerxst and Dirk. Purell lowered his head and slammed his fist into his chair, breaking off the arm of the chair. Kel walked toward the doors of the bridge and exited into the lounge, she looked back at everyone without saying a word before the doors swooshed open for her.

42(w)

Marcus looked down at Neb's body; he gave his side a little kick. Well, this isn't how I would have wished for you to die but nonetheless, good riddance. I had so much planned for your death but such is life.

Livia sat silently, wiping tears from her eyes. This made her resolve to kill Marcus even more resilient. She felt for the dagger that she had concealed beneath her dress.

Marcus turned to Livia, "That was sort of fun… wasn't it?" he grinned.

He then looked up to The Anvilus, "We have a shuttle to catch," he said to Livia.

"No, you don't," Eno said, emerging from his hiding spot.

Livia stood up. The voice was familiar but she could not quite make it out. It sounded almost slithery.

Marcus knew who it was and fired off his phaser, though in the wrong direction. He destroyed two columns and blew a large gap in the wall. A flying piece of concrete flew out at Marcus, knocking his phaser out of his hand. Marcus tried to retrieve the phaser but a scaly foot stepped on the phaser, crushing it.

Standing there – all four feet of him – was Eno. He had disengaged his mobile tranfiguror.

Livia could not believe what she was seeing, a lizard man draped in a toga. She almost ran away but this was too good to miss, she thought.

So the hen who had flown the coop – or in this case, the lizard – had returned. Marcus inched forward towards Eno.

"I wouldn't if I were you," Eno had his own phaser pointed directly at Marcus.

"Eno!" Marcus said in a soft-toned voice. "It's me, your master..." he paused, "... and friend."

"Master? Friend?" Eno's serpent tongue spat out. "I thinkssssssssssssssssss not. I have learnt much about Rome's past, present and its future all these long years. And what I have found out is that despots such as yourself have a very short life span. Do you know what day it is Marcus?" Eno hissed. "Today is the day to settle all debts."

"Who cares what day it is?" Marcus bit back.

"I know," Livia said. She grinned evilly.

Marcus stood, flabbergasted. He didn't get it.

"Should I remind you, master?" Eno said, sarcastically.

Livia knew and loved it. *"The **Ides of March** is a day in our (the Roman) calendar that corresponds to the 15th* *of March. It's a day for settling debts. It is also the day that Julius Caesar was assassinated."*

" You did not go far enough back in time, master."

Eno lunged forward towards Marcus, dagger in hand, but before he could get to him Livia darted out and stabbed Marcus in the back. In return, Marcus pulled out his own dagger and stabbed Livia in the arm.

Eno then plunged his dagger into Marcus's side.

Marcus knifed Eno in his shoulder.

Livia stabbed Marcus in the stomach as did Marcus to Livia.

Back and forth the three stabbed each other. Blood soaked the floor.

Marcus drew his dagger once more, slicing Livia's throat and with a swift turn, he drove a fatal blow into Eno's heart.

Livia and Eno were no more.

Marcus collapsed onto his knees. His hands were blood-soaked and his breath heavy. Then, out of nowhere, Mika jumped in and planted a spike through Marcus's neck and down through his back.

Almost as soon as Mika appeared, he was gone.

Marcus looked over to Eno's and Livia's lifeless bodies as they started to disintegrate into thin air. He then turned to Neb but before he could make Neb out, he too started to fade into dust.

The engines of The Anvilus roared as it headed up and up into the atmosphere.

Aboard the Photon Ledger, John keyed in the final sequences as Phil Collins sang 'Take Me Home'. The frequency blared out into space, hitting the outer bubble at the precise same time as The Anvilus hit the inner Bubble.

Mr.Tict, a revived TeeceeFore, Purell and Kel (who now had returned to the bridge) along with John, Traep and all of Triopelia watched on the view screen as the Velexian Vortex Viper Reversal Bubble shattered outward into space, dissolving as it did so.

The Photon Ledger shook from its position stationed on the dark side of the moon as the Bubble's final shock waves hit the ship.

The mood was sober on the bridge.

Kel and Purell began to monitor Earth's transmissions. They found all was where it was supposed to be for March 15th, 1990 – the present day.

No signs of Marcus's Rome or any footprints at all were left behind.

John detected a small cloaked ship leaving Earth's atmosphere that was now hailing The Photon Ledger.

It was Komi Koop with the rest of his comrades, along with Professor Pheet, LeBeau, See-Ess and Kcils. Blulay and Ruban had stayed behind.

"Permission to board?" Komi asked.

"Permission granted," replied John.

"Do we have room in the docking bay for another ship?" Purell turned to John.

"You will find that Eno's shuttle craft is no longer present," John affirmed.

"Yes, of course," Purell acknowledged.

"I better go down to Earth and see Blulay and Ruban," Traep sighed.

"Do you want us to go down with you?" Tict asked.

"Thank you both but I will be fine."

TeeceeFore turned back to the screen and looked down at the Earth. It was a beautiful sight to behold, minus the Bubble. Tict soon joined her. They held each other, their thoughts resting on Neb.

"What is that?" TeeceeFore pointed out into space from the screen.

A shimmering light sparked on and off.

"Kel?" TeeceeFore asked. "Can you magnify please?"

"It might just be a particle of the Bubble dissolving," Kel replied.

"Yes but it seems to be getting closer and closer," Tict said.

"Interesting!" Traep rubbed his chin.

"Magnifying now," Kel responded.

"My gods!" TeeceeFore screamed. "It can't be, can it?"

"Engaging tractor beam." Purell pressed a couple of buttons on the consul in front of him, along with Kel.

As the shimmering light became more visible, a person could be seen encased in a transparent bubble.

It was Neb!

42(x)

Neb awoke eight days later in the Med Bay aboard Halley's Casino.

He opened his eyes slowly. He wasn't sure where he was. His vision was blurred and he blinked a few times, trying to figure out his situation.

"Nebula?" he heard his mother's voice and felt her warm hand in his.

"Mom?" Neb asked tentatively.

"Yes, Nebula, it's me," she kissed his forehead.

"But," he asked, "Where are we? In Triopelian heaven or something?"

He then heard his father's familiar laugh.

"No, Neb. You're aboard Halley's Casino in the Med Bay," Ruban said.

After a few minutes Neb's vision started to return to him.

"Mom! Dad!" he cried happily.

"Well, young man, you are quite the wonder," Traep stepped out from behind Ruban.

"Neb, this is your grandfather; my father," Blulay said.

Traep moved closer to Neb, he reached out with his fingertips as wisps of green yellow glided out from them, first touching Neb and then moving from Neb to Blulay and to Ruban.

As the flow of information criss-crossed to each one, Neb came to realise he had more in common with his grandfather than he would ever have thought and Traep was also amazed at Neb's volume of information. Knowledge that he had collected not just from Earth but everywhere. He had so much more at his fingertips than any Triopelian.

"Ok, ok. That is enough time, let the man rest some more." Dr. Vanquwippllle, the new Med Bay physician from Solaratic V who had recently joined the crew, shooed everyone out of the room.

"Now Mr. Yorker, you seem to be coming along just fine, a few more tests and you should be good to return to your post," Dr. Vanquwippllle said.

"You look somewhat familiar?" Neb said to the doctor and at that same moment Professor Pheet and LeBeau came into the room.

"He should," said Pheet. "He's my brother. Different father, same mother."

"Gabriel, didn't I tell you to wait outside until I said it was ok to visit!" Dr. Vanquwippllle shook his head at his brother. "And you!" The doctor turned his attention to

LeBeau. "I should have known you wouldn't be too far away."

"Nice to see you too, Doc," laughed LeBeau.

"Five minutes and that's it! He needs his rest for tomorrow evening," Dr. Vanquwippllle said and left the room.

"Tomorrow evening? What is he talking about?" Neb asked.

"It's a surprise!" Pheet said giddily, rolling his eyes.

"GP! You don't tell someone they are having a surprise party, it's supposed to be a surprise!" LeBeau gave Pheet a little playful push on the shoulder.

"Although… there is a surprise party for you tomorrow evening," LeBeau beamed. "How are you feeling, by the way?"

"Actually, I feel pretty good, but I don't understand why I am alive."

Then it dawned on him.

"Did we save the Earth?"

"We're standing here, aren't we?" Pheet replied. "And you just saw your parents."

"And Marcus?"

"Gone! Gone! Gone!" LeBeau said, happily.

"I still don't understand why I am alive."

"Perhaps I can answer that," John Lennon suddenly appeared.

"Where did you come from?" Pheet looked at John, a little ruffled.

"It's not where did I come from, but where am I going?" John replied in his Liverpudlian accent, with a grin.

"Let's go. Neb and John have a few things to discuss," LeBeau grabbed Pheet and hurried him out of the Med Bay.

"But what did he mean… It's not where did I come from, but where am I going?" Pheet was heard to say as the door swooshed behind them.

"He's funny; that Pheet guy is," John smiled.

"So?" Neb asked. "Why am I alive?"

"It's very extraordinary," John began. You see, you thought — and correctly so — that Marcus, Eno and yourself were the only ones from the same time frame but you were wrong."

"How so?" Neb enquired.

"You forgot Livia."

"Livia?" Neb asked, puzzled.

"Yes, Livia. Before Marcus enacted the parallel conundrum he put Livia in cryostasis in the same time frame that you first were a part of with Lafil, right before you left to go back to Halley's Casino, three years ago. When Lafil returned to the Earth and died on Earth, Marcus could not time travel back to the same point in time where you and Lafil were originally, so it was as if Lafil never existed but only Marcus, Eno and Livia did from this time frame. Eno, who was waiting for Marcus on the moon, encased in the time bubble, used the time bubble to venture back with Marcus to Rome of 12 BCE – before your appearance with Lafil. Thus Marcus was able to use the time bubble to enact the parallel conundrum."

"I am starting to hate bubbles," said Neb.

"In a way, you can thank Lafil – that he returned to Earth – otherwise I would be talking to an empty bed. Though it would have not been the first time but that is another story."

"But how does that explain why I am still here?" Neb asked.

"You can thank The Anvilus for that," John replied. "As she – The Anvilus – hit the Bubble, she engaged an air pocket that encased you and flung you out into space just as the bubble collapsed. It was a gift from her to you."

"But how did she know?" Neb again asked, confused.

"TeeceeFore said – and in her own words – it was 'a woman's prerogative'."

Neb sat silent. It would take him years to figure it all out.

"Well, if that's all." John turned to leave and said, "I have to rehearse for tomorrow night!"

42(y)

Neb sat upright in bed, rubbing his chin and scratching his head while thinking, thinking, thinking.

Dr. Vanquwippllle soon returned with the good news that all of Neb's tests and healing were now complete and he was free to return to his personal quarters — with the stipulation that he in no way was to do any work for the next three weeks.

"Perhaps take a vacation," Dr. Vanquwipllle suggested.

A vacation! Neb thought. What is that?

Neb made his way out of the Med Bay and walked gingerly along, following the familiar white curving walls of the Casino.

Guests were running in out of the Games Rooms. He thought he caught a glimpse of Fleece, entering the Backgammon Room.

Was that Gnits as well?

President Eno?

Shappledigger?

Neb chuckled to himself as he continued on his way to his quarters, passing Mr. Tict's office and the Green Room where strange musical sounds could be heard bumping up against the walls.

Neb was greeted by guests who recognized him from their previous stays on the Casino.

"Hello! Nice to see you again," Neb said.

Neb finally arrived at his quarters. It seems like years, he thought, as the doors swooshed open.

The first thing Neb noticed, laid out on his bed, was his clean and firmly pressed bright red Assistant Concierge suit, along with a white turtle neck, a new belt adorned with a shining new belt buckle, and by the bed, his black galaxy hopper running shoes.

An envelope with his name 'Nebula Yorker' on it, was pinned to the breast pocket of the suit.

Neb reached for the envelope and opened it.

It read:

Nebula Yorker, you are hereby cordially invited

to attend a Gala Spectacular and Dinner.

To be hosted by the entire crew and guests of Halley's Casino

> *in association with The Council of U and a grateful*
> *universe.*
>
> *Time – 8:00 PM sharp*
>
> *Don't be late!*

Neb laughed out loud. He had no idea what time it presently was.

"Interface!" Neb called out.

"Welcome back, Nebula Yorker," the Interface replied. "How can I be of service?"

"What time is it?" Neb asked.

"It is 5:45 PM," the Interface answered. "Is there anything more that I may assist you with, Nebula Yorker?"

"No, that will be fine, Interface," Neb replied.

I think I better take a shower. Neb smelt under his arms and let out a, "Phew!"

Yep. He said to himself.

Before Neb could take his shower though, his room comm buzzed.

"Come in," Neb answered.

In walked Pic and Pic-One.

"Greetings, Neb," they both said in sync. "We are very happy to see you again."

"As I you," Neb replied.

"We wanted to make sure your quarters were all in order as per Mr. Tict's orders."

"Yes, everything is fine, thank you."

"Very well," Pic said and bowed simultaneously with Pic-One. They then abruptly left the room.

Neb just shook his head. Androids, he thought, so much like puppy dogs sometimes.

He knew though, that in time those puppy dogs would be much more.

Neb was finally now able to take that long overdue shower, the warm light water soaked into every pore of his body.

It felt like months since his last shower.

He started to sing Eddy Money's 'Two Tickets to Paradise', for some reason it was a song he always enjoyed singing in the shower.

By the time Neb stepped out of the shower it was almost 7:00 PM.

He took his time drying himself off and then getting dressed into his double breasted red suit. It somehow felt different this time, as he slipped on his shoes. Perhaps he could just be the Assistant Concierge this time around and so enjoy the ride.

He had about an hour to burn so he decided to update himself on the goings on of the Casino while he had been away. He had already met the new Doctor and had noticed a few more new crew members. One in particular had caught his eye – Mot Yttep.

"What? Mot Yttep?" Mot had died in his encounter with the Ar-Den clone, so what was this all about?

As Neb thought about Mot, his room comm buzzed again.

"Come in," Neb said.

In came Kel, dressed in a long, metallic, shining blue dress, her blonde air falling down on her shoulders.

"Wow!" Neb said out loud, thinking he was thinking it.

He remembered how he felt when he met KEL-345 three years ago, before he knew she was an android and even after he did.

"You look marvelous," Neb gushed.

"TeeceeFore picked out this attire. I gather you like it?"

"Yes, very much," Neb smiled.

"Shall we go?" Kel asked.

"After you," Neb said as the door swooshed open.

"After you. I don't understand," Kel tilted her head.

And there it was. There was the KEL-345 android he had first met. Neb smiled to himself.

They left Neb's quarters; the hallway was bustling, with everyone finely dressed.

Of course not everyone would be able to fit into the Green Room, so a viewing party was set up in every Games Room and quarters throughout the Casino.

Word had spread that even Pratt, Lerxst and Dirk would be tuned in.

Neb could feel the rush of anticipation and excitement throughout the ship; the vibe pulsated so much Neb could feel it through the soles of his feet.

He really didn't know what to expect and was getting excited as they approached the Green Room.

"Here we are," Kel said, as they stopped in front of the doors to the Green Room.

Neb was about to say 'after you', but then decided not to.

Neb straightened himself out, coughed and then nodded to Kel as the doors swooshed open.

The doors opened to a boisterous crowd – the room was filled from top to bottom. It seemed as though Neb was entering the Green Room for the first time again.

Above each table, small balls of light hovered, much like the night that Neb had encountered when he first met Tict well over three years ago, though a little smaller.

Each of the balls began to change colour as they rose, humming as they floated upwards. They drifted up high enough to almost disappear from view before each ball exploded, sending down streamers of dancing fire towards the seated guests.

The dancing fire transformed into something resembling light falling snow then disappeared before it touched anyone's heads.

Android waiters and waitresses were busy as usual. Some of them turned to Neb to wink at him, which gave him a shock.

Perhaps this android evolution thing is moving faster than he thought?

Kel and Neb reached the winding staircase that lead up to the Green Room's balcony. It had been redone after the encounter with the Ar-Den clone. The room was now designed to hold more people than it previously had. The balcony was usually reserved for the Council of U's 15 chief delegates but when Neb and Kel reached the top of the stairs, Neb noticed that none of the Council were present. He thought that very odd but he was then greeted by an assortment of guests and old and new friends.

There was Professor Pheet, LeBeau, Shappledigger, Gnits, Kcils, See-Ess, Purell, Desfannie 417, Fleece, Komi Koop, his mother and father – Blulay and Ruban – and his grandfather, Traep, along with two of his uncles that he had yet to meet, named Yddeg and Xela.

And to Neb's further astonishment, Devo Shog and Mot Yttep were also present!

"What on Earth!" Neb shook his head.

John Lennon though, was nowhere to be seen.

There wasn't any time to ask any questions, which Neb wanted to do, because as soon as they all had seated themselves, a fanfare of music began as swirly spotlights raced across the room and stage.

"Ladies and gentlemen!" A voice boomed out of the Green Room speakers. "Let's give a warm welcome to the one and only Sy Dyloup"

The stage curtains flung open and out flew Sy Dyloup, dressed to the nines in a silver mirrored suit wearing a black cape with a red lining.

His hover shoes let out little wisps of blue smoke as he flew over the room and up to the balcony where he rested his butt on the railings.

"Well, well!" he said to the crowd. "How are we all doing on this fine evening on Halley's Casino?"

All in attendance cheered, not just in the Green Room but throughout the Casino's screening parties.

Those on Pratt, Lerxst and Dirk did not know what to make of Sy Dyloup and the ongoing festivities, as they watched.

"Tonight we have a show of shows, one that will make you jump up and dance the night away," Sy Dyloup said, as he hovered back down to the stage.

Neb and everyone on the balcony were in complete awe.

"Now without further ado, let me introduce everyone's favourite Concierge and his most beautiful wife... Mr. Tict and the President of Telvon Three—TeeceeFore!!!"

The crowd clapped once as was per normal when announcing dignitaries.

42(z)

Tict was dressed in his best black tuxedo, a white shirt and a yellow bow tie. And not to forget those shimmering, polished, red shoes! (The bow tie was something new, Neb noted and smiled)

"Good evening! Good evening!" Tict addressed everyone excitedly.

"Tonight we give thanks to all that are here," Tict looked up to the balcony and eyed Neb. Although the gala night was being held to thank Neb for saving the Earth and the entire universe, no one on the Casino knew what he had done for them except the Triopelians – and a few others of course.

Most everyone on the Casino knew only what they had been told – that a special announcement was to be made and that a party of all parties would be thrown, so dress up and have fun!

TeeceeFore now addressed the Casino.

"Tonight we celebrate the welcoming back of those who have for so long been so near but so far away. Friends, if you would turn your attention to the balcony, I give you Traep, Yeddg and Xela – our Triopelian delegation. Please join us in applauding their welcome return to the Council of U.

Traep, Yeddg and Xela all stood.

A hush crept through the entire Casino; no one said a word.

But the calm was followed by a tumult of applause. The ovation that took place that night at that moment, was like none that was ever seen or heard ever again on the Casino.

Everyone stood and cheered; some even cried.

No one had thought that this day would ever come, some had thought the Triopelians were a myth – but no more.

Pratt, Lerxst and Dirk were overcome with heartfelt joy – and also sadness for having been apart for so long.

After the applause had died down, Mr. Tict and TeeceeFore left the stage to join Neb and the others.

Soon Sy Dyloup was back on stage, the curtain behind him closed once again.

"Are you ready to sing and dance?" Sy Dyloup shouted.

"YES!" came the answering roar. Even those on Pratt, Lerxst and Dirk cheered "YES!"

"I give you the House Band!" Sy Dyloup screamed, as the stage curtain slowly opened to reveal...

Members of the Council of U, ready to rock!

There was:

Luapeyentraccm, Viceroy of Dregonion with a bass guitar strapped about him. Tregot the Dan of Lanoishull on steel peddle guitar. Mleh Novel, Premier of Sasnakra Prime on drums, accompanied also on drums by Snilloc Liph, Fifth Master from Oootopopah. Jonibleeuw, Duchess Samrajni of Ekaveo with an acoustic guitar and vocals. Queen Mercury, The White Sovereign of Chocxivxix on piano and vocals. Van Ohic, Ard RI the Tenth from Emerald Prime on saxophone and vocals. Notlen Hoj, Duke of Landanphishfri on synthesizer and vocals. Prince Cirderf, Esyparells Ish, Ellakeeper, Bac Roew and Messill Di then filed out and stood to the far right side of the stage, all dressed in light blue choir robes.

TeeceeFore, also one of the Council sat this one out but she was replaced by John Lennon who was standing front stage holding a beautiful white Gibson guitar.

One other member was missing, a Triopelian member, though that slot was soon to be filled.

John approached the microphone and said, "I would like to say thank you, on behalf of the group and ourselves. I hope we pass the audition!"

John then turned to the group and counted "1, 2, 3..." and started in, playing 'Whatever Gets You Through The Night'.

The Casino was jumping for the next two hours. Traep even took to the stage with a tambourine in hand and sang backup vocals to round out the number on stage.

Neb could not believe the evening. He was marvellously stunned, especially when Kel and Purell danced. The encore of the show, though, brought Neb to tears.

John now stood all alone on stage while all of the Council members joined Neb and the others with him on the balcony.

"You don't know how much I will miss all of you," John began.

"I don't know how all of this happened, who I was or how I got here but I do know where I am going. And I want to thank you all."

Over the years, John's presence on the Casino was that of just another guest to most, they did not know who John Lennon was or that he came from Earth. Not even Tict or TeeceeFore could figure it all out.

They trusted the Vegastriopelia who brought John's essence aboard the Casino in the first place and created a clone matrix body for him but now John's time and his essence awaited a new beginning, out beyond the Galactic Rim.

"As I was saying," John continued. "I would like to invite a few old friends on stage to close out the evening."

Again the stage curtain slowly opened and Neb almost fainted over in his chair.

Paul McCartney, George Harrison and Ringo Starr, with a full orchestra in the background appeared. Paul,

George and Ringo seemed a little dazed. They really were not sure if this was real or not. For all they knew, they were dreaming.

"This one is for Neb."

John looked up at Neb and gave him the thumbs up.

"Ready boys?" John turned to the lads and immediately started to play 'The Long and Winding Road'.

Neb cried all through the song, with tears of joy.

As soon the song was over the Fab Four bowed as the stage curtains closed around them. It was the last time Neb would see John Lennon.

Meanwhile, back on Earth, Paul was calling George, Ringo was calling Paul and George was calling Ringo – all with the same dream to tell of.

Ringo kept asking if they ever got paid for the gig.

After the festivities of the evening closed down and the Green Room emptied, only the Council of U, Neb and his family and friends remained.

The Council thanked Neb personally for what he had done in thwarting Marcus and restoring calm to the universe.

Neb watched Devo Shog and Mott Yttep from a distance across the room. He was afraid to go over and see them.

Tict was watching Neb closely and knew what was on his mind so he grabbed a couple of the very last bottles of impel berry wine and sat down beside Neb.

"Well my boy, you never cease to amaze!" Tict slapped Neb on the back and then poured each of them a glass.

TeeceeFore sat at the far end of the table and lifted her glass in salute to Neb. Neb likewise, in turn, raised his glass to TeeceeFore and smiled.

"I gather you're wondering about Devo Shog and Mot," Tict nodded towards the two.

"You caught that, eh?" Neb replied.

"It wasn't hard to notice, it was written all over your face," Tict answered.

"So, are you going to tell me?" Neb sipped on his wine.

"You can thank your grandfather and your uncles."

"Oh?" Neb replied.

"They took Devo Shog out of cryostasis after learning through TeeceeFore about the Ar-Den incident and they somehow revived him. Don't ask me how they did it. Perhaps that is something you can discuss with them; I will never understand Triopelian technology," Tict took a gulp of wine.

"And Mot?" Neb asked.

"Now that was interesting," Tict continued.

"It seems they took a strain of Mot's DNA that had been stored and cloned his DNA which was somewhat similar to what Ar-Den did with hers but not to the same extent. Hell, whatever they did to Mot, when they recreated him he remembered his encounter with Ar-Den. Can you fathom that?" Tict said. "How unbelievable you Triopelians are. As much as the Triopelians marvel at you Neb, I think both you and they have much to learn from each other. Don't you think?"

Neb raised his glass of wine and clinked it with Tict's. "You are a wise man, Archibald," Neb said.

"Of course I am," Tict laughed.

"Indeed," Neb replied.

Traep started to make his way over to Neb, bringing with him Neb's two uncles that he was about to meet for the first time.

"I will take my leave," Tict said and rose up to rejoin TeeceeFore.

"Nebula, I would like to introduce to you your uncles – Yddeg and Xela," Traep said to Neb.

"Please," Neb motioned for them to sit down and they were soon joined by Ruban and Blulay.

Tict and TeeceeFore watched all six Triopelians chat and laugh together.

"Isn't life amazing, dear," said TeeceeFore to Tict. "Who would have ever guessed – not one but six Triopelians here on the Casino. Traep tells me we will be seeing more of his fellow citizens and more often, in the near future."

"And why not?" Tict replied. "Everyone needs a vacation now and then, even myths and legends."

"What about Neb? Do you think he will stay with us on Halley's?" TeeceeFore asked.

"I think so, dear. After all, we need him as much as he needs us."

Tict gave his wife a peck on the cheek.

"Are we getting frisky Mr. Tict?" TeeceeFore giggled.

"I am, Mrs. Tict."

Epilogue

Three years had now passed since Neb's universe-saving last adventure.

He sat in the back of the Casino enjoying a rare day off, watching the stars zoom by and the holographic comet tails spin out.

Soon after the events of three years earlier, Neb and his parents had visited Pratt, Lerxst and Dirk. He loved getting to know his own and their heritage – his heritage. He had so many relatives he could not count them all. He had even met a girl named Karma of Dirk. It was nothing too serious – but who knew, Neb thought. They both liked each other and that was a start.

Blulay and Ruban returned to Earth under the Yorker moniker, much to the dismay of Traep but he understood; after all, they were scientists.

They invited Traep to visit the Earth for himself which he did and Neb's parents would return home to Triopelia every August.

Neb and the Vegastriopelia continued their relationship, minus John Lennon. Neb found the song that the Vegastriopelia sang to him much more soothing than when in its corporeal form.

The Triopelians themselves were more visible as guests to the Casino. Once every four months a delegation would visit and through all of this Neb kept his secret of his Triopelian heritage. At least for the time being – sooner or later everyone would know.

Professor Pheet and LeBeau returned to teaching on Marine, of all places. Neb promised to visit them.

Kel left the Casino for an undetermined sabbatical, along with Purell. They intended to unravel the schematics of The Anvilus with a few other fellow androids on a lush moon in the Bonicula Cluster, not too far from Repooc Ecila Six where President Eno promised he would keep an eye on them.

Mr. Tict continued his concierge duties on Halley's, though from time to time he left Neb in charge while he and TeeceeFore visited Telvon Three where, after all, TeeceeFore was the President. Though, she was thinking of giving it up as she found the excitement of the Casino much more to her liking.

Neb had been sitting for hours meditating and loving his life when he heard Mot Yppet call out his name. He turned around to see Mot carrying a package in his hand.

"This just came for you on the galactic mail shuttle," Mot handed the package to Neb.

In his six years on Halley's Casino this was a first – getting mail.

"How are you doing by the way, Mot?" Neb asked.

"You know me Neb, I am always working on the engines," Mot replied. "I would love to chat but Dasfannie 417 needs my help with his new upgrades!"

"Ok," Neb said, "but we're still up for dinner tomorrow evening, right?"

"For sure! See you then," Mot turned and left.

Neb could still not believe Mot was alive after all these years.

"Now Neb, what do we have here?" Neb said, ripping open the package.

He tore off the brown paper wrapping to reveal a box that read 'Lite Bright'.

Lite Bright? Neb mused.

Lite Bright was a toy from 1967 Earth. It consisted of a light box with small colored plastic pegs that fitted into a panel and were illuminated to create a picture or words in light.

What in the world? Neb thought.

He opened the box and pulled out the light box that was already lit up. It had two words glowing on its surface. They read: 'HELP ME'.

"What in the world?" Neb gasped, "Not again!"

Author's Note

This book is entirely a work of fiction. Certain historical events are here rendered, but in an entirely fictitious manner. At the same time, the real names of certain actual historical figures are used in this novel, but the characters themselves are fictional creations. In all other respects, this book is a work of fiction. Names, characters, places, dates, geographical descriptions are all either the product of the author's imagination or are used fictitiously. Any resemblance to actual persons, living or dead, or to actual events or locales is entirely coincidental.

The Wonderful Thank You List

First of all: To that which is and will always be. Amen

I want to whole heartedly thank all those of you who have supported me through these 3 novels. When I was about 12 years of age I would tell everyone and anyone that one day I would write a book. It took some time but here we are in 2019 and not just one book, but three… And I am not finished yet.

Thank you all for coming along on this ride, this fun, this pure joy of adventure!

Rosemary. Your spirit, love and presence continues to abound! We ALL miss you sister.

The Brothers:

Bryan & Maureen, Michael & Adele, Billy & Gayle, Leo, Tommy & Lynn and Kevin

The Cousins:

Nancy & Wayne Rainville - Steven & Bonnie Neale and Connie Butler

For your invaluable help:

Helen Durrant, Lynne Penner, Lanze Lee Langill, Jonathan Vermeire, Mary Taker Baskin

Lili O' Reilly, M.D. Woods and Gordon Demell

Author Bio

JG Fahey is not an alien, contrary to what you may have heard, though he swears he has been to space. Mark has dabbled in various undertakings throughout his illustrious career, from on-air hosting/reporter/stand-up comic to messenger for the Prime Minister of Canada. Mark also holds a degree in Restaurant Services. His  family and friends can attest to his excellent cooking skills. Born in Ottawa, Ontario, Canada, Mark was raised and still resides in Aylmer, Quebec, Canada. For now :-)

Return Trip is the 3rd book in the Halley's Casino trilogy.

Find updates at the following links; that is if Mark isn't too lazy to update updates.

www.markjgfahey.com

Twitter: @jg_fahey

Facebook: Halleyscasino (all one word)

Instagram: Mark JG Fahey - Halley's Casino

Brought to you by the letters

J & N

www.ingramcontent.com/pod-product-compliance
Lightning Source LLC
Chambersburg PA
CBHW070734120726
47910CB00001B/99